BLACK SUN RISING

ORDER OF THE BLACK SUN - BOOK 3

P.W. CHILD

Heiken Marketing

Edited (USA) by Joni Wilson

Other Books in this Series:

Ice Station Wolfenstein - Order of the Black Sun - Book 1

Deep Sea One – Order of the Black Sun – Book 2

The Quest for Valhalla- Order of the Black Sun - Book 4

PROLOGUE

escending from a clear blue sky, the
AgustaWestland AW119 sent waves of sand
scudding across the ground below. The woman
sitting by the window gazed out over the desert, lost in
thought. The end of the Grand Canyon spread out in the
distance, but it had long since lost its ability to impress her.
Too many years of traveling the world had taken their toll.
Now the world's geographical wonders were little more than
an inconvenience, standing between her and her latest
destination.

The chopper touched down. The woman uncrossed her
legs, smoothed down her flowing linen trousers, and stood. A
man with long, ash blond hair was approaching, ready to
offer her a steadying hand as she alighted. "Hey," he called,

over the noise of the propeller. "How was your flight?"

The woman replied with a one-shouldered shrug and allowed herself to be helped down onto the sand. "Is everything ready?" she asked.

Her lack of niceties and small talk did not offend the man. "You know it!" He followed as she strode purposefully away from the helicopter. "I knew you'd want everything to be perfect, so I've been keeping a super close watch on every detail. How are you feeling about it, anyway? I'm kinda invigorated, myself. If we pull this off, it's going to be bigger than anything we've ever done before."

She stopped abruptly and turned to shoot him an icy glare. "If?"

He raised his hands apologetically. "When."

"Exactly. When. Now, I know that we're setting up the surface area the same way as usual, and the entrance to the medical compound will be the same. I saw the developments over at the cinder cone a couple of weeks ago. All I need you to show me is the new installations here."

"Sure thing, S. It's all in place. The screening facility won't be fully functional until tomorrow, though. Some problem with the—"

She cut him off with an abrupt gesture. "Tomorrow? We agreed it would all be ready by today."

"I know, I know, and I'm sorry. It was working this morning and now it's glitching. I've got some people working on it right now. Tomorrow, I promise you—hey, where are you going?"

The woman had turned and was walking swiftly back toward the helicopter. The man ran after her, diving in front of her so that she had to stop. She sighed. "Don't get in my way, Cody," she said. "It's not ready. You have one more chance. I will come back tomorrow, and it will be ready then."

"It will, S, I promise." Perhaps it was the desert heat, but a thin film of sweat was beginning to form on the young man's brow.

"I'm sure it will." She stepped up into the chopper. As she turned to look at the man, her stony expression suddenly melted into a smile. "You know that I require nothing less than total commitment. I know you understand."

With no further conversation, she was gone. The man watched as the helicopter took off, shielding his eyes from the sand it churned up. He did not seem comforted in the slightest by her words.

CHAPTER 1

S am Cleave lay awake in his bed, glaring resentfully at the glowing red digits of his alarm clock, which were helpfully informing him that it was 4:17 AM. His thin summer blanket lay in a heap on the floor, the window was wide open, and the cheap electric fan was on its highest setting. Its whirring was getting on Sam's nerves and preventing him from getting to sleep, but he knew that if he switched if off he would have no chance of sleeping in this heat. Tired and irritable, he flipped his pillow over in search of a cool spot. Much to his annoyance, his pillow seemed to be warm all over.

Tossing the pillow aside, Sam hauled himself to his feet and stumbled through to the kitchen. In the dim predawn light he managed to find a clean-looking glass, but his plans to fill it with water were thwarted by Bruichladdich, who was asleep in the sink. Instead Sam turned and headed for his desk. For want of anything better to do, he opened his laptop and fired up the Internet. An email notification caught his eye.

Hey Sam,

Long time no see! Seems like no time at all since we were all in Ushuaia. What a crazy experience that whole thing was!

I don't know if you've seen much of Matlock lately, but if you have then maybe he's told you that I've gone in kind of a different direction these days. No more polar exploring for me— I think I've done my time out on the permafrost! I've been exploring a more spiritual way of life instead.

When I got home I was blessed enough to make contact with a group of people who run Vision Quests, and I've been spending a lot of time with them out in the desert in Arizona. Have you ever been there, Sam? It's a whole different world, and when you're out in the playa or in the valleys where there's nothing but sand, it does something to your mind. It makes everything clear.

You're probably wondering why I'm telling you all this. Well, as you can probably tell, my time in the desert has been an important experience for me. Life-changing, I would say.

I'm really eager to share what I've learned with the world, so I want to write a book about it. I had someone who helped me with my books about the Arctic and Antarctica, but I think this book's going to need a totally different flavor, and I was hoping you would be able to help me.

If you're interested, I think you'd need to experience the desert for yourself. There's no way anybody could capture it without living it for themselves. And of course I would need you to spend some time interviewing me and working on a structure.

So what do you say? If you would be prepared to come out here for, say, six weeks? I would pay for your flights and all your living costs, along with your fee. Whatever you want to charge, I can pay it. It's worth it to me to know I have the right man for the job.

Let me know what you think. It would be great to see you again, and I think I can promise you that this will be a life-changing experience for you, just like it was for me!

Jefferson

Sam blinked a few times and stared blearily at the screen. The words squirmed before his tired eyes. He squinted as he reread them, trying to wake his brain enough to process the message. Was Jefferson Daniels really proposing that Sam should drag himself to America and join him for a bit of navel-gazing meditation in a teepee somewhere?

"I've only just got settled in after last time," Sam thought aloud. Bruichladdich leaped into his lap and shoved his ginger head against Sam's cheek. "What do you think, Bruich? You don't want me disappearing again, do you? And I can't say I fancy it much." As the cat curled up on Sam's lap and began a ragged purr, Sam's eyes wandered to the half-empty bottle of Lagavulin standing on the bookshelf. It was easily within arm's reach. It would help him to sleep. Or if it didn't, it would at least take the edge off of being awake, just as it had so many times before. He leaned in and closed his fingers around the comforting shape. The glass was cool against his palm. He pressed the bottle against his forehead and felt a brief moment of relief from the oppressive heat. "If I'm too hot in Edinburgh in August, I'd probably melt in Arizona."

He set the bottle down. It sat tauntingly next to an invitingly empty tumbler. For a long moment Sam looked at it, then tore his gaze away and reread the email. "What is a Vision Quest, anyway?" he wondered. Reaching over the cat, he typed the phrase into his search engine and hit return. A split second later he had a screen full of results, telling him about everything from Native American Indian rites of initiation to the recent trend for wealthy people with no cultural connections to the Native Americans to pay large sums to become dehydrated in search of spiritual enlightenment. Somehow Sam was unsurprised that this kind of thing had appealed to Jefferson.

"This doesn't look like much fun at all, Bruich," Sam said, scanning a list of recommended preparations for a quest. "Fasting, meditation, solitude . . . no, I can't say I fancy this in the slightest. Even the fancy version aimed at white people with more money than sense doesn't look great. Look at this . . . 'purge your body of all toxins, learn rituals of incorporation'—what the hell is a ritual of incorporation?

'The threshold of the unknown' . . . Seriously, Bruich, can you see me lasting five minutes at one of these things?" He reached for the whisky bottle again and poured himself a generous measure.

"Keep your judgment to yourself, cat," he muttered as Bruich stared up at him with eyes full of feline reproach. "If you'd read what I'd just read, you'd be drinking too."

✠✠✠

The life raft rocked and nearly tipped as the wave crashed against it. Sam grabbed hold of the side and felt his fingers fail to grip the wet, slippery rubber. He forced his eyes to stay open despite the stinging salt. The destroyer was getting closer by the second, churning the water so that the raft and its occupants were tossed about helplessly. He saw Purdue leaning over the edge, yelling at the destroyer. Sam could not make out the words, but he could see that Purdue was about to lose his footing. He opened his mouth to scream a warning, but then the next wave crested. It broke over them and the water choked the words out of him, so all he could do was lunge across the raft and hope to pull Purdue back to safety. But as he reached out, he felt nothing in his hands.

As he heard Purdue's voice in a watery hell of beckoning, he turned to see that he was standing on the oil rig, Deep Sea One. From all sides came Aryan giants, stalking toward him, each of them armed with replicas of the Spear of Longinus, the battering waves rising behind them.

He called out to Nina, but she only wept somewhere in his mind, her whimpers echoing like peals of demon laughter while the tidal wave swallowed the platform. From the sea arose the face of the shrine that sheltered the Godwomb, and it lazily stretched its stone mouth to suck him in.

"Sam?"

Sam opened his eyes. Slowly he again became aware of his surroundings—the overstuffed, low-slung chair in which he sat, the gently clinical scent of the therapy room, the late afternoon sunshine streaming in through the window. A soft-spoken young man sat opposite him, watching Sam with professional concern.

"Would you like a glass of water?" he asked. It was not really a question. He was already filling the glass even as he asked, and he pressed it into Sam's hand without waiting for a response. "Before we finish, I just wanted to check—how are you getting on with the drinking?"

It wasn't an unexpected question. In fact, sitting in the waiting room before the appointment began, Sam had debated how honest he ought to be. He felt sure that his unshaven face and bags under his eyes told the true story.

It could not, he was sure, be that difficult to figure out that he had lulled himself to sleep in the arms of mistress usquebaugh last night.

His plan was to be straightforward about it. This young man had not seen half the things that Sam had. He could not possibly understand that sometimes drink was the only thing that would soothe his aching mind. Well, Sam intended to make him understand. He would be clear and concise, and let the therapist know that he did not require any help managing his drinking.

"Yeah, not bad," Sam cringed inside, as he heard the words leave his mouth. He felt his head bob involuntarily in an enthusiastic nod, which made him acutely aware of the tender, underslept feeling plaguing the backs of his eyeballs. "The odd dram now and then, you know. Nothing to worry about."

The therapist smiled. "Good. Now, I'd like you to take it easy for the rest of the day, Sam. Don't worry if you feel a bit shaky during the next couple of days, it's perfectly normal when you've been working through this kind of trauma. You might feel a bit sick or have a headache. If that happens, just check in with what's making you feel that way, drink plenty of water, and let yourself rest. If there's anything you're not sure about, you've got my number. Now just take your time."

Sam sipped the water, feeling idiotic. He had no idea how he was supposed to take his time drinking it when there was someone watching him.

The hypnotherapist was a nice enough lad, but there was something about his bland smile and relentless caring that made Sam uneasy. How are you supposed to take your time drinking your water when you know there's another appointment right after you, and this guy probably just wants you to get out so he can have a quick smoke before the next person's due in to cry about his problems, Sam wondered. Losing his nerve, he knocked back the rest of the water in one gulp and handed the glass to the therapist. He muttered a brief word of thanks and then fled.

✠✠✠

The elegant streets of the New Town were bustling with tourists, shoppers, and the first office workers to make their escape for the day. Sam wandered along George Street, trying to stave off the moment when he would have to head home and get back to work on the latest local interest story assigned to him by the Post.

After a couple of trucks plowed into a low bridge up at Cameron Toll, the Edinburgh Post had begun a campaign to have the bridge rebuilt. Sam had conducted the usual weary round of interviews with concerned residents eager to have their say.

His next task would be to weave those words into an article that struck the right balance between tolerable journalism and the kind of righteous indignation that would sell the paper. It was not the kind of work he relished.

After returning from the nerve-wrecking experience on the platform of Deep Sea One, he had elected to hold on to his records of the expedition until Purdue contacted him. This profound discovery had to be carefully exhibited at the risk of luring the wrong attention toward the owner of such a relic. After all, he thought, this was Purdue's expedition, Purdue's money, and, ultimately, Purdue's relic.

After he had disappeared with it a few months before, there was no knowing of what had become of him or the artifact. Releasing any sort of report on it would be futile, as he did not have the actual item as proof. For now he had to maintain his run-of-the-mill routine.

As he strolled toward Princes Street and began the steep walk up the Mound, which separated New Town and Old Town, Sam glanced up at the distinctive skyline of Old Town. This had been an eventful city, he knew.

Battles had been fought here. Edinburgh Castle had been besieged and conquered and besieged again.

Bloody murders and all sorts of sinister misdeeds had been carried out in the densely packed closes. But now there's nothing more interesting going on than a couple of idiots driving their trucks into a bridge, Sam thought. This city's come down in the world.

Still, at least his therapist assured him, his dissatisfaction with the lack of interesting events in his hometown was a good thing. It was a step in the right direction, apparently a sign that he was no longer feeling quite so apathetic and depressed as he had in the previous years. Whether his most recent experiences in Antarctica and Tibet had helped to restore him to his old self or whether it was just the passage of time making his grief less acute, neither Sam nor his therapist could tell. All they knew was that he seemed to be taking a little more interest in life these days, and this was considered to be a good thing.

Sam knew full well what most of his dreams conveyed, what their recurring purpose was. He knew what they were based on and that the images he suffered during his clawing nightmares were indeed not entirely fantastical, but he dared not reveal this to anyone in the real world, let alone a mind-probing, know-it-all, like his therapist.

Imagine such a thing, telling your shrink that you had your hands on the only true Spear of Destiny and that the object had powers that controlled the ocean, among other things.

And that under the North Sea a sinister organization was actively hatching plans to take over the world now, after failing in the 1940s.

Sam scoffed as the thought became a scenario. Across his face a silly smile peeked at the absurdity of it all—but he had been there. He tried to soothe his paranoia, *Thank god there aren't people like that influencing the world anymore. Imagine if the Nazis had access to today's technology! Wouldn't that bring about a clusterfuck of epic proportions?*

It had been nearly six months since Sam's return to normal life after he and Nina barely survived the collapse of Deep Sea One. It was long enough for him to get over the feeling of strangeness at being home again, and long enough to become disgusted with his home and his job once more.

He reached the top of the Mound and made his way along George IV Bridge, heading for Southside, which meant battling his way through an army of fresh-faced young actors who were in town for the Fringe Festival and desperate to hand Sam flyers for their shows. He jammed his hands into his pockets and stared fixedly at the ground in front of him, refusing to make eye contact.

It's amazing how quickly the boredom sets in, he thought. Maybe Purdue had the right idea. Maybe being a mega-rich thrill seeker is the way to do things. I should give the mad bastard a call and find out what he's doing—see if he still wants me to write that profile on him. Purdue had not been seen since the chaos on his offshore oil rig, but word of mouth dictated that Purdue had been busy. The last thing Sam had heard was that Purdue was developing some complicated new piece of technology that he was unable to talk about, but which would, of course, revolutionize the entire world.

In all honesty, Sam believed him. Anyone who had done research on Dave Purdue knew that the man had been responsible for some incredibly important advances in software and nanotechnology, and, despite wanting to write him off as nothing but a techno-geek turned billionaire playboy, Sam found himself gripped by a sneaking admiration.

Despite the danger Purdue had dragged him into, Sam liked him. There was a part of Sam that hoped he would someday get to finish writing the profile that Purdue had requested—although as long as it remained unfinished, Sam's editor would continue to salivate at the prospect of it and give him a certain amount of leeway.

For some reason Purdue had been keeping his possession of the ancient religious relic under wraps and Sam could only imagine that the questionable visitors to Deep Sea One had something to do with his need to hide such information for now. There was also an element of curiosity for Sam, because it was difficult not to wonder what exactly made a man like Purdue tick.

The route home led Sam straight through Edinburgh University's Bristo Square—the heart of Fringe Festival territory, making it a seething, crowded nightmare to cross. As always, Sam fixed his gaze straight ahead and pretended that he was not surreptitiously scanning his peripheral vision for glimpses of petite women with bobbed dark hair and an impatient stride. He knew that in a city this small, it would only be a matter of time before he and Nina ran into each other, but they had been doing a good job of avoidance so far.

In fact, they took great care to not have their paths intersect.

After returning from the frightening adventure in Tibet and the subsequent turmoil on Purdue's offshore oil platform, Nina gave him a call. It was a strange request, but out of respect Sam adhered to it as he had promised.

For her to ask him to keep his distance for a little while until she had "composed herself mentally" was not preposterous in the least, although he was disappointed by it. It was understandable, and, quite obvious by the state Nina was in on returning to Edinburgh, she needed some serious quiet time away from anything that reminded her of the incidents following their discovery of the Spear. Sam did not ask what she was planning to do, but she assured him that she was going to be unavailable for a few months. He trusted that she would resurface when she was ready.

Sam did not like to admit that he was secretly disappointed each time he crossed the square without encountering her. She never came into Dagda anymore. He wondered where she drank now.

CHAPTER 2

W hat the hell do you do on a Vision Quest, anyway?" DCI Patrick Smith asked, with his usual tact and subtlety, taking a swig of his pint. "Isn't it just a bunch of hippies in the desert taking drugs?"

"Mostly." Sam picked up the little water jug and added a dash to his whisky. "I mean, I can understand it if you're an actual Native American Indian, and it's something you do as part of your religion or because that's your tradition. But what Jefferson's doing . . . it just looks like someone's figured out a way to take ten grand a pop off of middle-aged men for taking them on a little camping trip. And the really clever bit is that they don't have to worry about getting complaints about it being too hot, or too uncomfortable, or the food being terrible, because that's the point. Everyone's there to fast and be uncomfortable." He sipped his drink, and then gave a satisfied sigh. "Wish I'd thought of it first."

"You don't fancy doing it, then?"

Sam shook his head. "Can you see me lasting five minutes in a setup like that, Paddy? I'd get kicked out for drinking or telling the warrior leader to fuck off."

"The shaman, Sam. They are called shaman," Paddy smiled into his glass as he took a swig.

Sam paused with an indifferent leer and carried on, "Mind you, there's a little bit of me that wishes I had the self-control to do it. The money that Jefferson's offering is really damn good. Still, it's not for me."

"So what's the plan instead?" Paddy asked. "Are you staying here?"

"I don't know," Sam replied. "Probably. I've had enough running around to last me a lifetime, and it's about time I started trying to build something permanent. You know, maybe I should buy a flat or something—think about the long term."

Paddy's jaw nearly hit the table. "Sam Cleave thinking about the future? Is all that therapy starting to show? What have they done to you, Sam?"

"You can get straight to fuck," Sam grinned, as Paddy dissolved into helpless laughter. "You bought your house when you were twenty-five, you prematurely middle-aged bastard. It's just time, that's all."

"Sorry, Sam," Paddy gasped for breath and tried to get his laughter under control. "I'm happy for you, really I am. It's just . . . I wish you could see the change in yourself. The state you were in a year ago, I didn't think you were going to make it. I was forever worrying that you'd walk under a bus or something. And now you're actually talking about buying a house!"

"A flat, Paddy," Sam corrected. "Let's not get carried away. It's just that I've got the money I got paid for the Antarctica trip sitting there, and it's enough for a deposit with a little bit left over, so I thought I might."

"The Sam Cleave I knew a year ago would have blown it all on single malt and binged himself to death. That's what you told me your plan was."

Sam smiled wryly at the memory. "True. And the man I was three years ago would have spent the lot on a trip around the world with Trish."

He waited for the melancholy drop in his stomach that he always experienced when he mentioned her name, but it did not come. Cautiously, he continued.

"It still pisses me off that we never got to do that, you know. She'd been saving for years. The plan was to start in Paris and just work our way east until we found ourselves back there." Still the gut twist of grief did not happen. Instead, Sam felt a swift pang of guilt, like hundreds of tiny, simultaneous knife wounds, brought on by being able to think about her in such normal terms.

Unable to resist inflicting a little more pain on himself, Sam reached into the recesses of his mind for the memory of Trish, a little bit tipsy on her thirty-second birthday, explaining her travel plans with all the careful detail of inebriation. She—they—would cross Russia on the Trans-Siberian Express, she had informed him. Faithfully he recalled her leaning across the table, too intent to notice the puddle of spilled beer soaking her elbows, pushing a loose tendril of hair into her customary messy topknot.

It was a gesture that always made Sam want to untuck the strand again, just to see the flicker or amused annoyance that crossed her lovely face when he did.

He could picture everything—the ring she wore on the middle finger of her right hand, the tiny scar on the tip of her nose, and the way she tapped the table to emphasize her points.

What he could not find, though, was her voice—not clearly, at least. It was muffled in his head, as if he were listening for her from behind a thick pane of glass.

"Sam?"

With a sudden, fierce shake of the head, Sam dragged himself back to reality. "Sorry, Paddy, I was miles away."

"So I could see. Are you ok?"

"I'm fine."

Paddy sat back, but Sam could see the concern on his round, normally cheerful face. "Good. So do you know where you're going to look for a place?"

"Probably just around here," Sam said. "I like Southside. Something like the place I've got just now would do nicely. And if I don't look too far then I won't have to get a moving company, I can just borrow a shopping cart from Tesco and wheel everything from place to place in that. Or I could get some chump with a car to help me shift stuff. There's bound to be some big ginger bastard who'd do it for a few pints and a pizza."

"Aye, there probably is." Paddy downed the last of his peanuts, crumpled the packet, and threw it at Sam. "But I know you. If I help you move, I'll end up buying the pizza."

Sam considered denying it, but both men knew it was true. "Probably," he said. "But you never know. Maybe I'll surprise you. And I haven't even started looking yet, so I've got time to save up. Maybe Mitchell's calling me to give me a raise— then when the time comes I'll be able to get you extra pepperoni."

✠✠✠

"So, what can I do for you, Mitchell?"

In the two years that Sam had been working for the Post, he had managed to avoid most of Mitchell's "little chats." They were notorious among the journalists as well-intentioned wastes of time.

Since Mitchell's nepotistic appointment as assistant editor, he had been desperately trying to make the little world of the Edinburgh Post a better place, and Sam knew he was not the only seasoned journalist to take advantage of this.

Mitchell was constantly torn between his desire to keep supposed "star" journalists like Sam happy and the need to keep sales figures high to please the demanding father who had appointed him to the job.

When Sam felt bad about giving Mitchell a hard time by turning in pieces a little after deadline or half-assing the less interesting stories, he rationalized it by reminding himself that a little sweat was a small price to pay for the considerable privilege and security that the young man enjoyed.

"Good to see you, Sam!" Mitchell wore his customary desperate beam. "I, er . . . I wanted to have a little chat. Have a seat."

Sam dropped into the low-slung armchair facing Mitchell's desk and shuffled around a bit, unable to get comfortable, conscious of his legs being too lanky for this kind of seat.

"Coffee? I can send someone—"

"No, it's fine." Sam tried stretching his legs out, but that was even less comfortable than having his knees jutting upward like denim foothills.

"Well, if you're sure." Mitchell perched on his desk in a failed attempt at casualness and picked up his own cup, clearly freshly fetched from the Starbucks across the road. He took a lengthy swig of his chai latte, then replaced it and fixed his gaze on the cup. "The thing is, Sam—I'm going to come straight to the point. The thing is . . . I'm sure you're aware that the paper's not doing so well just now. It's a tough time for print media. We're struggling to keep the figures up. We're going to have to tighten our belts a bit."

Sam nodded. This "little chat" was not entirely unexpected. Sam had been aware of rumors flying around for some time about the paper's impending move to new, cheaper premises and a heavier focus on content for the website rather than the print edition. Everyone had been expecting the breaking news of the move and for the staff to have their workload increased while the pay remained the same.

"Fair enough," Sam said. "So where are we moving?"

"Moving?"

"Isn't that what's happening? A few of the people have been taking bets on where we'll be going. Mine's on the old office buildings at Meadowbank. Am I right?"

For a moment Mitchell said nothing. This was clearly not how he had intended this conversation to go, and Sam could see the wheels in his head turning as he tried to figure out how to get it back on track.

He took a deep breath, then retreated behind his desk and sat down. "Sam, I think you've got the wrong end of the stick," he sighed. "We are moving, it's true—but that's not what I needed to talk to you about. It's—well—we're downsizing, Sam, quite considerably. And we've got to let some people go."

Having finally come to his point, Mitchell plowed on full speed. "I'm so sorry, Sam. You know I'd keep you on if I could, but the decisions come from higher up. What we're hoping for is that the savings we'll make will pull the paper clear and then once we're on a better footing we'll be able to bring you back in. Maybe even on a better deal!"

It took a few seconds for Sam to take in what he had just heard. He stared blankly at Mitchell, pink-faced and perspiring as the lad smiled a smile that pleaded with Sam not to hate him. Meaningless words washed over him as Mitchell began to babble about redundancy packages, severance pay, and the difficulty of maintaining a print newspaper in the age of print media. The phrase "last in, first out" made an appearance, accompanied by vague expressions of Mitchell's fear for his own job. None of it sank in. When Mitchell pushed the papers terminating Sam's contract across the desk, Sam took up the chewed pen he was offered and signed without a word. He laid the pen down with uncharacteristic precision, lining it up against the text of the redundancy agreement.

As Mitchell showered him with thanks for being so cooperative, Sam began to wonder how many others were going to suffer the same fate that day.

A glance at the clock told him that this "little chat" had taken fewer than ten minutes. In that short space of time, Sam had gone from being a man with a plan to put down roots to a redundant drifter. Next to the clock Mitchell had hung a collection of framed photos, each showing him with someone he considered important.

His father, the lord provost, the first minister, a couple of high-profile writers and artists . . . and Sam, looking bemused and a little disheveled as Mitchell shook his hand enthusiastically. He had never noticed that photo before, perhaps because it was hard to spot among the others, or perhaps because Sam so often dodged Mitchell's chats. He recognized the event—it was a party hosted by the Clarion just after Sam had received his Pulitzer. He had shaken hands with many enthusiastic young journalists that day. He had never realized that Mitchell had been among them.

And now he's giving me the boot, Sam thought, half-amused and half-annoyed. He allowed Mitchell to grasp his hand once again and give it his best firm handshake before holding the door open for Sam to leave. He was halfway through it when a thought struck him and he turned.

"Mitchell?"

A flicker of dread flashed across Mitchell's face, anticipating awkward questions or recriminations. "Yes, Sam?"

"Before I go—where are the new premises? I need to know if I won the bet while I'm still here to collect on it."

CHAPTER 3

The money that Sam collected from the other journalists for winning the bet paid for several pouches of Whiskas cat food for Bruichladdich, a final round at Dagda, a trashy airport novel, and a small packet of mini pretzels on the plane to America. It had been no surprise that the severance package offered by the Post was not particularly generous, and it was equally unsurprising to learn that there were no newspapers within commuting distance of Edinburgh currently looking to expand their staff.

With unemployment looming just a fortnight away, Sam had found himself facing a choice between living off his savings, while he pursued a probably fruitless quest for a new job, and taking Jefferson Daniels up on his offer. The money was excellent and the work looked likely to be easy, so Sam bit the bullet, sent the cat on his holidays to Uncle Paddy's house again, and booked a flight.

As annoyed as he was by the situation, Sam had to admit that it was not all bad. Jefferson had been keen to get going and wanted to immediately bring Sam to where he lived in Montana. When Sam had demurred, citing the additional expense of plane tickets bought on short notice, Jefferson had added a clause to the contract stating that he would pay all of Sam's travel and living expenses for the six weeks they were to spend working on the book. "It'll be worth it," he had said, flashing his toothpaste-commercial grin while they Skyped. "If you're here for the Mind Meld, you'll get a real flavor of what I've been doing. I think it'll really add something to the book."

So Sam had agreed. The plan was that he would fly to Great Falls and spend some time with Jefferson and his family, observing them in their natural habitat, then accompany them to Arizona to watch Jefferson's initiation as some kind of official within his little group of New Agers— or FireStormers, as this lot preferred to be called. Sam shook his head as he recalled the conversation.

It had been difficult enough keeping a straight face on Skype, and he was concerned that during his five weeks in Arizona he might accidentally allow his cynicism to show through. It would certainly be a test of his professionalism.

"Ladies and gentlemen, we are now beginning our descent into Great Falls, Montana!" The voice of a flight attendant crackled over the speaker, perkily dictatorial. In accordance with her demands, Sam flipped his tray table back into place, kicked his rucksack under the seat in front, and then looked idly out of the window as the voice reeled off the local time and temperature. The landscape was a patchwork of brownish fields, broken up with frequent canyons that put Sam in mind of scarred, puckered skin. The Missouri River, immense and blue-green, snaked its way toward Great Falls.

Well, it might not be what I had in mind, Sam thought, *but it sure as hell beats sitting around the flat all day trying to job hunt.*

✠✠✠

"Mr. Cleave?"

Stumbling out of the international arrivals gate, Sam glanced around in search of the owner of the voice calling his name. Standing at the opening, waving delicately, was a tall, willowy woman with carefully highlighted caramel blonde hair and perfectly subtle makeup.

She was dressed in a pale blue cashmere sweater and gray slacks, with a pearl necklace and pearl ear studs. Sam knew at once who she was. A woman such as this could only be Jefferson's wife. She had clearly been born and raised to sport a name like Paige.

"I'm so pleased to meet you at last, Mr. Cleave." Paige Daniels extended a slender hand for Sam to shake. He could not help but feel clumsy and slovenly next to her, especially considering the state of his clothes after a full day's travel. "My husband has told me so much about you. Jefferson will be here any minute; he's just gone to bring the car around. How was the flight? You must be exhausted. Jefferson told me that you wouldn't let him upgrade you to business class, though I simply can't imagine why not! This way—he's picking us up right out here."

Sure enough, just as they stepped into the warm evening air, a dark blue Lexus SUV pulled up, Jefferson at the wheel. With blithe indifference for the No Stopping sign, he leaped down from the driver's seat, strode round, and pulled Sam into a hearty bear hug. Were we this friendly? Sam wondered.

"Sam, buddy!" Jefferson boomed. "Good to see you! You've met Paige—isn't she great? Wait until you see what she's got on the stove; she is just the best cook! Oh, honey, let me get that for you."

He turned around to open the passenger door for Paige, then took Sam's luggage and swung it into the back seat. Sam climbed in after it and dutifully answered Jefferson's questions about what he had been up to since they had last seen each other, naturally withholding the more intense events.

He thought he detected a hint of disapproval from Paige when he confirmed that the Post had, indeed, let him go. She suppressed it quickly, and Sam wondered whether he had read too much into her tone. Fortunately, Jefferson changed the subject at that moment, pointing out a few local sightseeing spots along the route to their house.

Mile after mile of pale beige farmland stretched out under a pinkish sky. Sam watched for the falls that gave Cascade County its name, but saw none. Instead they headed toward what Sam took to be nearby hills, gradually realizing that he was in fact catching his first glimpse of the distant Rocky Mountains. Jefferson chatted away about Freezeout Lake and the local nature reserve, and how a man could just walk for hours and forget about everything.

Sam could imagine that it was true. The land certainly lived up to all the "Big Sky" hype. Sam had dismissed that at first, because the sky could hardly be different sizes in different places, but now that he saw the place, he felt the difference in perception.

After an hour, just as darkness fell, they sped past a sign reading "Welcome to Choteau: Gateway to the Rocky Mountain Front." Sam caught a brief glimpse of the town up ahead before the car swung off down a road with a sign marked "Deep Creek." Sam thought Jefferson had gone crazy and driven them off the road, before he realized they were on a dirt track.

"It's a short cut!" Jefferson assured him, catching sign of Sam's perplexed expression in the rearview mirror. "This way we don't have to go through Choteau to get to the cottage."

Hearing the word "cottage" in their earlier discussions, Sam had prepared himself for living in close proximity with the Daniels family. He had braced himself for cheek-by-jowl living, despite never wanting to do that again after those nights spent in a tent in Antarctica. He had not considered that Jefferson's idea of a cottage might be different from his own.

When the car stopped it was not a cottage that Sam saw, but a sprawling farmhouse with a handful of outbuildings.

There was a barn that had been converted into a triple garage, a paddock and stable, and along a short path stood a small house that was more in line with Sam's idea of a cottage.

"I hope you're ok with the guest suite," Jefferson said, pointing to the small house. "It's small, but it's kind of cozy. I'll drop your stuff in there. You go with Paige and she'll get you a drink."

Obediently Sam followed Paige into the house. It was immaculately presented, with fresh flowers in crystal vases on every surface.

A tall trophy case stood in the hallway, surrounded by carefully curated family photographs, so that any casual visitor would be immediately impressed with the family's high achievement levels.

Set slightly apart, just far enough to be conspicuous without being distasteful, was a perfect candid shot of Jefferson and Paige, apparently sharing a joke with George Bush Sr. in the White House Rose Garden.

"Nice glasses," Sam said, as Paige pressed an Old Fashioned in a monogrammed tumbler into his hand.

"Thanks," she smiled sweetly. "They came from my grandmother.

Those are her initials, Mary Hammersmith Cassidy. She always believed in the importance of good crystal." At once, Sam felt under immense pressure not to drop the glass or accidentally grip it too tightly.

"Hey, Mom, where's mine?"

Jefferson's daughter appeared in the doorway, slouching against the doorframe. She was as tall and slim as her mother, though her dress sense was certainly different. She wore layer on layer of wispy black garments, and her messy blonde ponytail contained a couple of clipped-in strands of red and purple streaks. Sam tried to suppress a smile as he caught sight of Paige's pursed lips.

"Henley, dear, we have company. Why don't you go and put on something more appropriate?"

"What's wrong with this?" Henley demanded, striding across the room so that her trailing sleeves and scarves fluttered behind her. "You said no skin. I'm not showing skin. Now can I have a drink?"

"Henley, we've discussed this." Paige turned to Sam apologetically. "I'm so sorry, Mr. Cleave. My daughter thinks she's an adult already. Henley, you are seventeen years old."

"Dad lets me drink." She reached for the nearest bottle in the liquor cabinet, but her mother slapped her hands away.

"Dad lets you have one glass of wine with dinner." Jefferson walked into the room and ruffled his daughter's hair. "Stop tormenting your mother. Have you said hello to Mr. Cleave yet?"

"Please, call me Sam," Being addressed so formally was starting to make him feel uneasy.

Henley grudgingly accepted the glass of lemonade that her mother handed her before retreating to the kitchen. She reached for a breadstick from the plate that sat in front of the liquor bottles, placed it between her perfect teeth and looked Sam in the eye as she bit down. "You're the guy who's going to write my dad's next book?" She frankly looked him up and down. "Cool. Let me help you with that. These FireStorm freaks? They're crazy. Like, worse than Scientology. Mom and Dad like it because it's like going to the country club but with added spirituality, but it's totally insane. One big money spinner with a side order of social control."

"Hey, Henley!" Jefferson laughed and threw an arm around his daughter's shoulders. "Whoa there, honey! Isn't she great? She's my little warrior for justice—aren't you, sweetie? But you'll see for yourself, Sam.

It's a really interesting new way of thinking. But you don't want to hear about all that right now!

You just relax tonight. Tomorrow we'll go out for dinner, just the two of us, and we can make a start then."

Henley rolled her eyes hard. "Daaaaaad, you're not taking him to that stupid mermaid place, are you?"

"Sssshh, honey, you'll ruin the surprise! Now come on, let's show Mr. Cleave through to the dining room. You know your mother won't appreciate it if we let the pot roast get cold."

✠✠✠

The "stupid mermaid place" turned out to be a kitschy tiki bar by the name of Sip 'n' Dip, where the daiquiris were accompanied by the sound of live jazz piano and the walls were lined with large fish tanks with attractive young women in mermaid costumes swimming around.

"It's not really Paige's kind of place," Jefferson said, slipping the bartender a generous tip. "But I kind of love it. My dad brought me here on my twenty-first birthday; bought me my first legal drink! I thought I was in girl heaven." He watched appreciatively as a mermaid with long dark hair and a red tail performed a lazy flip in front of them. "Now, let's get down to business. Did you get a chance to look at the information I sent you about FireStorm?"

Sam nodded. He had spent much of the previous day's plane journey looking through printouts of the FireStorm website. It was not yet live, but Jefferson had sent him screenshots of the "About FireStorm" section. In truth, he had struggled to understand it. All he had seen was a page full of platitudes about the Age of Aquarius, heightened consciousness, and the bringing together of peoples and cultures. So far there had been nothing to set it apart from any of the multitude of fashionable beliefs espoused by wealthy individuals. However, Sam was surprised that it had appealed to someone so conservative in his views as Jefferson, and he had spent the small hours of the previous night plagued by jet lag and trying to figure out a tactful way of phrasing the question.

"It was really interesting material," Sam erred on the side of diplomacy. "There's going to be a lot to discuss as we go forward, just so we can make sure everything's absolutely clear. But the first thing I'd like to know is exactly how you got involved. Things seem to have happened really quickly. You weren't involved with this group before you went to Antarctica, were you?"

"That's correct, I was not." Jefferson sighed deeply, staring at his drink. "I haven't spoken much to my family about this, Sam, but you were there, you'll understand.

Something broke inside of me in Antarctica. I mean, I'm used to harsh environments, and I've been in some situations where I didn't

think I was going to get out alive, but . . . nothing like that. I've never felt so . . . powerless. Like I didn't know what was going on, and nothing was what it was supposed to be. I decided I was done with polar expeditions before we even got home from Ushuaia.

I thought I'd come home and maybe try something new, stay here and make a difference, maybe go into politics. I'm getting a little old for exploring." Sam caught him sneaking a glance at his reflection in the mermaid tanks. "So I started spending a lot more time at the country club, building up some old friendships with people who could help me, and that's how I met Sara Stromer, the mind behind FireStorm. She was in town doing the groundwork for the Montana base. We got to talking, and I was able to introduce her to a few people who helped her find a site, and then got her applications and licenses fast-tracked. And as she told me more about what she was doing, I just kind of got interested and thought this might be the new purpose I was looking for.

Then I introduced her to Paige and they got on really well, so we flew down to the main base at Parashant and spent a weekend doing an introductory Mind Meld.

It really worked for us, so I got initiated and we've kept going back. Then eventually Sara asked if I wanted to get involved with running the Montana base. I said yes, and now they're going to give me an official role. It's really straightforward.

You'll pick it up quickly. Boy, I can't wait for you to meet Sara! She's great. You'll like her!"

"Can't wait," Sam said, with as much sincerity as he could muster. His mind conjured up an image of a dowdy, schoolmarmish middle-aged lady, trying desperately to look bohemian and New Age in a hot pink caftan with orange scarves tied round her neck and wrists. Or perhaps some wispy youngster, barely older than Henley, luring older men with the power of a killer midriff. Either way, Sam was sure, he would be unlikely to be taken with Sara Stromer.

CHAPTER 4

As it turned out, Sam was quite relieved to meet Sara. She and her second in command, Cody, arrived just as Paige and Henley seemed to be settling in for one of their longer and more involved arguments. Unlike the previous spats that Sam had seen, this one did not involve issues of appearance or behavior, but Henley's desire to delay college in favor of pursuing her winter sports career.

Sam knew that Sara was due any moment and was schooling himself to be polite and professional, but the longer the fight went on, the more tempted he became to feign illness just to get out of the room.

"Henley, for the last time, you are not skipping college!" Paige's sweet smile was still in place, but there was an unmistakable look of fury behind her eyes. "Take it from me, you don't want to be the oldest girl in your class—how will you ever meet anyone worth marrying if you're older than everyone around you? Now, the matter is closed—we have company."

Unwilling to concede entirely, Henley began questioning whether Sam truly counted as company or whether the fact that he was receiving payment from her father meant that he was help. She came close to succeeding. Paige was at the point of losing her temper completely when Jefferson emerged from his study to tell them that Sara's car was approaching. Sam breathed a hearty sigh of relief.

The slick black Cadillac cruised over the gravel and came to a halt just outside the house. It was driven by a man, who wore a ponytail, with an air of carefully studied coolness. In the passenger seat was the kind of expensively groomed woman whose age could never be guessed. With her perfectly cut hair, falling past her shoulders like the darkest liquid chocolate, and skin that had certainly had the benefit of a good dermatologist (if not a plastic surgeon), her birth date was as much a mystery as her past.

She's completely constructed, Sam thought. There's not one thing about her that gives away where she comes from or what kind of person she is when she's not working.

Dinner itself was a polite affair. Paige was a truly excellent cook and had put out an impressive spread—clear tomato soup with homemade spelt bread, a roasted guinea fowl with sage and blood orange, and finally a chocolate marquise, so rich that it had to be served in tiny portions. By the end of the meal, Sam was suffused with the pleasant sensation of having eaten far more than he actually required.

The food also served as an excellent means of keeping the conversation flowing. Seated with Paige on one side and Henley on the other, all Sam had to do was keep asking Paige about her many engagements as hostess and her time spent learning fine cooking, while protecting her from occasional barbs from her daughter. He had little occasion to talk at all to Sara and Cody. It seemed as though the room had split into two separate diner parties, with Jefferson talking FireStorm business at the far end of the table, while Sam kept Paige and Henley entertained.

Seems like a bit of a weird way to do things if I'm meant to be writing a book about these people, Sam thought. But mine is not to reason why. There'll be plenty of time to spend with them once we're out there. No sense in overdoing it.

✠✠✠

By the time dinner was done and the brandies had been drunk, Sam was in urgent need of a cigarette—not just for a nicotine fix, although that was always welcome, but to escape from the small talk. It was not hard to keep a trained hostess talking, but it was a little wearing after a while.

During his chat with Paige, Sam had eavesdropped snatches of Jefferson's conversation with Sara and overheard a few too many references to communal sharing of emotional experiences and to something called "The Hunt," which sounded more physical than Sam usually cared for. He was beginning to wonder whether accepting this job had really been such a great idea, even if the money was good.

"Ach, you're just winding yourself up," he said to himself, walking back toward his cottage. "You'll be fine. It's not for long. Besides, you could be doing with a nice, quiet, boring job after—"

A sound caught his attention. It was something familiar, he knew, made unfamiliar by the cold, dark night.

Sam listened intently—whistling wind, a faint chirp of crickets, rustling grass, and his own shallow breathing, nothing else—then something.

Footsteps. Slow, careful footsteps. Then . . . a click. Sam held his breath. He waited for the gunshot.

It did not come. Instead he heard a soft thump—and then, a few moments later, a louder one.

It was, he realized, a door—a car door. The unseen person must have tried to close it silently, failed and tried again.

As stealthily as he could, Sam crept toward the source of the noise. I must be insane, he thought. If I had any sense I would get Jefferson. He's bound to have a gun, and even if he doesn't, at least there'd be two of us, rather than just me and a lighter.

There was just enough moonlight for him to make out the shape of the car. Sam dropped to a crouch, wondering what he was going to do next. He settled on the idea of finding a place to hide and waiting to see what the intruder would do next, but to do that he was going to need more light. Shielding his lighter with his hand, he flicked the spark wheel.

The gasp from the car told him that he had misjudged the angle. In a heartbeat Sam was on his feet, ready to run—but even quicker, the car door swung open and a figure leaped out.

"I'm sorry!"

Sam heard the voice ring out from behind him. Its vulnerability caught him off-guard and he turned, holding the lighter up.

"I'm so sorry, I didn't mean to—look; please don't call the police, ok? I'm not trying to rob the place or anything, I swear. Oh, please, I'm so sorry, I'm really, really sorry—"

The woman was young, maybe twenty-five at most, and looked more terrified than anyone Sam had ever seen. Her hands were raised in a classic gesture of surrender. Sam had no idea what she was doing, but he was absolutely certain that he did not want to raise the alarm—at least, not yet. Raising a finger to his lips, he beckoned her to follow him back toward the guest cottage. She hesitated, clearly aware of the dangers of following strange men into strange houses, but the sound of the front door to the farmhouse opening made her rethink. She fell into line behind Sam, and the two of them hurried quietly toward the cottage door. As soon as they were inside Sam silently pulled it shut, and they both froze and waited until Sara and Cody's car was out of earshot.

"Wait," the woman said, looking closely at Sam. "You're not Jefferson Daniels. This is his place, isn't it? So who are you?"

"You're asking me?" Sam hissed back, still with half an ear listening for any further movement on the dark driveway.

"I'm someone who's got an invitation to be here, that's all you need to know. I take it you haven't?"

She looked away, abashed. "No," she said. "But please don't call the cops. I'll get in so much trouble, and I swear I'm not here to do anything wrong."

Sam could not help but laugh. "You're sneaking around someone else's property in the middle of the night, begging me not to get the police, and you expect me to believe that you're not doing anything wrong? Come with me." He led the woman, now looking more alarmed than ever, into the den. Jefferson was a good host and had furnished Sam with a decent bottle of Laphroaig, from which Sam poured two glasses. He handed one to the woman. "There. Now, have a seat. If you're not doing anything wrong, tell me what you are doing here. In fact, even if you are doing something wrong—especially if you are." He dropped into one of the overstuffed armchairs.

Tentatively, the young woman perched on the edge of the other seat, clutching the tumbler. "Ok . . . I'm not casing the place, I promise. I'm a journalist. I'm working on a story about Sara Stromer."

"What kind of story?"

"About her and this thing she runs called FireStorm. It's kind of a religion, but there's a lot of other stuff going on, such as land acquisition and links to major companies. No one knows a lot about it—it's really secretive—I'm just trying to learn more about it, and her."

"By sneaking around here at night?"

She looked down at her hands. "I've been following her since I heard she was in Montana. Rumor is that she's trying to set up a base here and I would love to break that news, but

I need details. I know she was meeting someone up by the Ear Mountain State Game Refuge today, but the car drove into a gated area and must have come out another way, because I lost her. But I'd heard her talking to that guy who assists her about dinner at Jefferson Daniels' place, so I tracked it down and waited here. I know it's a little unethical, but I don't think I'm doing anything criminal. I certainly don't intend to. It's just—"

Sam raised a hand, silencing her. "No explanation needed," he said. "I know. Sometimes you've just got to do these things. I've been a journalist for years, and you don't want to know about some of the things I've done. What's your name? Whom do you write for?"

With a small sigh of relief, she took a sip of the whisky.

"It's Julia Rose. Julia Rose Gaultier," she said, then hesitated for a moment before adding, "and I don't really write for anyone just now. I have a blog—yeah, I know—but I'm trying to use it to catch a break. Something like this could really help me. How about you?"

"Sam Cleave." He stuck out a hand for her to shake. "I used to write for the—"

"Sam Cleave?" Briefly forgetting to keep her voice down, Julia Rose uttered Sam's name with a cry of excitement. "From the Clarion? You're the guy who broke the story about the arms ring?"

The delighted expression on her face made Sam feel bad that he could not muster more excitement. He wondered if he had ever been so young and enthusiastic. If he had, that version of him was impossible to call to mind now. "Yeah, that's me."

"Oh, my god!" Julia Rose stared at Sam as if she was carefully memorizing every detail of this meeting for posterity. "Oh, listen to me—you must think I'm just some stupid blogger fan girl. I'm not really. But I've read so much of your work, and it's been a big influence on me. I never thought I'd actually meet you!"

In an instant her elation gave way to anxiousness and she crumpled.

"Oh, god. And you just caught me trespassing. Are you friends with Mr. Daniels? Because I'd really appreciate it if you didn't tell him I was here. I'll go right now, I won't come back. And I won't come here again."

"Don't be daft," said Sam. "I'm not going to tell on you. Yes, I know Jefferson. He hired me to help him write a book. If you like, I can introduce you some time—not just now, obviously, but while I'm here. He likes to talk about all this FireStorm stuff to anyone who'll listen, so you'll definitely get something out of him. In the meantime, we'd probably best get you home. Are you from around here?"

Julia Rose shook her head, "from Minneapolis."

Sam racked his brain, trying to remember where Minneapolis was in relation to Montana. Quite far east, he seemed to recall. "Not going home tonight then, I take it? Where are you staying?"

"Well, I . . . " Julia Rose would not meet his eyes. Her voice dropped to a mumble. "In my car. Oh, don't look at me like that, it's not so bad. I couldn't afford to do this any other way. There are plenty of places to wash around here, if you don't mind cold river water. And I don't. It's the heat in Arizona that I'm worried about."

"You're planning to follow her down there?"

"I have to. I don't know how much you've heard about this Mind Meld thing, but it's going to be huge. Word is that most of Silicon Valley's going, and there are plans to unveil some new tech gear that will . . . actually, I don't fully understand what it's meant to do. People have been saying that it's going to bring together spirituality and social media, but I don't get how that's supposed to work. But I guess I'll find out. I hope I will. Although I'm probably just going to wind up getting myself arrested, if I can't even sneak around here without getting caught."

Sam could not deny that this was true, or that being caught trespassing in the FireStorm compound was unlikely to end well for a young African-American woman. Still, that was a less-pressing problem than the issue of what to do with her tonight. "Look, do you want to stay here tonight?" he asked. The look of apprehension crossed her face again. "Don't worry, there's a spare room. It's got a lock on the door and a separate bathroom. You might as well. But you'll need to leave before anyone gets up and sees your car."

She glanced toward the open door and spacious hallway beyond, leading toward the expensively refurbished, lavishly decorated bedrooms. Her hand went unconsciously to the nape of her neck, her fingers testing the cleanliness of her hair. She was evidently tempted.

"Come on," Sam said. "Stay here. There's a little kitchenette through the back—there's not an awful lot in it, but you're welcome to whatever's there."

At the mention of food, she visibly relaxed. Sam wondered how much she was eating, while living in her car. He knew he had almost won her over and that he would sleep much more easily knowing that he hadn't kicked her out into the night to take her chances by the roadside.

But there was something that she seemed to be uncertain about. She kept glancing toward her backpack, slouched on the floor at her feet.

"I hate to ask you for anything else when you're already being so generous," she said. "But . . . may I charge my laptop?"

CHAPTER 5

"Mom! Mom, I can't find my iPod!" Henley yelled from the top of the stairs. Paige, who was busy checking the labels on the family's luggage, did not even look up before yelling back that she had no idea where it was and perhaps Henley should take better care of her belongings. As mother and daughter launched into the beginning of a full-blown argument, Sam tried to make himself inconspicuous.

The past few days had been somewhat tense in the Daniels household.

The peace and quiet of Jefferson's study, where Sam had been conducting the interviews for the book, had frequently been shattered by the sound of Henley's protestations.

It was her opinion, frequently and vehemently stated, that FireStorm was a cult, spirituality was nonsense, and she had no interest

in being torn away from all her friends and her snowboard training to spend two weeks suffering in the Arizona heat. Julia Rose could not arrive to collect Sam soon enough.

Jefferson appeared from the driveway, his chiseled features twisted in suppressed frustration. Catching sight of Sam, he plastered a smile on his face. "Hey, buddy," he said, grabbing the first of the bags. "Both our rides are here. I really wish you'd let me buy you a plane ticket, though. Your intern's car is, well . . . it's kind of old. Have you seen it?"

Grabbing his bag, Sam strolled out to meet Julia Rose. It was true, he had never actually seen the car in daylight. It was a 1999 Toyota Camry that had clearly seen better days. Much better days. The red paint was shot thought with little sections of rust and discolored patches where old scratches had been touched up with spray paint that did not quite match. Julia Rose had clearly tried hard to make the car look less lived in, but Sam suspected that even if it had been freshly detailed it would have given that impression. There was little she could have done to reverse the damage done by several not-so-careful owners who had the car before her.

"That's your ride?" Henley appeared behind Sam, a tiny designer backpack slung over one shoulder. She peered over the top of her sunglasses at the car.

"Cool. Can I come along with you? If I have to spend five hours on a plane next to my mom, someone's going to die."

She stooped down to give Julia Rose her most winning smile through the driver's side window.
"Hey. I'm Henley Daniels. You must be Sam's intern. You seem cool, may I get a ride?"

"Sorry, Henley," Sam said, placing a hand on her shoulder and gently steering her back toward the cab that was waiting for the Daniels family, "nothing doing. I don't think your mom and dad would be happy with us kidnapping you. First class awaits. Off you go."

As Henley slouched toward the cab, Sam threw his bag in the back of the Camry. "Sorry about that," he said, pulling a large bag of Jolly Rancher candies from his jacket pocket as they pulled out of the driveway. "Were these the ones you said you liked? They'd better be good—I've got three more bags after this one."

✠✠✠

"I still can't believe you managed to get me into this thing," Julia Rose said, as the car clanked and groaned its way past signs for Wolf Creek and onto the Interstate. "How the hell did you do it?"

Sam shrugged and shifted his lanky frame, looking for a comfortable position for the long drive. "I didn't really expect it to work, to be honest with you. I'd have thought it was the kind of thing we had to arrange ages ago. I just said to Jefferson that there was a young American journalist that I'd been mentoring through email, and it occurred to me that it would be really beneficial if you could tag along with me for the experience and give me a hand. I told him that at such a big event, it would be handy to have a second pair of eyes to make sure I got a really clear sense of what was going on. Jefferson said he'd give Sara a call, and the next thing I heard was that you were in."

"Wow. I guess they must want his money really bad."

Sam thought back to that dinner with Sara and Cody. Yes, he thought, that must take a lot of cash to maintain. He tried to imagine the cost of Cody's exquisitely cut suit, and Sara's immaculately styled hair with her subtle, expensive perfume.

He imagined that the aura of prosperity must be a key factor in promoting FireStorm—this was not a religion that welcomed the poor and underprivileged.

It was a belief system that preached the rewards and righteousness of material wealth. For all their focus on "connection," Sam was yet to see the few FireStormers he knew connecting with anyone who did not at least appear prosperous.

The image of Sara Stromer danced before Sam's mind's eye.

He could understand why she was so successful at what she did.
Even just thinking about her made him think that he ought to be listening to her, following her instructions and letting her enlighten him. There was something about her that invited confidence, even obedience. An air of authority . . . she reminded him a little of Nina. Or, at least what Nina might have been if she'd had a little more gloss, a much better controlled temper, and a more manipulative, and perhaps more cynical temperament.

He wondered what Nina would make of these people. A small, mischievous part of Sam wished that the two women would meet, and that he would be there to watch. Many of his fondest memories of Nina were of her attempting to stifle her annoyance with the people around her.

"Coming up for Helena," Julia Rose announced. Sam snapped back to reality. If they were already close to Helena, his little reverie must have taken up the better part of an hour. "We'll make a quick coffee stop there," Julia Rose continued, "and maybe grab some breakfast. Then we'll just keep going until we hit Pocatello."

"How long's that?"

"Five hours? Maybe a little more. If we hit any holdups we might stop a little earlier, maybe around Idaho Falls or somewhere. We should get to Las Vegas before midnight."

Sam gave a long, low whistle. "Where I come from, if you drove for that long you'd end up in France. Does the radio work?"

"It's not great. Mostly it'll just pick up one station and the options are listen to it or turn it off. Shouldn't be too bad around here. There'll be some music or talk radio or something. Just wait until we get to Utah—bet your bottom dollar it'll only pick up some crazy Mormon religious show."

"Can't wait," said Sam. "At least the times when the radio isn't picking up anything good will give us a while to get our stories straight, if we're supposed to have been corresponding for months."

"You mean we're not just going with 'this is some crazy chick I found trespassing outside Jefferson Daniels' house'? Kinda disappointing." Julia Rose took a couple of sweets, deftly unwrapping them with one hand. "We're gonna have to come up with something just as interesting. I think we should tell people that we met on FetLife or something." Sam's head spun in disbelief, until he caught sight of her wide, wicked smile. She glanced over and burst out laughing at the look on his face. "You've got to loosen up, Sam! Ok, we'll figure it out. What did you have in mind?"

✠✠✠

By the time they reached Salt Lake City, the radio had indeed started picking up only a minor religious station broadcasting nothing but the Mormon Tabernacle Choir. For a while they listened, but soon enough Julia Rose became bored and complained that it was not good driving music. They drove in silence, not a sound except the quiet munching as they continued to work their way through the large stockpile of snacks that Sam had picked up when they stopped in Pocatello.

After a couple of weeks of hearty, healthy meals at Jefferson's, Sam intended to make the most of this opportunity for a junk fix before setting foot in the FireStorm compound.

During the previous eight hours, as they had rushed past nearly 600 miles of forest and farmland, they had agreed on a version of events that would, they hoped, convince anyone who asked that they had known each other online for months. Julia Rose would claim that she had approached numerous prize-winning journalists, sending out emails asking for any hints or tips they might have for a new graduate trying to make her way in the world of journalism. For the most part she had received no response or a form reply containing the standard recommendations that she work hard, hone her skills, network, and try to break an interesting news story.

Only Sam Cleave had come back with a proper, personal response—because, Sam claimed, her email had caught him in a moment of half-drunk nostalgia. He had told her what he could, but he made it clear that times had changed considerably since he had started out.

He had read her blog posts, offered her writing tips, and given her permission to keep in contact and send him any major pieces to critique.

When he had realized that he would be traveling to Montana, he had let her know and she had made plans to drive from Minnesota to Montana to meet her idol turned mentor.

The bit that Sam was most proud of was an idea of Julia Rose's, that he should claim it was meeting Sara and Cody and learning more about FireStorm that had prompted him to offer her this impromptu internship. "Tell them that they inspired you to give back to the journalistic community that made you what you are," she suggested with a smirk. "Say that they opened your eyes to the importance of connections. They'll eat it up."

Sam was increasingly glad that he had followed his instincts and taken a chance on Julia Rose. He was rapidly coming to the conclusion that she was a smart, savvy young woman.

Peachy keen and a little egocentric, as all aspiring journalists tended to be, but with the spark of intelligence that made Sam think she'd press on even after reality started to bite.

He had admired her tenacity from the moment he had learned that she was living in her car in pursuit of a story, but that was only the start of it.

She had a slight chip on her shoulder about what she perceived as her "late start" in the field—at twenty-five, she had just graduated. She evidently saw this as a serious disadvantage, but Sam thought otherwise. She had worked like hell to secure a place at the Missouri School of Journalism at the University of Missouri in Columbia, one of the best journalism programs in the country. But even with financial aid and her customary frugality, the cost of college had been high. In order to manage the size of her mountain of debt, she had held down two jobs and reduced her studies to part-time, sending money to her mother in Minneapolis to help support her younger brother.

Talking about her family had caused Julia Rose to make an unexpected stop somewhere in the vicinity of American Falls, Idaho. What had started out as a casual mention of her mother, while explaining her unusual education, had quickly become the story of what had happened to Julia Rose's father, which had left her shaking so hard with rage that Sam had suggested they pull over.

"I'm sorry," Julia Rose had said, trying to lay her hands in a flat, calm, steady gesture on the wheel.

"This is why I don't usually talk about Dad. I get too angry. I'll give you the short version—he was a construction worker who got killed in an accident at work when I was thirteen. He was hit by a collapsing wall. The insurance company found a way to say it was his fault, so they only paid us a tiny compensation. Mom was pregnant at the time and ended up with all sorts of health problems, probably due to the stress. She lost her job, and we didn't have health insurance, so the money got eaten up by medical bills. It was really shitty all around, but it's kind of what got me into journalism. I had this big idea that I was going to be a ball-busting, take-no-prisoners, investigative journalist, and that I'd bring the company that killed my dad and the insurers who stiffed my family to justice."

"Is that still the plan?" Sam had asked.

She shook her head vehemently. "I grew out of that shit—got older and stopped reading comic books. But I'd put a lot of time into finding out how journalism worked and it looked like something I could do to make some money and have a decent life, so I stuck with it. Yeah, I know.

There's no money in journalism any more. It's still better than flipping burgers or being someone's maid. And maybe I can do some good with it, even if that doesn't mean some stupid Batman shit about avenging my dad.

So now you know why all this means so much to me.

But if I sit here and indulge this crap all day we're never going to get to Vegas. So that's it. I don't want to talk about it anymore."

That had been her last word on the subject. Sam was intrigued—he wanted to know more about how she had managed to keep her head above water and what he could do to help her to catch a break. To hell with getting to Vegas on time. He was quite prepared to spring for a night's accommodation if she needed to stop. Yet every time he tried to gently raise the subject again, she would deftly change it. Before he knew it, they were approaching Cedar City and their cover story was in place.

"Last stop before Vegas," Julia Rose said, preparing to pull in at a gas station. "It shouldn't take us more than an hour-and-a-half from here; it'll be real quiet by now. So that means we'll get there at, what, eleven-thirty? Not bad going. Kind of sucks that we're this close to Parashant and we're just going to have to drive past it."

"True," said Sam, "but who's going to turn down a free trip to Vegas? You might make your fortune. I'm going to get a drink. Should I get you a coffee?"

"May I get a Red Bull instead? And maybe some aspirin, if that's ok. Do you want some cash for that?"

"No bother. It's all going on the Daniels account."

"Oh, ok. In that case, let's make it Advil!"

✠✠✠

They rolled into Vegas slightly ahead of schedule. Julia Rose's feet seemed to be getting heavier on the gas pedal as they got closer to their destination. Sam consulted his scribbled notes for the address of their hotel, the Verbena. It took only a moderate amount of circling and swearing at each other to find it, at which point life suddenly became considerably easier. Despite Julia Rose's protestations that no hotel in Vegas would valet park her car, she handed the keys to Sam and let him toss them to the attendant. If the attendant judged them for arriving in a rust bucket, he did not let it show on his face but accepted Sam's tip, slipped behind the wheel, and told them to contact the reception desk when they wanted the car again.

At the reception counter they completed name tags identifying them as part of the FireStorm group and were handed keys to rooms 1850 and 1851.

"Dinner service just got finished," the receptionist informed them, her smile unwavering, "but we have an extensive room service menu, so if you see anything you like, we'll send it right up. Your rooms are on the eighteenth floor. Are you sure you don't want someone to show you the way? Ok! Well, turn right as you get out of the elevator."

The elevators, like the rest of the Verbena, were a confection of white plastic and highly polished chrome.

There were even a couple of glass lifts, like little bubbles that faced both the interior and exterior of the building,

offering guests the opportunity to ride in full view of the lobby and the Las Vegas skyline. Sam could see why Sara had chosen this place as a meeting point for the Silicon Valley delegates. It felt like the whole place had been built out of iPhones. Selecting a floor could be achieved with a mundane push of a button, but there was also the option of speaking your destination to a voice recognition system, which cheerfully repeated Sam's words back to him.

"I see that you have just checked in!" the elevator voice said. "Please don't forget to check out our in-house casino, our award-winning restaurant, our world-famous champagne bar, our state-of-the-art gymnasium and spa facility, or any of the other extraordinary features we offer here at the Verbena! If you require anything during your stay or wish to personalize your Verbena experience, just speak into the microphone beside your bed and a member of our team will be right with you!"

Sam bit his tongue. He promised himself he would get through this first night, at least, without swearing at the technology. He thought fondly of some of the run-down bed and breakfast places he had stayed at through the years, places run by surly old couples who viewed their guests with anything from suspicion to open hostility. It seemed friendlier, somehow, than this mechanized place that offered a "personalized experience" while being utterly clinical.

He stepped out into the hallway of the eighteenth floor, Julia Rose behind him, and turned right as they had been instructed. Just as they set off down the corridor, another elevator pinged behind them. Instinctively, Sam turned around and saw the doors open to let out a well-dressed couple. The man was tall and heron-like, wearing small glasses and expert tailored clothing. Sam recognized him at once as Dave Purdue, the same thrill-seeking billionaire who had dragged him and Jefferson all the way to Antarctica in search of lost Nazi treasures. The obsessed magnate who had plummeted him into the dangers of sneaking into Tibet and desecrating temples to acquire the location of a religious item that drove men mad in its pursuit.

And the woman beside him was none other than Nina.

CHAPTER 6

The Verbena had nothing as low-tech as a normal alarm clock on its bedside tables. Instead, pale blue digits were projected onto the stark white walls. These read 03:07 when the faint tapping on the door began.

Sam was not asleep, of course. Even after a week in America, his sense of time was yet to catch up. He was sprawled diagonally across the vast bed, staring at the ceiling, half-listening to the news on the giant plasma TV, while he sucked despondently on the end of an electronic cigarette. Quietly, he rolled off the bed and crept across the floor. For all its gadgetry, the one thing the room did not have was a peephole in the door. He glanced around to see if there was something he should be pressing or whispering at to bring up information about who was on the other side of the door.

The tapping came again. It was soft, so soft that it would not have woken even the lightest of sleepers. Someone wanted to know whether he was awake. Sam wondered whether the person would be able to see light under the door or hear the sound of the TV. Then again, he thought, I could have fallen asleep with the TV on—and the lights too. It's no guarantee of anything. I could just—

"Sam? I would be surprised if you are not both in the room and currently awake. Please let me in."

Purdue. The voice on the other side of the door was Purdue. Sam pushed the button beside the door, making it slide open to let Purdue in.

"Thank you, Sam. I knew you would be up, I remember well your habits." He strolled into the room, examined the layout, then walked straight toward the far wall and pressed his palm against it. A panel swished out of sight, revealing the mini bar that Sam had searched for in vain a few hours earlier. Purdue took out two miniature bottles of vodka, complete with tiny chilled shot glasses placed over the top, and handed one to Sam. "Insomnia can be so useful when I am at home and have things I can work on. In a situation like this, I simply find my wakefulness incredibly tedious. Nina is no help at all. I have never known a woman to sleep as soundly as she does."

Purdue's words hit Sam like a sucker punch to the gut. Ever since he had run into them in the corridor, Sam had been trying hard not to think about why Nina was here. That Purdue was here for the Mind Meld was obvious—in fact, Sam was kicking himself for not figuring out sooner that Purdue was likely to be here. Nano-technology and software were two of the disciplines that had made Purdue so rich, and the world was small where such wealthy men were concerned. But Nina . . . Sam knew that she must either be working for him or sleeping with him, and deep down he knew that no personal assistant would have been so well-dressed for dinner with her boss.

Despite himself, his mind conjured up an image of Nina lying prone across one of these massive hotel beds, the tangle of sheets around her body, the pale white skin of her slim back, her dark hair fanning out over the pillow . . . He could imagine her breathing, heavy with slumber, exhausted after a long session of strenuous—

Enough of that, Sam told himself, none of my business. He popped the top off the vodka bottle and took a swig, not bothering to pour it into the little glass. He racked his brain for some suitable small talk, anything that would not lead back to a conversation about Nina.

"So, have you been in Vegas long?" Sam tried, then cursed within the confines of his head. How was that a question that would lead away from Nina?

"For six days," Purdue said, folding himself into one of the complicated seats by the coffee table. "I wanted to give myself time to acclimatize before the Mind Meld begins. I would hate to be at a disadvantage due to jet lag. Fortunately, Nina was available at short notice to accompany me. In that respect I am rather grateful to her department in the university. If the department head had been a little more appreciative of her talents, she might still be employed there and I might be here alone."

Sam thought that he was doing an admirable job of controlling his face, but Purdue must have picked up on something. "Am I being insensitive?" he asked. "I'm sorry. I hope you realize that I am not attempting to crow over you, Sam. I was aware of a previous attraction between you and Nina, but she assured me that there was nothing between you. I would be lying if I said to you that I would not have invited her here if there had been something between you, but knowing her as I do, I am sure it would have made a difference to her response."

"It's fine." Unwilling to risk the fancy half-kneeler, half-chairs, Sam perched on the edge of his bed. "There never was anything, really. I thought about asking her out once, but it never happened. So you and she are . . . well, that's great. Good. I hope it's all going well."

While uttering the words, it did cross Sam's mind that Nina could not possibly have asked Sam to distance himself purely to be able to pursue Dave Purdue, even after all she and Sam had endured together. The Judas kiss of the whole affair burned in his chest and scorched his heart, but his face remained unhindered by the bite of it.

For a long moment Purdue stared quizzically at Sam, one eyebrow raised in disbelief. However, he did not push the matter any further. Instead, he relaxed in his chair and allowed Sam to draw him into a little inconsequential discussion of Las Vegas, the Verbena, and America in general. Purdue asked about Julia Rose, and Sam, remembering Purdue's sense of humor, told him the truth about how he had acquired his "intern."

They laughed together at the thought of Sam's mild abuse of FireStorm's hospitality, and as they worked their way through the contents of the mini bar, Sam remembered how entertaining Purdue's company could be.

Yes, he was intense and a little crazy—but he had few boundaries, and he was exciting. An excellent drinking buddy —just the sort of man you could down vodka with until the first hints of daylight made their presence felt over the Nevada skyline.

✠✠✠

"Now, god knows I'm not a man to stop anybody having a good time," Jefferson Daniels addressed the table, "but there has to be a few limits in place. I mean, shouldn't a man be able to take his family out for dinner without having to worry what his teenage daughter's going to see?"

A few seats away, Henley groaned and slumped across the table, picking at a bowl of granola. Despite his fuzzy head, Sam smiled. Jefferson had been holding forth for a good twenty minutes about the disreputable state in which he found Las Vegas.

The FireStorm delegates had been seated in a private dining room for breakfast, full of large round tables designed to encourage people to start mingling and "connecting.

In practice, people had split into small groups where they already knew one another, so Sam, Nina, and Purdue were sitting with the Daniels family.

Sam and Nina exchanged brief glances. He figured Purdue must have offered her some comfort, some nudge in her career, for her to have finally submitted to his advances. He wondered if it even bothered her a little that she did not have the courage to just say it to his face—Listen, Sam, you have been with me through so much, but unfortunately your friendship is not enough to buy me a private jet,—he imagined harshly.

Nina, always groggy until the second caffeine hit of the day kicked in, winced every time Jefferson resumed his monologue. By contrast, Paige sat at her husband's side looking perfectly groomed. Sam would not have been surprised to learn that she had already visited both the hotel's gym and its spa that morning.

At the far end of the room, Cody was beginning to work his way around the tables with a personal greeting for each delegate. In his carefully casual shorts and shirt, his ash blond hair in a long ponytail, he looked right at home among the Silicon Valley types currently sucking down cup after cup of strong coffee.

"What the fuck actually happened?" Nina muttered under her breath. She turned to Purdue. "Do you know? I missed the bit where he told us all what upset him so much."

"He took his wife and daughter out for dinner in Vegas and was surprised when there was a floor show," Sam leaned across Purdue to explain. "He thinks Henley might have been traumatized by the sight of pasties."

"Seriously?" Nina's face contorted with a contempt she could only manage first thing in the morning. "Did he think they call this place Sin City just for kicks?" She looked as if she was about to settle in for a rant, but then she had a moment of sudden realization that she was talking to Sam, whom she had made a personal mental note to keep as far at bay as possible, and she went quiet.

Jefferson was far from finished. He was now discussing how he had heard that Vegas had cleaned its act up and become family friendly. "If you ask me," he said, gesticulating with his fork as he worked his way through a plate of bacon and eggs, "it still has a long way to go. Paige, honey, I can't apologize enough. You know I'd never have chosen a place like that if I'd have known. Henley, I know you're a smart girl. I hope you'll remember that those young women are not role models. I'm not going to tell you that they're doing something wrong. Sometimes circumstances can drive a woman to do terrible things, and it's not for us to judge those who are less fortunate than us.

But I hope you'll remember that you are more fortunate, and it falls to those of us who are to lead by example and turn our backs on places such as that."

It was clear that Jefferson had really hit his stride, and he was not planning to conclude for some time. Sam wondered whether he was practicing for his political career.

"Dad, stop," Henley raised her head, her eyes still streaked with the remnants of last night's eyeliner. "Seriously, this is so stupid. It doesn't matter, I've seen tits before."

"Henley Caroline Cassidy Daniels!" Paige shot to her feet. "How dare you! And in front of company! You apologize to these people this minute."

Dropping her head, Henley mumbled an apology. "But it's true," she grumbled, as her mother sat down. "Anyway, you can't police their bodies that way. They're adults. They can do what they want. And I don't see how it's any different to Dad taking guests to Sip 'n' Dip. Would it have been ok if those girls last night would have worn tails?"

Neither of Henley's parents replied, but Jefferson had the decency to look somewhat sheepish. Presently Henley rose, leaving her granola almost untouched, and disappeared upstairs.

"Where's the girl you were with last night?" The caffeine was clearly starting to work its magic.

Nina had woken up enough for her voice to take on an acerbic quality as she spoke to Sam.

"Checking out the swimming pool, I think," Sam replied with a level of cheerfulness carefully calculated to irritate her. "That's Julia Rose, by the way. Julia Rose Gaultier. My, er . . . intern."

He could see the wheels turning behind her eyes as she tried to figure out to what extent he was serious and to what extent he was winding her up. There was residual annoyance, a little judgment building, in case Sam really was taking advantage of a keen young journalist, a slight amusement, a large amount of curiosity that she was trying to contain. Her eyes narrowed slightly as she watched him over the top of her coffee cup.

"Sam is provoking you, Nina," Purdue looked from one to the other with his usual cool, appraising gaze. "He told me about Julia Rose last night, and while it's an unusual story it does not appear to be a romantic or sexual one."

"Last night? When last night? I didn't notice you were gone."

"I had difficulty sleeping," Purdue said. "So I paid Sam a visit. I didn't want to wake you."

Sam fidgeted in his seat, battling the impulse to abandon breakfast and retreat to his room.

Seeing Purdue and Nina discussing this little domestic detail was making him decidedly uncomfortable. When did this start? he wondered. That day when I went to interview Matlock, I thought . . . Maybe I was wrong. I could have been, I suppose. I thought that was water under the bridge. She never said anything during out last time together, which I might add, was extensive. Or maybe it was just after that, after almost getting crushed by the ocean in a small room just before being rescued? Her need to be away from it all, perhaps? Do they look like it's a new thing? I don't know. Would Nina go on a trip like this with someone she hadn't been seeing for long? She went to Antarctica on next to no notice . . . But that involved her work. Hunting tenure pushed her into the Tibetan trip. Maybe this does too? But how? She's a German history specialist; what would there be for her to do out here?

Fortunately he was spared any further discomfort—of that nature, at least—by Cody pausing in his greetings to address the whole room. He had noticed Henley's departure and decided to talk to everyone before they began to finish their breakfasts and scatter.

In his confident, charismatic manner, he reminded them that they had a whole day to spend in Vegas before that night's welcome dinner, where most of them would connect with Sara Stromer in person for the first time. The following morning, as soon as breakfast was done, transport would be waiting to take them to Parashant to begin their Vision Quest.

"So I would encourage everyone to make the most of the dinner tonight and breakfast tomorrow," he beamed at them. "Because after that we'll be following the kind of diet that the Paleo-Indian might have enjoyed—and that means no microwaves or takeout places where we'll be going! I can't wait! Can you?"

Somewhere over to his left, Sam heard Nina mutter, "I bloody can."

CHAPTER 7

Sam did a quick spin around in front of Julia Rose. "Just about presentable?" he asked. She looked appraisingly at him. "Black tie isn't really your scene, is it? Yeah, you'll be ok. You won't be the only guy in a room who clearly never wears a tux."

"What? What's wrong with my tuxedo, you cheeky thing?" Sam gave himself a quick once over in the mirror. The suit had seen better days, it was true. He had bought for his sister's wedding and only worn it a couple of times since then. It didn't have any holes in it, at least none that he was aware of, and it still fit. He had polished his shoes and had a proper shave especially for the occasion—not a hint of his usual five o'clock shadow. He had drawn the line, though, at trying to slick his hair. He had run a comb through it. That was surely good enough.

Julia Rose was looking stylish in a yellow Alexander McQueen dress that fell to her knees and was gathered by a gold belt at her waist. "Can you believe someone just left this here?" She clearly could not believe her luck. Earlier that day she had ventured down to the front desk and explained her situation to a sympathetic-looking young man, telling him how she had come to cover the Mind Meld but had never expected that a lowly intern would be invited to the black-tie welcome dinner. He had shown her a closet full of garments that had been forgotten by guests. These were the items that had been there for so long that they could reasonably be assumed to have been forgotten, but were also expensive enough that the hotel thought them worth hanging on to, just in case. As long as she was extremely careful, brought it back by morning and did not tell his boss, the young man had said, Julia Rose was welcome to borrow anything.

Sam strolled over to the mini bar. "One quick thing before we go," he said, reaching in and taking out a little bottle. He poured its clear contents into two shot glasses and passed one to Julia Rose.

"What's this?"

"Don't know," said Sam. "Booze of some kind." He necked his swiftly, and then smacked his lips.

"Ah, grappa, I think. It's a little bit of an acquired taste, but I'm really sure this is the kind of event you should line your stomach for."

Julia Rose shrugged. "Ok, then." She knocked hers back and pulled a face. "Ugh. You weren't kidding. Wow! That's strong."

"Yup," Sam said. "Now let's go and see how much free champagne we can get through before they figure out we're a pair of liars and kick us out."

✠✠✠

The entrance to the dining room had been draped with a pristine white curtain with the FireStorm logo emblazoned on it—an image of the sun with its rays bursting out to reach the far edges of the cloth. It looked disturbingly like the symbol in the boardroom where the order had congregated under Deep Sea One. In keeping with the image of the room, it had been picked out in an elegant monochrome. As Sam and Julia Rose approached, part of the curtain was swooped aside by a tall, imposing member of the security team. He nodded politely as they passed through.

Behind the curtain was a long room with a high, vaulted ceiling, lined with long tables draped in black linens, laden with huge, white covered dishes.

Expressionless wait staff stood at ease behind the tables, waiting for the order to step forward and serve, while cocktail waiters wove their way through the ranks of the guests, passing out colorful, exotic-looking drinks in long-stemmed glasses. At the far end hung another set of curtains bearing the FireStorm logo.

Sam accepted one of the intriguing cocktails and looked around for Purdue and Nina. Though he would not admit it to himself, he was hoping to catch sight of them before they saw him, to see how they acted together when they did not know he was watching. He took a sip of the bright blue drink. *What the hell is this?* he thought, as he swallowed. *Someone needs to show these people how to make a proper cocktail! I haven't tasted anything as weak as this since I was ten years old and nicking tiny nips of my dad's whisky to put in my lemonade. It's as bad as American beer. Practically water.*

He was just about to go in search of a proper drink when the sound of a gong reverberated throughout the room.

In front of the curtains at the far end of the room stood Cody Cignetti-Dwyer, his long hair loose and flowing down the back of his tux. He waited for the noise in the room to die down, then smiled around at them.

"Hi!" He let one hand slide casually into his pocket. "Everyone having a good time? Great! That's just great. I know this is going to be a little difficult with glasses in your hands, but I'd like you all to make some noise to welcome the lady who brought us here today, the woman with the vision behind FireStorm—ladies and gentlemen, this is Sara Stromer!"

As the crowd around him erupted into whoops and cheers, Sam felt a little uncomfortable. Applause he could manage, but shrieking like a 1960s teenager at a Beatles concert had never been part of his repertoire. Politely, he patted the hand holding his glass with his free hand and smiled in the direction of the platform.

The curtains parted to reveal Sara, tall and statuesque in a columnar white dress, her dark hair swept into an elaborate updo. She posed for a moment, taking in the ovation without directly acknowledging it, then stepped forward. She raised a slender hand, silencing the room in an instant.

"I feel a tremendous sense of connection with everyone present tonight."

Her words rolled slowly from her lips, her enunciation clear and her tone warm. "Thank you. I thank each one of you for joining us. I can hardly believe that this dream of mine, the meeting of minds, is finally happening—and I am grateful to all of you for allowing that to happen. If you take nothing else away from the Mind Meld, you can at least take this: you have made me unutterably happy."

Under normal circumstances, her words would have left Sam fighting to stifle a laugh. His tolerance for this kind of thing was low, and it would not have been the first time that he had needed to fake a coughing fit to cover an involuntary snort of derision. But there was something about Sara Stromer that gave him pause. He was sure that a part of it was the precision and control in her delivery.

Yet there was something else, something Sam could not quite put his finger on. It was something to do with the fact that she really appeared to believe herself. Cody had "snake-oil sales" written all over him, but Sara . . . Sara was wholehearted. When she shifted her gaze around the room, making eye contact with one delegate after another, it no longer felt like a cheap trick being used to sell an idea. It felt personal. It felt real.

Her eyes locked with Sam's from across the room and for a moment he froze, seized by sudden alarm.

Can she tell what I was thinking? he wondered, then dismissed the thought immediately as she moved to the next person. Of course she can't. She's just good at what she does, that's all. I should be taking notes. I could do with being this persuasive when I get home and start looking for a new job.

"Before I officially welcome you to this dinner," Sara continued, "I would like to make sure that everyone is on equal footing. In this room we have the technologists: the software developers, the engineers, and the programmers. We have the leaders: the politicians, the state representatives, and the chief executives.

We have the visionaries: the designers and the spiritually advanced. And we have the people who inhabit other disciplines or who defy categorization altogether.

You know that we have brought you here in search of new ways of thinking, doing, and being.

You know that I strive to bring people together, to forge and strengthen connections among different types of mind. Look around this room. Take a few moments to make eye contact with people you have never met. Let yourself question who they are, what they do, and what they have to offer this meeting. Resist any temptation to guess how the worth of your own offering compares to theirs. If you are here, in this room, we hold that you are equal."

Does that include the waiters? Sam watched the little army of staff members, who had retreated to the background for Sara's speech. He expected to see a few eye rolls, surreptitious checks of watches or phones, or just blank, indifferent faces. Instead, the whole line of waiters was rapt. They hardly even blinked as they hung on Sara's every word. Sam had never seen anything like it.

"To the outside world, people such as you are seen as the elite—high achievers, high earners, and perhaps even household names. To us, you are all those things—but you are also neophytes. No doubt some of you have been through a period of spiritual experimentation. Maybe you've done some meditation, you might even have done a Vision Quest before—but believe me, there is no journey quite like this one.

During the next ten days, we are going to work together to turn simple concepts into radical ones. Concepts such as openness, acceptance, and honesty.

Everyone believes that they understand these words. Most people would even claim that they practice, or at least they try to, these things in day-to-day life. But we believe that we can all go further. We can do more. We can really live these claims."

Something drew Sam's eye across the room full of still listeners. Perhaps it was a tiny flicker of movement or perhaps just an awareness of a reaction. Whatever the reason, he turned his head a little and caught sight of Nina in a shimmering blue cocktail dress. To the casual onlooker she might have seemed to be listening with polite interest, but Sam had learned a little about the facial expressions of Nina Gould. That careful politeness was accompanied by a slight raise of her left eyebrow, always a sure sign that in the privacy of her own head she was eviscerating the arguments being made by the speaker.

Sara extended a slender arm in a sweeping gesture toward the buffet. "The first step in your journey will be to free your bodies from the many poisons and inhibitors that we are guilty of consuming. To help you on your way, we've designed tonight's dinner to reflect the diet of our ancestors. Everything you'll eat tonight is natural, free range, and organic. It's hunted, gathered, and prepared by hand—we know the origins of this food from start to finish and can provide that information if you like. Your journey into FireStorm begins now. Enjoy!"

The gong sounded again and the curtains swirled back into place, concealing Sara.

As one, the servers surged forward and lifted the lids on the oversized dishes, filling the room with the mouthwatering aromas of braised meats and vegetables. Sam had taken the precaution of remaining close to the tables, so he was one of the first to grab a plate and start loading it. There were whole fish baked in salt, chargrilled chicken cooked with lime and mango, along with roasted beets, carrots, and squash. Slabs of pink steak were piled next to a vast volcanic stone, so hot that the air above it shimmered. One by one the servers threw the steaks onto the stone and seared them exactly to each person's satisfaction. Sam took his well done, with a hearty scoop of avocado salsa on the side.

"Blue, please." Sam heard Nina's voice behind him, just as he was about to move away from the steak server. He decided to wait until she had her food, then ask her what she had made of everything they had just heard.

"Really standard nonsense," she said, taking a bite of the barely cooked meat. "Mmm, this is good. This would be absolutely perfect with a decent glass of red wine. I'm not impressed by all this fruit juice."

"Is that what it is?" Sam examined his newly refreshed blue drink. "I thought it was a bit weak."

"Did Jefferson not tell you what to expect, or were you just not listening? This is how the whole thing's going to work.

The entire Vision Quest. No booze. It's a toxin that you can't allow into the temple of your body or some such shit. Same with anything starchy—no bread, no rice, and no potatoes—nothing agriculture or processed. If you can't just stab it or pick it off the tree, you won't be eating it until you're home."

Sam's shoulders drooped. "Damn. Jefferson said something about purifying ourselves, but I thought he just meant meditating and stuff. I thought getting off your face on fermented fruit was an accepted spiritual practice in ancient religions."

"Depends on which ones you're picking and choosing from, I suppose. Where's your protégé?"

Realizing that he did not know, Sam scanned the room until he spotted Julia Rose at the other end of the tables, heaping her plate with grilled asparagus and courgette and chatting to Cody. "Over there," he said, nodding toward her. "On the case, by the looks of it. How about Purdue, where's he?"

"Upstairs ordering room service. He has a migraine."

They lapsed into an awkward silence. The natural next step should have been for Sam to dig for a little more information about Nina and Purdue's relationship, but he couldn't quite bring himself to do it, and she couldn't quite bring herself to volunteer it.

Instead they picked at their food and watched the other delegates. Some had splintered into little groups of people they already knew. Others were clearly feeling more isolated and either standing alone, feigning interest in the catering or the draperies, or attempting to start desperate, socially anxious conversations.

Sara had reappeared and was gliding among the delegates, pausing for brief conversations in which she would lay a delicate hand on the subject's arm or shoulder, or clasp their hand in hers. Her exchanges with them were intense, her gaze locked with theirs, and then in a moment she would be gone, moving to the next person. To Sam, it looked like a lot of hard work. He found himself speculating about what a life like hers must be like, with every aspect of her work persona so carefully cultivated and so well performed. He was extremely glad that no one expected him to be so poised or so groomed in everyday life.

"Sara! Hey, Sara!" Cody's nasal Valley twang sliced through the gentle babble of small talk.

"We have a question over here that I think you should answer—and I think everybody would want to hear it."

All eyes turned in the direction of his voice. Julia Rose was cringing next to him, her hands half-raised as if she had tried and failed to stop him from attracting the attention of the entire room. Sara strode toward them, the crowd parting before her.

"A question?" her voice remained smooth and gentle, though it carried to ever part of the room. "By all means . . . Julia Rose, isn't it?"

Julia Rose's eyes widened. Evidently she had not expected Sara to have any idea who she was. "Um, yes . . . " she gulped, then took a deep breath and tried to recover her composure. "I don't mean to be rude, Ms. Stromer—"

"Sara."

"Sara. Ok. I don't mean to be rude, Sara, but I was just asking about the rumors about FireStorm. You know. The ones about people not being allowed to leave once they get involved and having to give really personal information and money if they want to progress to higher levels."

For a long, long moment, no one made a sound. Sara, smiling beatifically, tilted her head to one side in apparent contemplation of the question.

Then at last she straightened and spoke. "Thank you, Julia Rose—not just for asking those questions in the first place, but for having the courage to ask them openly, in front of the whole group. That was a brave thing to do. Before I answer, I would like you to do something for me. I would like you to drink with me. Will you do that?"

Julia Rose nodded with a confidence that Sam was sure was false. Sara snapped her fingers and one of the servers scurried off and returned with a small stone bottle and two carved obsidian glasses.

Into these, Sara poured a creamy white liquid. She held one out to Julia Rose, then locked eyes with her while they drank. It's just two people drinking, Sam thought. It's funny how making it a bit ritualistic gives it power. I can see it's affecting Julia Rose—she's totally caught up in all this, I can tell. Poor girl can barely stand up straight. Still, she'll learn a lot.

"Now, to answer your question," Sara continued. "Of course, we don't force anyone to stay in FireStorm. Joining us is entirely voluntary, and there are some people who come to our earliest courses and decide that what we offer is not for them—at least, not yet.

Once people have joined, they tend to stay. It's not through any coercion, but through a simple lack of desire to leave us. As for the sharing of personal information . . . What we do, what we encourage our members to do, involves a high level of self-awareness and trust. Those things can't be achieved without getting a little personal—but again, these are free choices that our members make."

She turned in a slow circle, taking in the whole room. "No doubt there are plenty of you who have questions just like Julia Rose's, but who felt less able to ask.

Or perhaps she simply beat you to it. Either way, this is why we have brought you here. The best way to understand FireStorm is to experience it.

There are questions to which you'll never have a satisfactory response without living the answer. That's what we have chosen to give you. We hope that you'll choose to give us your trust in return."

As she finished, she stepped toward Julia Rose and enfolded her in a tight embrace. Julia Rose froze briefly, taken by surprise—then, to Sam's astonishment, wrapped her arms around Sara and allowed herself to be held close.

CHAPTER 8

As dawn broke the following morning, Sam joined the line of FireStorm delegates staggering out of the Verbena into the first rays of Las Vegas sunshine. It was too early to be up, and judging by the amount of squinting and groaning that was going on, Sam had not been the only one to retreat to his room and drain the mini bar following the welcome dinner.

"Mr. Sam Cleave?"

Sam lifted his head to see one of the hotel's perky young employees flashing her perma-grin at him. She was one of three people standing a little way outside the Verbena, between the doors and the waiting luxury coaches.

Two others were holding large trays full of Starbucks cups. The girl who had spoken picked up one of the drinks and held it out. It had his name written on the cardboard.

"Breakfast tea with a little milk and three white sugars, is that correct?" She pressed the cup into his unresisting hand, then a look of horror flashed across her face. "Oh no! It's four, isn't it? Four sugars. Oh, I'm so sorry, Mr. Cleave. Here!" She dived into the pocket of her blazer and pulled out an extra packet of sugar and a long wooden stirrer. The smile returned. "You have a great trip, now!"

The young woman turned her attention to the person behind Sam, greeting him by name and reciting the type of drink she had anticipated he would require. He wanted to stop and ask how they had learned what he liked to drink, especially because he never frequented coffee shops, other than greasy spoons. Jefferson could have told them, I suppose, he thought, eavesdropping as the person behind him was given a triple latte with hazelnut syrup. But still, it's a lot of effort to go to.

Drink in hand, he allowed himself to be marshaled onto the coach. It was nothing like his previous experiences of buses. There was nothing resembling normal bus seats— instead the interior was ringed with leather couches.

At the far end, a large screen showed landscapes from around the world, accompanied by a gentle ripple of soothing string music.

Out of habit, he looked around to see if any of the others were aboard the same coach, but they were not. Jefferson and his family were visible in the coach parked parallel, and Sam saw Purdue and Nina being ushered aboard the same vehicle. Of Julia Rose, there was no sign. Sam guessed that she must be aboard the third coach. Grateful for the peace and quiet, he dropped into a corner and rested his eyes, just for a moment.

✠✠✠

Nina had succeeded in getting her cup of weak, milky tea changed for a double espresso. The tea tasted wrong here, but the coffee was strong and the caffeine hit welcome. Or at least it had been at the time. Now she watched the other passengers beginning to nod off within minutes of being assigned their seats on the plane, and she envied them. She was now alert, her nerves jangled, and her body tense. Sticking to a single espresso might have been a better idea, she thought.

The North Las Vegas Airport stretched beyond the windows toward the distant mountains. It hardly seemed worth loading everyone on the Boeing 737 SX-VIP for such a short journey, though Nina could imagine that she would feel otherwise if faced with the prospect of traveling the whole way by coach

—and she could not deny that there was a certain decadent delight in taking such a brief flight in such a fancy aircraft. She stretched out in the spacious seat, luxuriously upholstered in soft white leather, and spread a cashmere blanket the color of butterscotch across her lap. Even in the cool breeze of the cabin's air conditioning, it was nowhere near chilly enough to warrant a blanket, but it seemed a pity not to make use of it.

This is crazy, she thought, as she settled her head on the small white pillow. I'm not one of these people. They're rich, successful, and used to stuff like this. And I'm . . . not. I'm an under-employed, underpaid academic—well, ex-academic, I suppose—and before I met Purdue I'd never experienced anything like this. Damn it! I have got to get used to calling him Dave. It's been a month now; it's ridiculous still to be thinking of him as Purdue when we're—

Her train of thought was abruptly derailed by Purdue's sudden appearance beside her.

He had been looking around the plane and was enthusing about it, babbling happily about its technical specifications and the ways in which it could be modified to incorporate all sorts of new software. Every single word of it went over Nina's head. "I thought your professional field was software and technology, not engineering?" she said.

"Oh, yes," Purdue nodded. "That's my primary area of expertise. Aviation is merely a hobby! But it is a fascinating one. I can't say that I've ever flown in this particular model before, but the pilot has kindly agreed to talk to me about his experiences."

"Let me guess—you're spending the flight in the cockpit? Again?"

Purdue dropped a kiss on the top of Nina's head. "You'll have company this time," he assured her. "I took care of it."

Before she could ask any questions or raise any objections, Purdue strode up the gangway and disappeared into the area marked "Cabin Crew Only." Nina hardly had time to register her annoyance before a flight attendant materialized to show another passenger to the seat beside her. She didn't even need to look up.

"Hello, Sam."

✠✠✠

Damn you, Dave Purdue. Damn your stupid, twisted sense of humor. Nina was torn between laughing and swearing under her breath as Sam slumped into the seat next to hers. She noticed that he looked around first to see whether any of the other seats were free, but he was the last person to board and there was no chance of his being reseated.

"Where's Purdue?" Sam asked eventually, when it became clear that the cabin crew was not going to tell him there had been a mistake and ask him to swap seats. "I'd have thought he'd be sitting here."

Nina shook her head, carefully keeping her face neutral. "He's in the cockpit."

She watched with increasing amusement as Sam tried to find the right way to phrase the questions he clearly wanted to ask. At length he gave up his search for something tactful, subtle, or original. "I thought that you and he were . . . er . . . that you were, you know . . . together? Was I wrong about that?"

"Oh, no!" She smiled sweetly, unwrapping a mint and offering one to Sam as the plane began its path along the runway. "We're here together. I wouldn't be attending this shindig if he hadn't invited me. As for whether we're together in the sense of, you know, together . . . I have no idea."

"Has it been going on for long?" Judging by the tone of Sam's voice, he was equally curious and reluctant to know the answer.

Nina sighed. "For fuck's sake, Sam, you know it hasn't. When's the last time we saw each other? March? April?

And you knew I wasn't seeing anyone then. I actually didn't cross paths with him again until July, if that's what's troubling you.

If you want the details, I was teaching at summer school, he was giving a talk at some STEM event, we were both at the same drinks reception, and he asked me out. I said yes. And here we are."

"Look, I'm not judging," Sam's tone was, to Nina's ears at least, a little defensive. "What you do is entirely your business. I'm just trying to make sense of it, that's all."

"Christ, you and me both."

In a display of unusual tact, Sam did not question Nina further. She felt a little bit bad. That response had been snappier than she had intended it to be, and she was irritated with herself—partly for sounding like a teenager trying to be enigmatic and partly for letting Purdue's little joke get to her.

The last thing she had expected was to run into Sam in Las Vegas, and the prospect of spending the next couple of weeks in close proximity to him, with Purdue engineering opportunities to leave them alone together just to see how they would react, did not make her happy.

I don't know why he thinks it's so bloody interesting anyway, she thought. It's not as if anything really happened between me and Sam. One kiss, that's all. I didn't think anyone was even paying that much attention. But then, Purdue never seems to miss a damn thing.

With a muffled roar, the plane glided smoothly from tarmac to air. Nina's fingers closed around the arms of her chair and dug in deep. Her mind with images of screaming passengers, of flashing lights, of the white hot fireball that the plane would surely become when it inevitably crashed. She had not always been such a terrible flyer. For a long time she had been able to keep her claustrophobia under control when traveling by air, but it had taken a turn for the worse after her experiences in the submarine during the Wolfenstein expedition, followed by a turbulent flight home from Ushuaia and then the disastrous confinement of Deep Sea One. She had not flown again until this trip to America. In retrospect, I should have done some short flights first, she thought, and got my hand in again. Doing another long-haul trip was insane.

She jumped as she felt a hand cover hers.

"Sorry!" Sam took his hand away again. "I just thought you might want—I remembered that it used to help you, having a hand to hold. I didn't think. Sorry."

"No, it's ok," she said, holding her hand out to him. "It's fine. You just took me by surprise, that's all. It does help. It really, really helps. I just hate feeling that if the plane goes down, I'm going to die alone."

"Well, you're not. All of these nice people will be right here with you, keeping you company. And if we're going to die, I promise you that I won't hold it against you if you break my fingers." He smiled. Despite herself, Nina smiled back. She wanted to hold onto her reluctant distance from Sam. Damn it, he was not supposed to interfere! He wrote that feature on Frank Matlock, advertising his book, knowing full well that Dr. Matlock had shafted Nina by stealing her work. It had damn near killed their friendship for good.

It took perilous experiences well beyond her acceptance and surreal terror under the thrall of an ancient relic to mend their fresh camaraderie. Then her subsequent emotional collapse ripped her from Sam's friendship and she had to make the harsh decision to distance herself long enough, to keep her episode utterly secret from all who knew her, and retreat into the drudgery of devising her next move in life.

And with all her plans in place, finally working out, Sam had to plummet back into her life.

The plane finished its steep ascent and settled into a comfortable cruise. Little by little, Nina relaxed her grip on Sam's fingers. She wondered whether she was being unreasonable. Leaving the faculty was a welcome blessing to freedom disguised as a suicidal move at the juncture her career had reached, at the time a bold decision while in the throes of severe emotional trauma and unsound resolve.

Besides, she had already been uncertain about her academic career. The harder she tried to be angry about her missed opportunity after Wolfenstein, the more certain she became that she had not lost anything that she really wanted. There would have been other opportunities, if she had really wanted them. And there were. The hunt for the Spear of Destiny was as equally glamorous as revealing the existence of a secret Nazi ice station. Besides, plenty of people managed to forge successful careers based on less momentous material. She could have continued along the tedious path she had been on, churning out publications just for the sake of it, going to the right conferences, and kissing the right asses.

It's just a bit of a funk, she told herself. Everyone goes through it at some point.

I'm sure that once I've had some time away from academia, I'll remember why I once thought it was my vocation. All I need is a different route to the same goal. God, I hope this is the right one this time.

The captain's voice came over the speaker, announcing the plane's descent. Nina realized that she still had not let go of Sam's hand. It had been a short flight, barely forty-five minutes, but still, she should not have left her hand in his the whole time.

She wondered whether it would be more awkward now to remove it or to leave it where it was. She decided in favor of leaving it where it was.

Taking it away would only draw attention to the awkwardness, and she did not want to risk him offering it again to comfort her during the landing.

✠✠✠

"Nina?" Sam touched her arm as she stood up to disembark.

"Yeah?"

"About the material we gathered on Deep Sea One . . . "

Nina shook her head as she slung her bag over her shoulder. "Not yet, Sam; soon, but not yet."

Sam was uncertain what that meant, but her tone was polite and serene and he trusted her to return later to that statement. A brisk nod was all he got from her, but he smiled, nonetheless, as she walked down the passage. Purdue had emerged from the cockpit. He smiled and greeted Sam as he passed, then Nina took his hand and they left the plane together.

CHAPTER 9

Welcome to Parashant!" Jefferson beamed, striding toward Sam with his heavy-looking, artfully rugged backpack held on one shoulder. "Looks like we'll have a nice cool day for building our camp! That's good. It's a lot more work getting it all set up when it's hot."

Sam, wilting in the Arizona heat, made no reply. All his energy was currently being divided between lugging his holdall and staying on his feet without dissolving into a puddle of whisky-flavored sweat. It might have been a cool day by Jefferson's standards, but at 22° C, it was far too hot for him.

After disembarking from the plane at Grand Gulch, the group had been met by a fleet of Jeeps and ferried along winding dirt roads. They had passed the signs for Parashant National Monument some time ago and were now far off the beaten track, leaving the edge of the Grand Canyon far behind. They found themselves in an expanse of parched wilderness, sparsely populated by scrub vegetation. Some way off, Sam thought he could make out the shimmer of water—he assumed that they must be close to a river, because they would need some source of water. However, he was not sure. In the blinding sunlight, with nothing to shield his eyes, the thing he took for water could just as easily have been rising heat.

The group of delegates contained a variety of people, such as Sam (clearly not use to the heat and exertion and already starting to feel dehydrated) to glossy, fit, and well-prepared individuals (looking as if they just stepped out of an air-conditioned gym). Among the latter group, Paige Daniels was clearly the leader.

Her crisp cotton shirt was not white, since Labor Day had passed, but it was such a pale shade of pink that it made little difference. Navy blue shorts revealed toned, tanned legs that could just as easily have belonged to her daughter.

Henley, however, had refused to shed her black attire. She was dressed in what appeared to be a partially destroyed ballet tutu and boots from Doc Martens. Her eyeliner was smudged across her left cheek.

"Dad, how far do we have to go?" she moaned. "Where's the base?"

"It'll be around here soon!" Jefferson lifted his daughter's wheeled suitcase. "Just as soon as we've built it. This wasn't the greatest choice, was it, honey? Why didn't you bring the backpack your mom gave you?"

"I'm not carrying that thing. It's butt ugly." She took the case from her father. It was a little too heavy for her, but she was determined not to concede that the backpack might have made her life easier. "So, are there going to be tents or something? Where are they?"

"Right over here, Miss Daniels," Cody called from a little way off. He was posing on a rock, well aware of the figure he cut in his stone colored shorts and white T-shirt with the clear blue sky as his backdrop. He looked like some kind of advertisement. Sam's dislike for him deepened just a little further, but he joined the delegates in moving obediently toward the pile of tent materials to which Cody was pointing.

As much as Sam hated being given orders and was not keen on physical labor, he was happy to pitch in and help with anything that would afford the group some shade from the intense sun.

His attitude was shared by many of the delegates. Within minutes everyone's belongings were heaped in a pile and hands that had not touched anything less refined than a keyboard in years were gripping long wooden tent poles and wielding spikes and mallets. Sam had decided that he would prefer to stick with the devil he knew, so he had sought out Purdue and chosen to work alongside him. There were no instructions telling them how to erect these tents, but he was willing to bet that Purdue would either know, or he would be swift to work it out.

Sure enough, Purdue had assembled a small team and was busy issuing instructions. He had found Nina and Julia Rose, but he had also recruited a stocky man with close-cropped, dark hair and a man, with a long, mopey face and a slight, premature paunch, whom Sam took to be one of the programmers. There was no time for introductions, not with the sun getting increasingly hot overhead. Purdue flitted among the members of the team, working out angles and making suggestions. He seemed to have had the foresight to fill a small notebook with instructions. Sam caught glimpses of it concealed in his palm as he moved around the group.

They were not the first group to finish. That honor went to a team led by Dylan Thoreau, the CEO of a massive social media network.

From what Sam had heard about him and succeeded in eavesdropping, it seemed that he had previously participated in several sweat lodges and presumably had experience in putting up these teepee-style tents. Nevertheless, it was too hot to care about finishing first. As soon as they were certain that the tent was stable, Sam dived gratefully into the shade.

Soon Cody appeared at the flap of the tent with an armful of empty waterskins. He carried out a swift head count of the little group and left a skin for each person. The stocky man, speaking in a heavy eastern European accent that Sam found difficult to place, gathered them and offered to fill them at the river.

"Anyone know who that guy is?" Sam asked in a whisper, as soon as he thought the man was out of earshot. "I haven't seen him before. Is he one of the FireStorm people?"

Purdue shook his head. "Not at all, Sam. He's my new bodyguard—well, reasonably new—no more than a couple of months. Kai is his name. Kai Gretzsky."

"Wait—your bodyguard?" Nina said. "How is it possible that I didn't realize you had a new bodyguard?"

Flashes of Calisto Fernandez, his last bodyguard, seeped into Nina's mind. She briefly remembered the woman who saved her from getting shot in the face by a Norwegian henchman. She realized that Purdue was on his third bodyguard in as many years.

"I asked him to keep his distance, because you didn't get on with the first one." Purdue's tone was bright, but Nina shuddered at the memory of Ziv Blomstein, the first bodyguard to protect Purdue, some time ago during the Antarctic trip. Much taller and more physically imposing than his current successor, Blomstein had been a silent, threatening figure who had been ready to kill Nina during their time on the submarine as they escaped the ice station. Despite his eventual act of self-sacrifice that had saved them all, Nina had good reason to feel uneasy at the mention of Blomstein's name.

"We tried to find a way for him to continue protecting us from a distance while we are out here," Purdue continued, "but it simply proved too difficult. Straightforward enough in a hotel, but considerably less easy in the desert. Here, he will simply have to share my accommodations."

"Remind me to stay near you," the young man chimed in. "Oh, right. I haven't introduced myself. Sorry. I'm Hunter Sherwood. I'm a programmer for Kari. You've probably seen my boss, Sakura, around."

"Sakura Ito?" Julia Rose asked. "Oh, my god, she's amazing! I was so excited when I saw she was here. How come you're with us? No offense, but if I had a connection to Sakura Ito, I'd be right there trying to impress her."

Hunter grimaced and shifted a little closer to the door, fanning himself with the flap of the tent. "Hmm. She's ok, but I'm avoiding her right now. If she'd picked one of the people who actually wanted to be here instead of doing random selection, I'd be at home right now. Sorry. I know you probably really want to be here. I'm just not really into this kind of stuff."

As Kai returned with the waterskins and everyone proceeded to quench their thirsts, Hunter held forth. He quizzed the others about what they knew of the organization and was delighted to hear that none of them knew anything that had not come straight from Sara, Cody, or Jefferson. Sam shot a questioning look at Julia Rose, wondering why she was not telling Hunter about her research, but she replied with an almost imperceptible shake of the head and he did not push it further.

It seemed that Hunter was extremely skeptical about the claims that FireStorm was making about "bringing the world together." He believed that there was nothing to the organization but marketing—packaging spirituality and wisdom in fancy ways so that they could be marketed as luxury goods.

"It's bullshit," he stated flatly. "These people who buy into it, they're the ones with a ton of time and money, right?

They've got time to sit around worrying about whether they're connected to other people's unique special snowflakeness, or whatever it is. The rest of us . . . do we care? I don't know about the rest of you, but I don't have time to care. And if being spiritually connected is going to cost me tens of thousands of dollars, I can't afford it. I'll just have to settle for being disconnected.

"But you know the worst thing? It's not even about that. People have been selling this togetherness stuff for years, ever since the hippies, maybe even earlier, but these people have taken it to the next level! Word is that they're trying to get people to integrate or some shit, and you have to get all their software and products to do it. I've never before heard of any religion that needed an app."

"But plenty of religious apps exist, don't they?" Nina was constitutionally incapable of letting a badly formulated argument slip by. "When I set my phone up, the most popular free apps available were the Bible and the Quran."

Hunter's pudgy face rounded into a smug smile. "They exist," he said, oblivious as Nina bristled at his condescending tone. "Of course, they exist. But they're not mandatory. You can be a Christian and not have a Bible app on your phone. But you can't join FireStorm without using the company app, which means going through the complete sign up. And yeah, it's free . . . but did nobody ever tell you that if you're not the paying customer, you're the product?"

It was clear from Hunter's tone that he believed that he had just delivered the slam dunk that would leave Nina with no possible retort, but before he could bask in his victory, Purdue gave a gentle chuckle.

"That might be true of certain types of apps," he said, pushing his round glasses back up the bridge of his nose. "Indeed, there are many that serve no other purpose. But I think you are mistaken where FireStorm is concerned, Hunter. If there is a mandatory app to which all members are expected to subscribe, it is certainly a small part of a larger package, and you will find that its users are paying for it in other ways. To run such a large operation as this, simply in order to mine data . . . I simply can't see how it would be financially viable."

"Dude, do you even know how much people are willing to pay for that kind of data?"

Sam couldn't help himself. He laughed aloud. Hunter looked deeply offended and started to pull himself up onto his knees, preparing to leave in search of a more sympathetic tent.

"Sorry, pal," Sam said, laying a conciliatory hand on Hunter's arm. "No need to go. I'm not laughing at you. It's just that if you knew this man, you'd know that he's probably the one person who knows the exact retail price on people's data, because he's the one who pays it. He's a mad bastard who likes to know everything about everyone, and he's probably done his homework on you too."

Julia Rose looked shocked. A couple of days in Las Vegas had not been sufficient for her to figure out the dynamics between Sam, Nina, and Purdue. She did not yet know how they worked, or how far Sam could go without provoking Purdue's ire. If truth be told, Sam himself did not know—but he was interested to find out.

Not a flicker of discomposure showed on Purdue's face. He merely nodded in acknowledgment. "Sam is quite correct," he said. "When I require information about someone, I pay well for it."

Hunter looked as though he did not want to believe that he was sharing his space with someone who would perpetuate data mining. Sam had never seen anyone look at Purdue with such evident judgment. "Well, at least you won't have much on me," Hunter spoke with absolute certainty. "I dedicate a lot of time to making sure my online footprint is minimal. So if you've been paying someone for information about me, you've been wasting your money. Now I'm going to go and find out what's happening next. Excuse me."

With as much dignity as he could muster while dressed in Bermuda shorts that should have been left in the 1980s, Hunter ducked through the flap of the tent and disappeared in search of Cody. "Oh dear," said Sam. "I don't think that's the response he was expecting."

"What was he expecting?" Nina wondered. "You can't come to a place like this and expect to find a sympathetic ear for stuff like that. I mean, he's probably right, there probably is something incredibly cynical about all of this. I'd be more surprised if it wasn't an attempt to fleece people, to be quite honest. But still, I wouldn't have thought that being quite so loose-lipped about the idea that it's some kind of conspiracy is a great idea."

"As far as I can tell, what we just saw was the latest in a long line of ill-advised choices made by Mr. Sherwood," Purdue said, consulting what Sam had thought was a notebook. Instead, it turned out to be a small device resembling a tiny tablet computer, but extremely thin and capable of being folded.

When Purdue produced it from his pocket it was the size of a matchbook, but he deftly unfolded it until it was the length of his hand.

His strokes on its surface as he searched for information were more of a caress than a swipe.

"Hmm. Yes. If Hunter's everyday intelligence were equal to his programming ability, he might be a dangerous man.

Certainly he would be running KNCT in Ms. Ito's place. And he would surely realize that refusing to use Facebook is considerably more effective if you don't spend a great deal of time blogging about how you don't use Facebook."

CHAPTER 10

A dozen small tents peppered the desert sand, their poles reaching up toward the clear blue sky. These had been designated as the delegates' sleeping areas, four or five to a tent. A little way off, they had cleared an area of scrubby vegetation to erect a larger structure, more akin to a yurt in shape than to a teepee, though still constructed of the same red cedar and bison hides as the sleeping tents. This tent, large enough to contain everyone, would be the focal point of all meetings, rituals and "connections." Sam had cringed a little when Cody had said the word "connections" with no apparent awareness of how incredibly vacuous the whole thing sounded, but he had played his part in raising the tent without complaint.

Jefferson had led the building of the connection tent.

Flashing his dazzling smile at the assembled delegates, he threw himself heart and soul into motivating and guiding the group. When they needed an outside eye to instruct them in where to place a pole or how taut to pull a rope or a hide, he stepped back and called out to them in his best public-speaking voice. Whenever they would benefit from another pair of hands, or when the mood of the group threatened to sour and turn against their current leader, he would be right there working alongside them, putting his back into the heaviest of work and encouraging his family to do the same.

Based largely on her put-together appearance and her precise, regulated manners, Sam had not expected Paige to embrace the kind of work they were doing. Seeing her in action, though, he had to admit that he had misjudged her. She matched her efforts perfectly to her husband's. Her smile never wavered, and her contribution to the work was far from negligible. Even Henley seemed to be in good form.

For all her teenage cynicism and the little rebellions that Sam had witnessed at close quarters, she had spent a lifetime being trained by her parents to behave well when people were watching. Sam began to see how they would function as a political family, if Jefferson pursued his ambitions.

He wondered briefly whether the family's involvement with FireStorm would help or hinder them, but before his mind could wander too far down that path he was called on to help shift the central pole, and the physical exertion to which he was so unaccustomed demanded the entirety of his attention.

✠✠✠

As soon as the tent-building was finished, there was a mass migration down to the river. It had been hot work, and most of the delegates were now sticky with sweat. Sam's hair was plastered to his head and his throat was like sandpaper. He had emptied the contents of his waterskin before work on the main tent had even begun, and now he wanted nothing more than to down mouthful after clear, cool mouthful of river water. He cupped his hands and scooped it into his mouth, over and over again, until his thirst was quenched and he was ready to go downstream and join the others who were already wading to cool off. The water was brackish and cold despite the beating sun, and Sam plunged into it gratefully.

By the time he surfaced he was a little giddy from the change in temperature and the roar of the water in his ears. He took a step toward the bank, but his foot landed on a slippery rock and he lost his balance, collapsing sideways into the water.

As he fell he was vaguely aware that he had barely missed a collision with someone next to him, and he scrambled to his feet to apologize.

"Don't worry about it, Sam," Sara's melodious voice washed over him.

She stood up to her hips in the water, her long, dark hair soaked and glistening in a long braid down her back.

Her long, loose cotton shift clung to her golden skin. "Are you suffering in this heat? This is tame for Parashant, but I remember that you mentioned how warm you were finding Montana. I can only imagine how you're finding it here."

"It's . . . it's fine." As hard as he tried, Sam was struggling to maintain eye contact. "I know this must be really mild for you. I've read about how hot it gets out here. But where I come from, this is heat-wave temperature. This is when Scottish people just lie in darkened rooms with a fan pointed at them. Or we strip off and bake ourselves until we're pink, but I always favored the darkened room, myself."

"I believe you," Sara smirked, looking him up and down. "I'm sure you'll get used to it soon enough, but until you do, here's a hint—pure cotton is your best friend just now. If it's thoroughly soaked, it won't provide any insulation at all.

It'll just trap all the moisture, which will keep you cool, and it'll dry slower than that blended fabric that you're wearing, buying you a few more precious minutes of cooling. If it's a loose garment, it'll work even better. Something like . . . mine, for instance." She smoothed the drenched cloth over her body in a gesture so unsubtle that Sam was extremely glad that he was standing in deep, cold water. "If you don't have anything with you, talk to Cody. We always bring a few spare shirts along for anyone who needs them. You'll be glad of it, especially at night."

As she strolled off downstream, Sam plunged back under the water. When he reemerged, Nina was watching him with an amused grin on her face. "Was that you getting converted?" she inquired politely.

"Something like that," Sam said. "I might yet be convinced about all this connection malarkey."

✠✠✠

As he headed back toward the connection tent, a delicious aroma of cooking hit Sam's nose. His stomach growled urgently. He had not even noticed that he was getting hungry, not while he had been so busy attending to his other needs, but now he found himself ravenous. He joined the line of people filing into the tent and gratefully accepted a bowl of some kind of stew. He had no idea what it was.

There were definitely lentils, and as he took an eager mouthful he could taste herbs that his uneducated palette was at a loss to identify. All he knew was that it was food, and it was delicious, even if it was vegetarian.

Once he had scraped the last remains from his bowl, he set it down on the reed-strewn floor where he sat cross-legged. Only then did it occur to him to wonder where the food had come from. It was being served by Cody from a large cauldron suspended over a fire pit near the center of the tent, but Sam could not imagine that so much food could have been prepared by one man, with apparently no counter space or storage for ingredients, in such a short time. It had been less than an hour since the connection tent had been finished, and at that point the fire pit had not even been constructed.

Or had it? Sam leaned over to get a better look at it. Beneath the rough hewn stones he could just make out a base of breeze blocks. As the fire began to burn a little lower he could see the soot and carbon markings on the stone, darker and more deeply ingrained than he would have expected to see on a newly constructed pit. I suppose they built it for a previous Vision Quest, he thought.

Makes sense. If they always bring their groups to the same place, it would save time and material just to have this already built and covered up.

I'm still not sure where they conjured up the food from, though. It tasted fresh, but what do I know? That's probably just because it was healthy. That must have been pre-prepared. There's no way Cody could have made this much so quickly.

"Ok, people!" Cody clapped his hands together, calling for everyone's attention. "Thanks for all your hard work today. It's been great to see everyone bonding so quickly—you did a great job of getting the teepees up real fast! Isn't this place great? I love Parashant, I really do. I think I love it a little more every time I come here. Isn't it just the most beautiful place?" He waited for a response. A ripple of nods and murmurs went around the room, punctuated by a few more emphatic agreements.

"Now, here's what's going to happen, ok? First of all, we're going to come around and collect all your phones, tablets, computers, watches, and anything else you can use to communicate with the outside world or subscribe to the concept of time. Don't worry, you'll get 'em back! This is just for the first few days, while you get use to being out here and focusing on communicating and connecting with one another.

Once you're all accustomed to making true, genuine connections with the people here in front of you, it'll be time to start integrating that process into how you interact with the outside world. By the time you leave Parashant, if you commit to what we're doing here, you'll be perfectly capable of connecting openly, honestly, truthfully, and fully with anyone you meet. The divinity in you will be able to meet with the divinity in them, no matter what means of communication you're using."

Sure enough, two of the FireStorm acolytes had started moving swiftly but discreetly among the delegates, carrying wicker baskets in which they collected the devices that people surrendered. "Don't you worry if you don't have your gadgets on you," Cody reassured them all. "We'll send someone to your teepees a little later on. Everything will be kept under lock and key, and that key will be on my person every minute of the day."

Sam's ancient brick of a phone was still in his backpack, but as the basket passed his way he took the opportunity to have a quick look at its contents. He guessed that the cheap, bottom-of-the-range smart phone that stood out among the brand new iPhones must belong to Julia Rose.

There was no sign of Purdue's tiny folding tablet, but Sam was not sure whether that was because it was buried under the larger devices, the basket had not been passed to him yet, or Purdue simply had not handed it over. Considering that it was likely to be some one-of-a-kind invention of his own, Sam was not sure whether Purdue would willingly hand it over.

"Later this evening," Cody continued, "right about sunset, we'll bring everyone back here and introduce you to this special, spiritual place. That's when we will start the first stage of our process. Now, I should warn you, it's not going to be easy.

Do any of you know how to start a fire? I mean, without matches or paraffin or pressing an ignition switch?

Friction. Friction is how you start that kind of a fire. It's hard work. It takes a while. It has to be done just right. Despite what you might have learned in Boy Scouts, you can't just grab a couple of random sticks, give them a little rub together, and expect something to happen. You've got to apply the friction in just the right places, blow gently at exactly the right moment, and give it just the right amount of space to breathe.

For some of you, tonight will feel easy because you've done something like this before—you've practiced mindfulness or meditation maybe, and you've got used to sitting with your fears and discomfort. For the rest of you, it's likely to feel like friction. But trust us. We know what we're doing, and we'll guide you through this. Let us help you through the friction, and we'll get you to the point where we generate the spark and kindle the FireStorm that will ignite your whole life and bring you into contact with the divinity in you."

CHAPTER 11

The horizon glowed a deep orange as the sun descended toward it. There had been no word about the exact time at which the evening's introductory event was due to begin—not that it would have mattered, because all devices that could be used to tell the time were now in Cody's keeping. Sam had asked a couple of people if they knew. Only one, CEO Ethan McCluskey of a social media start-up named Synergize, had seemed to have a clue. He had taken part in Vision Quests and other ceremonies before.

"You're supposed to just feel when the time is right," he'd said, with a finality that made Sam feel utterly stupid. How is that even possible? he had asked himself. How can an entire group of people just feel when the time is right, when they can't even tell what time it is? I'll just keep an eye on the others and figure it out that way.

It turned out that his concerns were unwarranted. As the light changed and began to tinge the valley with gold, the two young FireStorm acolytes emerged from the connection tent, each carrying drums. Sam wondered whether they were twins, they looked so alike—one was male, the other female, but their angular faces were nearly identical and it required a second glance at their athletic bodies to figure out which was which. They both sported long, loosely braided brown hair and wore matching white tunics. As one, they lifted the drums and began to walk around the outside of the tent, beating a rapid, energetic rhythm, an unmistakable signal that it was time for the ceremony to begin.

Unfortunately, Sam's vantage point was from behind one of the scrubby bushes uphill from the campsite, where he was attempting to answer the call of nature. By the time he had finished and scrambled back down the hill, the rest of the delegates were already inside. He looked around for his friends as he stepped inside, but before he could spot them he felt a hand on his shoulder. It was Cody. He pushed Sam down onto his knees like the other delegates and stooped to whisper in his ear "Deep breaths, Sam. Just match them to everyone else's and you'll be fine."

Sara walked among the kneeling figures in full ceremonial regalia. She was a spectacular sight to behold. Her long, white robe was streaked with red down the back and emblazoned with the same spiky, angular black sun Sam had seen on the curtains in Las Vegas on the front. Her feet were bare but her toes were decorated with gold rings. A long, heavy chain, hung around her neck and falling almost to her waist, had feathers and crystals suspended from it.

Her dark hair was loose, with flowers and more feathers woven into it, and a delicate filigree ornament encircled her head. She carried a tied bundle of herbs in one hand, which she held for a moment in the flames from the fire pit. It caught light, releasing a cloud of sweet, fragrant smoke. Slowly she circled the room, trailing the smudge stick through the air above the heads of the delegates, chanting gently as she went.

It was not in Sam's nature to feel at ease in this kind of environment, and he took his deep breaths with a certain self-consciousness. He listened carefully to the people around him and tried to synchronize his breathing with theirs, but they were slightly out of sync with one another.

He picked one to follow at random, feeling like a pillock as he half-closed his eyes and squinted at the others to see whether anyone else had their eyes closed.

He could not tell, so he closed his completely. At least I'll look like I'm getting into it, he thought, even if this isn't what I'm meant to be doing.

The drumming stopped. The tent was silent, apart from the gentle crackle of the fire, the rhythmic inhalation and exhalation, and the faint sound of Sara's footsteps through the sand. "Welcome," she said softly, her voice as warm and inviting as if it had been an individual address. "We find ourselves now in a place of harsh, unforgiving beauty. It is the perfect place to connect with the divinity within you—a place that can be as unyielding as you are toward yourselves, where we must rely on one another and on ourselves without distraction or assistance from the outside world. You will leave here stronger and also kinder, more self-sufficient and less alone."

"Long before the Native Americans, the Paleo-Indian considered this land to be sacred. Each year, as the seasons turned and the summer heat began to descend, the tribes who inhabited this place would move from the shelter of the Grand Canyon to the higher elevation to find the cooler, fresher air of the mountain forests. This area was part of their sacred route, and they documented it in the form of paintings, petroglyphs, that have been preserved to this day.

They show us images of gatherings, of the confluence of energy being focused on a central point.

"They suggest that the type of ritual we carry out on this spot might well have been part of their lives—that we are a part of a tradition dating back more than 13,000 years. They knew then that this place—this earth shaped by volcanic fire, torrents of water, and the ceaseless rush of air—was the perfect meeting point between the human and the divine. They might have believed that they were communing with gods who existed as external forces. We, however, know that there is no separation between the human and the divine—except that which we choose to allow and create for ourselves."

As she sent more scented smoke drifting gently across the still air, Sara told tales of the Paleo-Indian and later the Native American tribes who had occupied Parashant. It seemed a little convenient to Sam that the names of these tribes had been "lost to history" but that their mythology had been passed down perfectly intact. Nevertheless, even his natural tendency toward pedantry had trouble standing up against the spellbinding atmosphere woven by Sara's words.

"Legend has it that Parashant was once the territory of an angry god," she half-whispered, "a fire god.

He made his home in one of the volcanoes that once set the valley ablaze. A neighboring volcano was inhabited by a beautiful fire goddess, and she was his lover.

For a time they were happy, until a great storm came.

The lightning god fell in love with the fire goddess, and when she refused to be his, he lashed out in a jealous rage, sending a bolt of his lightning deep into her volcanic home. It struck her in the heart. She died instantly, and her volcano cooled and became nothing more than a mountain.

"The fire god was devastated. The explosive glory of his volcano brought him no joy without his lover to share it, and the best he could do was send thin streams of lava trickling downhill like fiery tears. So it remained for a thousand years, until the first condor chose this path for its annual migration. They call these noble birds California condors, but the evidence of their presence in Arizona predates that of California by millennia. This condor flew high above the fire god's home, saw the marks of his grief on the scorched earth, and called out to the fire god to ask the cause of his grief.

"The fire god was so accustomed to his lonely solitude that at first he was taken back, but as he told the condor the circumstances of his pain, he began to feel friendship for the kind bird. At last he ceased to cry, and the ground cooled.

But the lightning god, who still considered himself a rival to the fire god, was angry and jealous of their bond. He threw another bolt, which caught the tip of the condor's mighty wings and send it spinning to earth, where it crashed into the ground. The lightning god left the bird for dead, certain that the cold night would kill the condor and leave the fire god alone once again.

"The condor felt the chill of the night air on its feathers and knew that without being able to fly to safety, it would certainly die on the cold rock, either freezing while the sun was gone or becoming the prey of a coyote. The bird called out to the fire god that it would be sorry to leave him to his solitude. At the prospect of further loneliness, the fire god began again to weep. Trails of molten rock cascaded down the mountainside, warming the earth beneath the condor, warming its body so that the cold night could do it no harm. When coyotes dared to approach, the fire god spat at them, gobbets of liquid flame that sent them scurrying for the shadows. Day after day, night after night, the fire god protected the condor until its body healed and the bird was able to soar through the skies once more.

"Their friendship continued for many years. The condor's migration path took him back and forth across the fire god's territory, and they spent a great deal of time together.

There were no secrets between them. They knew the innermost depths of each other's hearts. But sadly, the condor was mortal and the god was not, so eventually the condor's life came to an end. When the bird realized the end was near, it flew to the fire god's home and lay once more on the warm volcanic earth, taking comfort in the presence of the fire god, and then it died.

"The fire god, in his grief, took a handful of his friend's feathers and consumed them so that a part of the condor would always live in him, and, for a brief time, his fire burned black. He sent forth a mighty blaze of black fire and magma into the sky to mark the condor's passing, and it is from this that we take the name FireStorm. We seek to emulate the example of the fire giant and the condor, who found closeness and connection, who knew true friendship, and who lived interconnected lives."

That explains the logo, then, Sam thought. It must have been easier to use the black fire than the condor. Sara had fallen silent. She bowed her head, one hand clasped over her heart as if the telling of the story had taken everything she had to give. Sam looked at Cody, expecting him to step in and take over the proceedings, but he did not.

He knelt close by, watching Sara intently, until she raised her head again.

He passed her a small cup of water, which she accepted gratefully and sipped at gently.

"I have shared with you the story on which FireStorm is based. I should now tell you a little about who we are, who I am. We are a comparatively new organization—or at least, we are a new iteration of an old set of ideas. FireStorm has been called a religion. I don't know about that. A belief system, certainly, nut it's a belief system based on connections made by living beings, not on blind faith and the idea that a better world awaits us when we die. We are concerned with bringing connection back to a disconnected world."

She began to tell her own story. It was the typical history of a high achiever—Sara was the child of a lower middle-class family. She had worked hard, won a scholarship to Yale, and then worked her guts out to pay her living expenses. She had graduated at the top of her class, then moved to England to do her MBA at the London School of Economics. By the time she was twenty-five, she had made her first million dollars. She had gone on to lead Fortune 500 companies, frequently being pursued for other leadership positions. She had considered herself an excellent networker and an extremely successful person. By thirty-five, numerous publications had named her as one of the world's greatest businesswomen.

Of course, like so many people experiencing great professional success, her personal life had been a disaster. Her dedication to her work had left her little time for any form of distraction.

She had assumed that eventually her meteoric rise would come to an end, and that when her career hit its plateau, she would find the time for a relationship, perhaps even a family. Until then, she would continue to work insane hours, sleeping only a few hours a night.

Eventually she had burned out. On her doctor's advice she had planned a holiday, but taking time off meant putting in some long days before her vacation began. After fourteen hours in her Manhattan office she had set off for the Hamptons, where she had located a beach house to relax in. She never arrived. Physically and mentally exhausted, Sara had dozed off at the wheel of her Lexus.

"I woke up in the back of an ambulance," she said. Her hand strayed unconsciously to the tiny scar on her cheek. "I was covered in blood. I had three broken ribs and a fractured collarbone, and also little cuts all over me. The EMTs kept asking me who they ought to call . . . and I couldn't give them an answer.

There was my mother, back in Indiana, but what could she do from there? Calling her in the middle of the night would only have worried her, and it wouldn't have given me a hand to hold as the doctors stitched up my cuts and reset my bones. There was no one in my everyday life whom I knew well enough to ask. That was a heartbreaking moment.

"I knew then that I had become completely disconnected from myself and from everything that really mattered, and that no amount of money or success was going to comfort me when I found myself in an early grave. Things had to change. When I recovered, I went in search of my spiritual path. Along the way I found FireStorm, back in its earliest stages, and I'm proud to say that I helped the organization to develop into what it is today."

For a moment, the tent was silent as Sara's speech came to an end. Then Cody began to applaud heartily, and the rest of the group quickly followed his lead. "Thanks, Sara!" he cried over the tumult. "Thanks for sharing such an inspiring, cautionary story with us! I've heard it plenty of times before, of course, but every single time I'm amazed and blessed by the honesty and openness you give to us. Now—who's going to be brave enough to do what Sara has just done and tell us about their own disconnection?"

CHAPTER 12

Oh god, Sam thought, not me, not me, not me, don't pick me. He shrank back into the sandy floor, hunching his shoulders and ducking his head as subtly as he could. He had not been so unwilling to volunteer since his school days, standing at the side of a freezing cold playing field, hoping not to be asked to captain a team. I've got nothing to say about my "disconnections." I'm not sure I want to hear other people talk about theirs, but if it means I don't have to talk about mine, that'll do me just fine.

Much to his surprise, the first person to raise a hand was Julia Rose. He was accustomed to her looking nervous, but this was a kind of nerves he had never seen her display. Rather than looking as if she was expecting to be thrown out, this time she looked as jittery as someone meeting an idol. At

Cody's prompting she got to her feet and told the group her name, then she spoke haltingly. "I, um . . . I don't have a long story or anything. I'd probably have to think for a little while to tell you about disconnection in my own life—I think I'm still just getting my head around the concept. But I just wanted to say, Ms. Stromer—that spoke to me. There's a lot about your story that I recognize, and . . . I really want to call my mom right now."

She sat down again hastily, her dark skin tinged with a deep blush, her eyes on the floor. Sara was only a little way from her, and she reached over to take Julia Rose's hand. That's twice now, Sam thought. I got the impression that Julia Rose's interest in Sara Stromer was more muckraking than hero-worshipping. Maybe I was wrong.

Others followed, sharing stories of their less proud moments. Some were common place—there were several who had realized that they seldom spoke to other people except online, or that they had forgotten their own birthdays until Facebook had reminded them. Others, such as Sara's, were a little more dramatic. Christopher Slack, a British MP still young enough to carry a layer of puppy fat that he had expected to shed after leaving Eton, told them of a long, dark night of the soul after his father had died.

He had missed the funeral due to his heavy workload, then visited the grave a few days later, when he had a horrible moment of epiphany. It hit him that his father was gone and his opportunity to say goodbye had passed.

As affecting as some of the stories were, Sam found his concentration beginning to wane. There was a certain element of repetition to what he was hearing, and after a while the stories simply blurred into a mass of first-world misery. The more he heard, the more convinced he became that he had never experienced real "disconnection." Even when Trish had died, he had felt loss and loneliness and pain, but he had always known that if he had really wanted companionship, he had a couple of people who would provide it. He wasn't close to his sister, but he knew that she would never turn him away if he needed her, and there was always Paddy.

"Sam, how about you?"

Sam's whole body tensed at the sound of Cody's voice. The gaze of the room turned on him, expectant, demanding. He cleared his throat a couple of times, feeling foolish. What am I doing here again?

"Er . . . " Desperately he searched the recesses of his brain, searching for anything, any memory or experience that could be turned into a story that would satisfy the group.

He had nothing. The closest match he had was Trish's death, and he would not twist that in order to fit in with this crowd. "I don't think I've . . . er, you know, when I stop and think about it, I don't think I've ever been through that—disconnection, I mean."

"What do you mean, Sam?" Cody's twangy voice was as perky as ever, but Sam thought he detected an edge of irritation. "It's really a universal experience. Don't you find that online communication and heavy workloads have taken over your life?"

Sam shook his head. "Not really. Sorry. I'm not trying to be awkward or anything—and I'm not saying my experience is typical. I'm just a bit old-fashioned, I suppose. I never really got into online communication. When I want to connect with people I tend to just go for a pint with them."

"Ah!" Cody seized on Sam's words. "But are you able to connect with them without using alcohol as a crutch?"

"I've never really tried," Sam shrugged. "It's just what we do."

"As a way of coping with how much you work?"

"Er . . . possibly? I don't know. For the most part I've always liked what I do, so I've never really worried too much about separating work and life."

Cody stared at Sam, torn between disbelief and a desire to start aggressively fixing him. He took a step toward him, but Sara raised a hand, stopping him in his tracks.

She gave a slight shake of her head, and Cody backed down. "Well, Sam," he said, "I think those were some important realizations right there.

Sometimes it takes a little while to get as far as being able to recognize your own disconnection.

It's not easy. That's why this part is called friction. For some people, friction comes from working through their disconnections. For others, it's a process of learning to recognize them. Yours is going to take a little longer . . . " he gave Sam a grin so warm that it made him uncomfortable. "But we're here to work through it with you!"

✠✠✠

"Sam. Sam. Sam."

At first Sam was not sure whether the sound was real or not. It reached into the edge of his dreams, pulling him out of sleep and into reality, where he found himself in pitch darkness. He waited, completely still, for the whisper to happen again.

"Sam! Are you awake?"

Nina. It was Nina's voice. They had all been asked to sleep in the tent that they had helped to build, leaving Sam to share with Nina, Purdue, Julia Rose, and Hunter, who had dragged his blanket as far from the others as possible within the contents of the cramped teepee.

"Well, I am now," Sam sighed, rolling onto his back. He tried to focus, but it was too dark.

"Do you want a cigarette?" She rattled the packet and Sam heard the comforting sound of sweet nicotine calling his name. He crawled out from under his blanket and followed Nina as they fumbled their way toward the tent flap and out onto the sand. A fat, waxing Moon cast an ethereal glow over the landscape, providing them with almost enough light to see where they were going. Nina had a light of some kind— Sam could not see what she was holding, but he could see the small pool of light cast in front of her. He walked carefully in her footsteps, eyes on the ground to avoid the treacherous roots and tumbleweed that might be hiding in the night.

She led him down to the river, far enough from the camp that they would not disturb anyone with their conversation or their secondhand smoke. "Watch out for rattlesnakes," Nina warned Sam as she opened the packet and held it out to him.

"Are they around here? Do you have a light, by the way? I didn't pick up my jacket."

"Yes, here you go." She pulled a lighter from her pocket. "I think there are snakes here. If not, there's plenty of other deadly stuff—coyotes and the like, scorpions. Don't sit on a scorpion, will you?" As she lit his cigarette, Sam noticed that the device he had assumed was a light was actually Purdue's little folding tablet.

"I thought we were supposed to hand all our gadgets in?" Sam said, taking a grateful puff.

"Fuck that," Nina settled herself on a large, flat rock by the river and pulled off her shoes to dangle her feet in the water. "It would take more than some vague nonsense about 'connection' to persuade Dave to go give minutes without this. It's his favorite toy just now." She paused, waiting for Sam to speak, and then it struck her that the topic might be a little awkward. "So what did you make of all that stuff this evening?" She reached for the first alternative subject she could think of. "I wanted to look over and see how you were taking it, but I knew if I made eye contact with you I'd end up laughing and get us both in trouble."

"What, you mean you weren't sold on all the 100 percent genuine, definitely not made up some time in the 1960s Native American mythology? You do surprise me."

"It just pisses me off," she said. "I'm not keen on the idea of making money by selling a watered-down version of someone else's culture. To be honest, I nearly balked at the whole thing when Dave invited me to join him for a Vision Quest. I came because I wanted to see whether it's possible for these things to be done with any kind of integrity or respect for the history that they're laying claim to."

Sam laughed gently. "Of course, you did. Spoken like a true history scholar, Nina."

She went quiet. It took Sam a moment to notice, because he was accustomed to lapsing into companionable silence with Nina, or breaks that occurred naturally while they both smoked. She picked up a stone from the shale bank beside them and lobbed it into the water. "Not anymore," she whispered.

Little by little, in between long drags and long silences, Nina began to tell Sam what had happened after their last encounter at the university. After Matlock's book had come out to great fanfare, it left Nina in the unenviable position of being asked about it by staff and students. Had she known about Matlock's expedition? Was it true that she had been there too? Had she worried about Matlock when he insisted on going alone into uncharted areas of the ice station in search of Nazi artifacts? Knowing that she had been a much more proactive member of the expedition party than her boss —indeed, knowing that he had actually attempted to ensure that she would not be part of the expedition—Nina had found this galling. The fact that Matlock had appropriated her research and a handful of artifacts that rightly belonged to her and Sam made things even worse.

Sam nodded. He remembered how upset she was by being done in and he still felt bad about helping Matlock with his book and causing a rift between him and Nina's possible romance. But he knew that they had put that behind them during the last collaborative journey. Still it vexed her, of course, because it was the genesis of her resentment.

"Then when my annual review came up, the bastard had the audacity to tell me that I wasn't an enthusiastic enough member of the team—as if we were ever a fucking team!

That department was a nest of vipers, not a team. And he said that the department wasn't happy that I'd taken a sabbatical before Wolfenstein! Never mind that if I hadn't, he wouldn't have his precious book.

Then he had all these shitty remarks about my shooting for tenure, of course disguising his smugness under a smooth delivery, which he thought sufficed as 'advice' . . . " she sneered and paused for a second, then continued her rant, "Anyway, he made all sorts of irritating comments about how I'd better start toeing the line a bit more if I wanted to have a career in academia, and said that maybe once my fellowship was up I should try a different university and maybe shift my focus to something along the lines of gender theory. It wasn't such bad advice, but coming from him . . . I'm not going to be told that I'm not allowed to write about anything other than the role of women in the Third Reich, especially not by him. I might not have been able to stop him cheating me, but I don't have to let him patronize me into the bargain." She looked up at the sky and under her breath she added, "Wish I could introduce that fucker to Calisto . . . "

Sam could not help but smile at the thought of Purdue's female ex-bodyguard leaping into Matlock's office, ripping his misogynistic face off in a comic book spill of justice.

Nina's anger spent, she took a deep breath and reached down to scoop some cool water in her cupped hands. She poured it straight over her head. It cascaded down her bobbed black hair and trickled onto her pale skin, catching the moonlight. "It's so hot," she said. "How are you coping? I'm melting out here."

Sam wondered about the new position he played in the Nina game. She was so nonchalant about it all, as if she had never noticed their closeness while working on the Spear of Destiny in Purdue's sinister laboratories. Alas, Sam decided to let it go and enjoy the fact that they were at least talking, that they were once more in each other's company.

"Where's your light? Take a look at this." Sam pulled up the side of his T-shirt to show Nina the heat rash that had been developing down his left side during the course of the day.

"Ouch. Well, I don't have that, at least. I might have no job; I might have torched any prospects I had of a career in academia by telling the head of my department to go fuck himself; I might have no clue what I'm doing with my life; but I haven't got a heat rash. Have you got anything to put on that? Of course, you haven't.

Try talking to Cody about it; he'll probably be able to give you something.

For a man who arrived here with nothing but a small backpack, that man's got supplies for everything.

"That Hunter guy managed to get himself bitten by something while we were all down by the river—I don't know what, probably a mosquito or something—and Cody disappeared for a couple of minutes and came back with a whole range of antihistamines. Pills, creams, capsules, drowsy, nondrowsy . . . he must have had a dozen different kinds. Who just carries all that around with them?"

"Sounds like a hypochondriac," said Sam. "Though I must admit, I wondered where all the cooking stuff came from. They got dinner ready in no time. Must be a chest freezer stashed away under a rock or something, chock full of frozen lentil dinners. He probably buys them in bulk from some crap catering company that pads them out with floor sweepings."

"Ha, probably." Nina stubbed out her cigarette, smoked right down to the filter, and carefully tucked the butt in her pocket. She tapped gingerly at Purdue's device until it flashed up a digital clock. "Christ. It's after midnight. That's, what, about 6:00 AM back home? I still haven't adjusted. I suppose we should head back and try to get some sleep." She trailed her hand over the smooth rock. "I wish I could sleep out here without getting eaten by something or getting baked alive when the sun comes up. The tent's a bit close for my liking."

"Well, you know, I'm always game for a midnight cigarette if you need company," Sam offered. "Especially because these people don't seem to take kindly to the idea of us pumping ourselves full of toxins on their time."

Nina snorted. "Toxins." She pulled herself up and slipped her wet feet back into her shoes, grimacing at the sensation. "Next time remind me to bring a towel," she said, then led the way up the gentle slope toward the campsite.

As they approached their tent, the desert silence was broken by a sudden clash. They froze. Sam squinted in the direction the sound had come from, trying to make out what it had been. It was probably just someone dropping something, though it had sounded a little more . . . precise.

The sound came again, harsh and metallic, like a muffled cymbal. It was followed by a faint, rhythmic sound, like a soft but intense drum beat. Nina squeezed Sam's arm to get his attention and pointed toward the connection tent. Sure enough, a sliver of light showed through the tent flap. Sam was not sure whether it was just residual light from the dying fire, but it seemed to match the direction from which the noise had come. Together, Sam and Nina crept over to the tent, where they peered through the flap.

What they saw was the exaltation of Jefferson Daniels.

CHAPTER 13

Inside the connection tent, the fire pit was heaped with glowing coals. Cody crouched beside it, drizzling the hot stones with water and handfuls of herbs so that the air of the tent was heavily wreathed with scented steam. His face was concealed by a mask of bone and his golden hair was released from its ponytail so that it flowed down his back and over his shoulders. His pale shorts had been replaced by a white linen robe. For the first time since Sam had met him, Cody's tattoos no longer looked like the trappings of a poseur. In this context, they looked like they signified membership of some sort of tribe.

The drums and cymbals that Sam and Nina had heard were in the hands of the twin acolytes. The two people were indistinguishable, their faces concealed by white masks like

Cody's and their bodies covered by loose ceremonial garments that revealed nothing of their shapes. They knelt together at the far end of the tent, where one caressed a cymbal with a menacing metal beater, filling the tent with a scratchy metallic undertone, and the other patted feverishly at a set of hand drums. Two large buffalo horns lay in front of them, presumably for use later in the ritual.

Sara Stromer stood in front of the twins, her arms flung wide in a gesture of abandon or perhaps communion. Her own robe was flaming red, shot through with strands of gold, and she wore a heavy cloak of black feathers that spilled across the reed floor behind her in a long train. Her mask was not a simple disguise, but part of an elaborate headdress. Its base looked like polished jet, perhaps obsidian. Sam could only imagine the weight of it. It was overlaid with a filigree of gold, the metal twisted into intricate, swirling patterns. It encased her head like a helmet, and the point where the shimmering stone gave way to her long dark hair was obscured by a cascade of golden strands.

Paige and Henley lay prostrate at Sara's feet, motionless as she chanted over them. Sam could not discern her words, or even the language in which she spoke, because she never raised her voice above a half-whisper.

The thick material of the tent prevented the sounds of the ceremony from carrying to the rest of the campsite, but Sara was making certain.

She knelt and offered one hand to Paige and the other to Henley, helping them to their feet. As they rose, Sam could see that they wore brown shifts that put him in mind of the sackcloth worn by penitent sinners of the past. Sara kissed each woman on both cheeks, and then beckoned to Cody. He reached for a large brass pitcher that stood a little way from the fire and set it down beside an obsidian bowl. A pair of metal tongs hung from the apparatus that he had used for cooking earlier. Cody took hold of them and lifted six hot coals, one by one, into the bowl. From a leather pouch hung at his waist, he took a handful of herbs. As he poured water from the pitcher over the glowing stones, he scattered the herbs into the flow.

The bowl was carried with slow steps toward Sara, Paige, and Henley. By the time Cody had reached them and knelt before Sara in an attitude of supplication, holding the bowl above his bowed head, the scent of the aromatic herbs had reached Sam and Nina. They saw Paige and Henley being invited to inhale deep drafts of the fragrant steam. Sam did not know what plants had been used, but as the scent filled his lungs he was aware of a sensation of lightheadedness.

The word "hallucinogenic" scarcely had time to cross his mind before he saw Sara dipping two small horn cups into the hot water. She offered one to each woman.

Paige wore no mask, but she hardly needed one. Her usual polite blankness did not waver as she sipped the contents of the cup. Henley made a valiant attempt to control her reaction as she tasted the liquid, but she could not help a slight wrinkling of her nose. Swallowing her desire to object, she closed her eyes and knocked the drink back like a shot, downing it in a single gulp. As she handed the cup to Cody, she staggered slightly before kneeling before Sara once again.

Sam's head was beginning to feel a little fuzzy. He looked away from the tent flap for a moment, hoping that he could shake his head clear in the cool midnight air. It did not work. By the time he looked back, Sara had produced two white bone masks and was fitting them over Paige and Henley's heads. She laid a hand on each of their heads and chanted over them, then stepped back with a smile and welcomed them into FireStorm. Their initiation complete, Paige and Henley took up places beside the acolytes, clearing the way for the ceremony to which theirs had been nothing but a warm-up.

Jefferson's robes were gold. His cloak was gold. His arms were circled with gold bands.

In the firelight he looked like he was ablaze. The only thing that was not of gold was the bone mask that covered his face.

He approached Sara in a slow glide, as the drumming began again, and then gracefully got down on his knees. She took his face in her hands and held it while she addressed him in the unknown language. To judge by her tone, she seemed to be questioning him, even imploring him. Jefferson's reply was as confident as it could be, but it was clear that his grasp on the language was slight. Nevertheless, his answer satisfied Sara, and she placed a kiss in the center of his masked forehead.

More chanting followed, and more smudging with the bundle of burning herbs. At intervals Sara would call out, her voice rising to the volume of normal speech, and wait for the others to chant the appropriate response. The rhythm of their speech grew more rapid, their tone more fervent, and the drumming more intense.

Cody reached for the obsidian bowl once again, but instead of giving Jefferson the horn cup to drink from, he passed him the bowl and helped him to hold it as he drank deeply from it, swallowing great gulps of seasoned water until he had emptied the bowl. As he did so, the acolytes picked up the buffalo horns and blew softly into them, filling the tent with a soft moaning sound.

When he released the bowl, Sara ripped off the bone mask and threw it aside, leaving Jefferson's face bare. His skin was pink with heat and streaked with sweat, as he sweltered in the steamy heat.

Sam was not even aware that Cody had moved, but suddenly he saw him appear at Sara's side to place a long, glistening knife in her hand. The blade looked wickedly sharp, even clouded with condensation. As the chanting rose to a frenzy, Sara offered the blade to Jefferson. His fingers closed around it as he raised his free hand, his left hand. He dragged the tip of the knife across it. Blood welled up in the line of slit flesh. The acolytes hissed and gasped in approbation.

The knife changed hands, passing back to Sara, who applied it to her own palm before throwing it aside. She brought her hand around in a swift gesture, as if to strike Jefferson, but instead her palm slapped against his and they clasped hand to hand, blood to blood.

When Sara released him, Jefferson held out his arm, his palm upward, his hand open. Cody was at his side, the tongs in his hand, with a coal fresh from the fire gripped in its sharp teeth. Jefferson stood perfectly still as Cody lowered the sizzling stone onto his bloody palm, though Sam could see the effort it cost him not to flinch.

His face was contorted in agony, but he did not cry out. The stone was removed. Sara trailed the fingers of her own cut hand down Jefferson's cheek while Cody fetched a fresh bowl of water.

As Jefferson plunged his hand into the cool liquid, he hissed gently. The buffalo horns reached a crescendo. It was only a tiny part of the volume of which they were capable, but its effect was chilling. Jefferson's legs were beginning to shake, collapsing under the immense pain he was experiencing. Creams and bandages had been laid out in readiness, and Sara reached for them now, smoothing ointment onto Jefferson's freshly cauterized skin and wrapping it carefully as the music and chanting began to wane.

By the time the sounds had died away to nothing, Sara was holding Jefferson close. She signaled the others to approach and join together in a strangely choreographed group hug, while she returned to speaking English and uttered a series of confirmations. Jefferson had supplicated himself to them in order to become an official rather than simply an initiate. He had worn and cast aside the mask of his initiation. He had joined blood to blood with the embodiment of FireStorm and had accepted fire into his blood as it sealed his wound.

Apparently from nowhere, she produced a gold mask that would mark Jefferson as an official at future ceremonies. She placed it on him, and then declared the ritual to be at an end. She stood back from the little group and admired the new official and his recently initiated wife and daughter. They were, she said, the perfect picture of the perfect family, and it would be FireStorm's pleasure to work toward their well-being and prosperity.

Sam realized that his head was still woozy from the scent of the smoke, but Nina was tapping his shoulder in a manner that suggested that she was keen to leave. She hissed at him that she was sure they were being watched and that they weren't meant to be here, observing this apparently secret ritual. He wanted to turn around, to creep back to their tent and process the things he had just seen. Perhaps he would be able to ask Jefferson about it in the morning, or perhaps in a couple of days, once he had thought about it. But he found himself barely in control of his feet, unable to stand as his spine chose not to obey him, and his vision was thrown off-kilter by the constant rippling of everything in his peripheral vision.

He turned, trying to follow here, and his legs made it clear that they had no intention of carrying him to where he needed to be.

He felt the soft whump of his body collapsing on the sand; he felt his tongue flopping thick and useless in his mouth. The last thing he heard before he lost consciousness was a familiar, but dreaded, voice saying "Well . . . this is a surprise. And what might you two be up to at this time of night?"

CHAPTER 14

Shhh!" Nina hissed, her finger pressed to her lips. "You'll get us caught!" She took Purdue by the hand and led him back toward their tent, then remembered that Julia Rose and Hunter would still be sleeping there. "Damn it, is there anywhere we can go for a bit of privacy? I'm fucking sick of all this communal stuff."

""After only a day," Purdue smirked. "Patience really isn't one of your virtues, is it, my darling? Might I have my device back now?"

Flushing slightly, Nina handed over the folding tablet. Purdue opened it to the size of his palm and reactivated the light, spilling a pool of illumination onto the sand. "This way," he said.

Nina followed him past their tent, away from the campsite —not toward the river this time, but in the direction of a rock formation about a hundred yards from the site. On the far side of the rocks, the ground dropped away to form a little hollow, large enough for them both to sit.

"How did you know about this place?" Nina asked. "Have you been out here before?"

"No," said Purdue. "There was no need. I am perfectly capable of remotely conducting all the reconnaissance I need on a place like this."

"But how? You can't exactly look a place like this up on Google Maps. I tried, back when you told me this was where we would be going. You can only zoom in far enough to get a distant aerial view, there's nothing at this level of detail."

"I think my methods might have been a little more sophisticated than yours, Nina. Look." He opened up the tablet to its full size, a little larger than a sheet of paper and about as thin. Nina had seen him do this several times before and she had wondered exactly what the device was made of. He had explained it to her, but Purdue always struggled to talk about his work in terms that a layperson could understand, and his talk of gelatinous properties, molecular scale electronics, and catalytic homopolymerization had gone over her head.

All she knew was that it was infinitely flexible, incapable of running out of battery life, and sometimes struggled to get a signal in some of the rooms in Wrichtishousis, Purdue's home near Edinburgh.

He whispered an instruction to the device, which began a slideshow of images of Parashant. They covered the entire area in high resolution, picking out the tiniest details. Looking at these, Purdue would have known the place like the back of his hand before his arrival. "I surveyed the area thoroughly," he said, with a hint of pride in his voice.

"But how? Did you get someone to come out here and take these for you?"

"Nothing of the kind. I took them myself, from my desk at Wrichtishousis. Remote photography is increasingly easy if you have access to the right technology." The tone of his voice had tipped over from pride to smugness.

"What, you mean like a drone or something?"

"Precisely."

Not for the first time, Nina stared at Purdue and wondered what it must be like to be him.

To have that perfect sense of entitlement, to live in a world where, for the right price, all problems had solutions, and to have the funds to take advantage of them . . .

Once again, the thought of it made her uncomfortable. She focused on the images on the device. The nook in which they were now sitting was depicted in detail, from one angle after another. The river was shown so clearly that she could discern every pebble on its bed. Then there was the campsite itself. Seen from above, it was clear that it had been used for these purposes before—leftover stones and stumps gave away the positions of previous connection tents and teepees, more or less where they stood now. The shape of the fire pit was visible, its thin covering of sand not quite concealing it. And close by, a line in the sand . . .

"Is that a door?" Nina asked, pointing to the suspicious line. "Look, just there—it looks like a trapdoor or something, doesn't it?"

Purdue repositioned his glasses and peered through them. "You know, it does . . . " he mused. "I am surprised that I hadn't spotted that."

"What do you think, Sam?" Nina turned to look for Sam and noticed for the first time that he had not followed them. "Shit. Where is he?"

✠✠✠

Sam was, in fact, right where they had left him—collapsed in the sand at the entrance to the connection tent. He had rolled onto his back and was now gazing at the stars, watching them squirm and dance. He felt as if he could reach out and touch them, so he gave it a try. First he plucked a single star from the sky (which, he was surprised to learn, had the texture of velvet.) Emboldened, he swept a large handful of them into his palm, then worried about the effects of messing around with the solar system and tried to reposition them. He tried to recall the layouts of the constellations, something he had not considered since his brief time in Scouts. Nothing looked right.

Oh well, he thought, nothing I can do about it now. Whatever it is, it'll just have to happen. He released the remaining stars, scattering them at random across the sky, and let his arm drop back onto the sand. He closed his eyes, suddenly exhausted, and let himself start drifting off to sleep. He felt a familiar, comforting weight on his chest. Must be Bruichladdich, he thought. How did he get here from Paddy's? Cats do that sometimes, I suppose. They follow their owners. I read that somewhere. They stow away. He's a good cat, coming here to find me. I wish he'd shift over a little bit, he's squashing my lungs . . . but he'll be so comfortable. I can't move him. I'll be fine. I'm so tired . . .

The next thing he knew, a black bird had swooped down and lifted him gently in its talons, cradling him as they rose into the air. It lifted him higher and higher, up toward the stars he had so recently rearranged. He could see them at close quarters now, much bigger than when he had held them in his hand, and was disappointed to see that they were nothing but large white buttons. But none of that mattered. The condor was carrying him into the brightness of the Moon. Soon the light would consume him, and he would be asleep, and everything would be as peaceful as the cat curled up on his abdomen.

✠✠✠

"He's not here!" Nina looked frantically around the campsite. "If he's not here and he's not back in the tent, where is he?"

"It's only speculation, but perhaps he chose to sleep in another tent. He might be giving us a wide berth in order to avoid any possible confrontation with me."

Nina looked at Purdue with curiosity. Was he really jealous? It was so hard to tell how he felt—not just about her, but about anything.

His anger was impossible to detect until it became white hot rage, which had never been directed at her but which she had seen at close quarters and been unnerved by. His happiness was likewise indistinguishable until it spilled over into childlike glee. Even in bed his reactions were difficult to judge. She always had the sense that he was constantly analyzing every experience, to the point where he could not simply feel an honest reaction to something without it being extreme.

"Look, Dave . . . " Nina twisted her fingers together awkwardly. "I know it probably looked a bit suspicious, waking up and finding that Sam and I were both gone, and then coming out here and finding the two of us together. But honestly, there's nothing going on. I just couldn't sleep and I was feeling trapped in the tent and wanted someone to go for a smoke with."

He nodded. "I know."

"You do?" She scoured his face for any clue that might tell her what was going on. She found nothing.

"Oh, yes. Or if there was, you would be concealing it remarkably well. It's true that your hair is a little disheveled, which could be consistent with an act of passion, but you do not seem guilty.

You aren't blushing, you have not been touching your throat, which you always do when you have something to hide. There is no flush across your chest, which I would expect to see if you were sexually aroused, and the smell of your sweat is unlike the scent that you give off in those circumstances."

Nina was perplexed. On the one hand, his analysis was absolutely accurate, and it was certainly preferable to an unwarranted jealous scene. She could only imagine what her ex, Steven, would have made of a situation like this. But on the other, it was infuriating to be read so calmly. Surely a normal human being would have at least a slight flicker of jealousy. She tried to imagine how she would have felt if she had caught Purdue out here with Julia Rose, or perhaps with Sara. She couldn't make the image work in her head. It was too unlike him. She had no doubt that if Purdue felt the need to look outside of their relationship, he would simply tell her. In all likelihood, he would probably ask her to join in.

This is not a helpful train of thought, she told herself firmly. Setting it aside, she gave Purdue a brief recap of what she and Sam had witnessed in the connection tent. "I don't know what was in the steam, but I've been to a couple of parties where people have been using poppers and the smell sort of reminded me of that.

They were throwing a lot of herbs around, but what I was smelling wasn't entirely natural. I think Sam got more of a lungful than I did—he was up a bit higher. I was crouched down with my head about here, where the air was clearer. What if he's wandering around somewhere, high as a kite? We should find him."

"I doubt that we can," said Purdue. "Look around. We have nothing but desert. You and I, searching together with just a single light source between us, would cover these dunes and hollows slowly. Besides which, Sam's reaction to the drug would have to have been considerably stronger than yours to send him off on such addled ramblings, and that seems unlikely. Come back to bed. I would be prepared to bet that Sam will reappear in the morning, having spent the night in another tent—and if not, we can mobilize the entire group to search for him."

He held out a hand to Nina. Suddenly she felt weary. Purdue was probably right. Things had been a little weird between Sam and her thanks to her relationship with Purdue, and it made sense that he would have made himself scarce. Dawn was just a few hours away. They would find out what had happened to him then. She let Purdue take her hand and lead her back toward their tent, where she lay in the darkness, his arm around her, unable to sleep.

✠✠✠

Sam, on the other hand, slept soundly and dreamlessly. When at last he woke up, he was drawn gently back to consciousness by a soft voice speaking his name.

He opened his eyes to see a white ceiling above him, lit by gently glowing white lights. He turned his head and felt a soft pillow beneath his cheek. As he shifted his body, he felt a light blanket move with him. The place smelled clean, slightly chemical . . . medical. The gentle voice belonged to Sara, who was sitting at his bedside dressed in a silk trouser suit in pale gold.

"There you are, Sam," she smiled, laying a cool hand on his forehead. "You had us worried! How do you feel? Cody, give him some water."

"I'm fine," Sam rasped, gratefully accepting the glass of ice water. The liquid soothed his parched throat as he swallowed. "I think."

"You were lucky," she said, and held out a handful of half-mangled leaves for him to see. "We found these in your hand. I would assume that you recognize them, but if you got the leaves from someone who didn't tell you what they were, perhaps you don't.

It's salvia. Salvia divinorum, to be exact. I guess you found them down by the river? Or did somebody give them to you?"

Sam's head ached as he tried to remember. He could not recall anything to do with leaves, and he said so.

"It's ok. People often don't remember what they've done when they are under the drug's influence, or recently released from it. Since these have obviously been chewed, I guess you were chewing them last night—in which case you were lucky to end up down here. A little while ago we had someone get high on salvia during a Vision Quest and he wandered out into the desert. By the time we found him he was extremely dehydrated and had to be airlifted to a hospital. So even though it's a legal high, we don't advise using it while you're here—or any other mood-altering substance, for that matter." She closed her fingers, crushing the leaves.

"Where is this?" Sam asked.

"This is our medical facility," Cody spoke up, leaning on the back of Sara's chair. "It's kind of basic, but we've got everything we need for cases such as yours."

"But . . . where is it?"

"Right beneath the connection tent!" Cody said. "No, it's ok, there's no need to look so weirded out. You didn't know it was here, and that's because we didn't tell you.

We try to keep this place a secret so that all the delegates can feel like they're getting the authentic Parashant experience, hundreds of miles away from anything. They're not gonna feel like they're out here on their own if they know they've got this right downstairs, are they?" He flashed Sam a conspiratorial grin. "So don't go telling everybody, ok?"

Still bleary and half-awake, Sam agreed to keep the secret. Cody and Sara left him for another half hour, with strict instructions to finish the pint of water on the table beside him. When Cody returned, he got Sam back on his feet and led him down a white corridor to a kitchen, and between the two of them they carried that morning's breakfast up to the connection tent, ready for the delegates to start filing in.

Well, Sam thought, as he looked at the ovens, fridges, and microwaves lining the kitchen walls, that solves the mystery of the food. Maybe at some point I'll figure out what the hell happened last night and solve that one, too.

CHAPTER 15

W here's Sam?" Julia Rose rubbed her eyes. Only a sliver of morning light had made it through the tent flap, but it fell right across her face, making her blink hard. "I didn't think early mornings were his thing. Nina, have you seen him?"

Half awake and not yet thinking straight, Nina looked to Purdue to see whether he could inspire an answer. She could think of no plausible lie, but she did not want to tell anyone that she was worried about Sam until she had had the chance to look for him. Unfortunately Purdue was still sound asleep, sprawled on his back on the reed mat, so no help was forthcoming. "Er . . . " Nina began, somewhat inauspiciously. "I think he's . . . he might have . . . " she trailed off into silence. "I don't know. Sorry. I'm going to go and look for him." She fumbled around in her backpack, looking for her clothes.

"I'll come with you," said Julia Rose, kicking off her blanket. "Just let me get out of my PJs."

Nina wanted to put her off, but in her bleary state she could think of no good reason why Julia Rose should not come with her. Turning her back, she quickly stripped off her nightshirt and threw on a pair of shorts and a tank top, then pulled on her hiking boots and aimed a few swift sprays of sun cream at her pallid limbs. By the time she turned back around, Julia Rose was already dressed and ready to go.

"He's probably dead."

Both women whirled round to see Hunter, flat on his back and staring at the roof of the teepee. Both had completely forgotten that he was there. Nina mentally kicked herself for not being more aware of everyone else in the tent as she changed, and hoped that she had not given him an inadvertent eyeful.

"If he went out in the desert, all by himself, in the middle of the night," Hunter droned, "yeah, he's dead. There's probably a whole pack of coyotes snacking on him right now. Or maybe like a rattlesnake or something. Or maybe he saw something he shouldn't have seen and someone dropped him at the bottom of the canyon."

Nina stared at him, somewhere between bemusement and disdain. "Well, aren't you just a little ray of sunshine? Come on, Julia Rose. We've got better things to be doing than hanging around cheerful bastards like this one."

"Don't be hateful just because I'm right," Hunter said, apparently unperturbed. "See you at breakfast—unless you're dead too by then."

✠✠✠

"What the fuck is his problem?" Nina raged, as they walked away from the tent. "Who says things like that?"

"Douche bags, mostly," Julia Rose replied. "Don't worry about him, he's just an ass. I'm sure Sam will be fine—he probably just couldn't sleep or something." She followed hard on Nina's heels, striding across the campsite. It was still early, and only a couple of people had emerged from their tents. Sensing Nina's growing concern, Julia Rose searched for the right thing to say. "For what it's worth, I think it's great that you two still care so much about each other. Were you together for long?"

Nina stopped in her tracks and looked round. "Sam and I weren't together. Why does everyone think that?

There's never been anything between us—well, one brief moment, but that's it—and another brief, brief moment on the last trip. Hasn't anyone else ever had a short-lived attraction to a friend? Why does it have to be such a big deal to these people who aren't involved and never were? He's my friend, that's all—don't people usually care about their friends?"

Before Nina's eyes, Julia Rose's confidence crumbled. "I'm sorry . . . " she said. "I didn't mean to upset you."

Nina sighed, pressing the heels of her hands against her hot, sore eyes. "Of course, you didn't. I'm sorry. It's just . . . it's hot, I didn't sleep much, I'm in desperate need of caffeine and there's a lot that I'm struggling to get my head around just now. I shouldn't have taken it out on you. It's just . . . a lot of people ask me that kind of thing about Sam."

"Yeah," Julia Rose half smiled, "I kinda got that. So where are we going? Where do you think he is?"

"I've no idea," Nina admitted. "I wish I had. He was outside the connection tent last time I saw him, so I was thinking that he might have come back down to the river for another cigarette and maybe fallen asleep down here. Or that . . . " she fell silent.

The mental images of Sam's possible fates that were currently tormenting her did not bear mentioning. Deep in the pit of her stomach, she could feel the grip of the irrational fear that speaking those possibilities aloud might somehow cause them to come true.

They walked down to the river and Nina paced the bank, scanning it for any possible places where Sam's sleeping form might be concealed. For the briefest of moments her eyes strayed downriver, alert for any sign of him in the water. I'll give it a few more minutes, she thought, and then I'm going back to the campsite to get help.

✠✠✠

As Nina searched, Sam was emerging from the underground facility with Cody escorting him. His eyes were covered by a thick blindfold, leaving him feeling vulnerable and ill at ease as he entrusted himself entirely to Cody's guidance. He was still not convinced that the blindfold was really necessary, but Sara had insisted that this was the policy —only initiates and officials were allowed to know the location of the entrance to the facility, therefore Sam would have to be led out blindly and his eyes must remain covered until he was a safe distance away.

Stumbling after Cody, Sam felt the change from steps to sand under his feet. He heard the soft thud of the door falling shut behind them, and the swish of sand as Cody covered it over, concealing it from view.

"This way, Sam!" The twangy, nasal voice set Sam's teeth on edge even more than usual. There was something about being reliant on Cody that made him even less bearable than Sam had previously found. He felt Cody's hands on his shoulders, steering him away from the door, walking him around in large, looping circles so that Sam would have no chance of finding his way back to the place from which he had been released.

When the blindfold came off, Sam was back outside his own teepee. "There you go, buddy," said Cody. "You've still got time to get yourself cleaned up in time for breakfast. See you in the connection tent!"

Still in a daze, Sam crawled into the tent. Only Hunter was there, apparently asleep. Sam rifled through his backpack in search of clean clothes. He had a vague memory of rolling around on the sand, and it clung to his hair and hid under his fingernails. Changing his clothes was not going to be sufficient for making him feel less grimy. He dug out his towel and headed down toward the water.

✠✠✠

"Sam! Oh, god, Sam!" Nina waded toward him as fast as she could, splashing madly. She threw her arms around him in a sodden hug that nearly overbalanced them both. "Where were you? I thought you were dead!"

Sam spluttered as he got a mouthful of Nina's drenched hair. "Dead?" he laughed. "Why would I be dead?"

"Why wouldn't you? I didn't realize you weren't following, and then when I came back you weren't there. Where were you?"

As always, Sam's first instinct was to tell Nina everything. It was not in his nature to keep things to himself, he enjoyed having a partner in crime. Despite his promise to Cody, he made up his mind to tell her later. It's just Nina, he thought. Telling her hardly counts. For the moment, in front of Julia Rose, he kept the secret. "Cody found me," he said, preferring a half-truth to a lie. "He took me into one of the other tents. If truth be told, I'm still a bit out of it. Excuse me a minute."

He gulped down a deep breath and plunged under the water, where he ruffled his fingers through his hair to shake out the sand.

A quick scrub down later, he was ready to pull on his clean (though wet) clothes and follow the two women in search of breakfast.

✠✠✠

"What the hell is this?" Sam scowled at his plate. Kneeling among the reeds on the floor of the connection tent, his bamboo plate in one hand and wooden spork in the other, he reminded Nina of a moody schoolboy.

"Breakfast," she said. "Didn't you listen when they were telling you what was what?"

"No," Sam harrumphed. "Enlighten me, then—because I take it you did."

"Nope." Nina scooped up a mouthful of the alien food and shoveled it into her mouth. "I didn't listen to a thing. All I needed to know was that it's breakfast. This is the important bit." She held up her tin mug in a cheeky salute, and then took a deep draft. As soon as the liquid hit her tongue she gagged and barely forced herself to swallow. "What the hell is this?" she demanded. "That's not coffee!"

"Nope," said Julia Rose, "it's chicory and carob or some shit like that. Look."

She pointed back toward the long table where breakfast was being served. At the far end, up by the loaves of bread waiting to be cut, there hung a sign which read "All foods are organic, and free of gluten, meat, soya, sugar, milk, eggs, caffeine, and animal derivatives."

"No caffeine?" Nina stared at the treacherous contents of her mug in dismay.

"That's right," Cody appeared beside them, walking around with a jug to offer more of the wretched coffee substitute. "I know it's a culture shock, Nina, but you'll get used to it really fast. It's a lot better for you, and it'll help you unblock your energies. You can't connect with the divinity when you're full of caffeine! Oh, by the way—if you want your cigarettes back at the end of the Mind Meld, don't forget to reclaim them. You probably won't need them by then, but some people prefer to throw away that last pack for themselves. Sort of a symbolic thing, I guess."

Before either Sam or Nina had time to reply, Cody had moved on, weaving his way through the cross-legged diners. Nina's face was a perfect study of horror.

✠✠✠

Neither Sam nor Nina was impressed to learn that the second day of their FireStorm experience would involve climbing the ancient rock that was said to have been the home of the fire giant.

After their sleepless night, neither was in the mood for physical exertion in the desert heat, and Nina was still outraged by the loss of their cigarettes. She sulkily trailed along at the back off the group, kicking at the tumbleweeds that occasionally rolled past.

"What I want to know is how he got our cigarettes in the first place," she ranted. Sam was paying scant attention by this time. He had heard these words two or three times already, and while he shared her anger, he was more concerned with sizing up the other delegates and trying to figure out whether any of them were likely to have a packet stashed away. He did not fancy the prospect of spending his remaining time out here smokefree any more than Nina did.

Just behind them, huffing with the strain of keeping up, was Hunter. He was dragging himself up the hillside with the aid of two walking poles, his T-shirt and ponytail already drenched with sweat. "Are you talking about your cigarettes?" he asked, a malevolent smile creeping across his doughy face.

"Yeah, I told Cody where to find them. He came around this morning when you were all out and said he had to collect any drugs that anyone had." He turned to Sam. "So if you're looking for those miniature bottles of Scotch, you know where they are. Nice job of not sharing, by the way."

The effort of walking and talking simultaneously became too much for him, and with a hacking wheeze, he came to a halt and fumbled in his pockets for an inhaler. Sam and Nina walked on, picking up the pace to leave him behind. "If I get through this trip without smothering him in his sleep, I'll be doing well," said Nina. "Why did we have to get stuck sharing a tent with such a tosser?"

✠✠✠

Despite their objections to the hike, neither Sam nor Nina could deny that the view from the top of the hill was stunning. By the time they caught up to the group, everyone was gathered around Jefferson, who was standing on a boulder pointing out the things they could see in each direction. The Havasupai Indian Reservation lay to the east, beyond Mount Trumbull and its wilderness.

To the north was Utah, and to the west they could see Nevada, where a shimmer of smog hung high in the air, marking out the location of Las Vegas.

In the distance, far to the south, the craggy beginnings of the Grand Canyon were just visible.

The ground dipped slightly toward the center of the hilltop, betraying the hill's volcanic origins and offering a little bit of shelter from the clean, chilly wind that took the edge off the desert heat. The sky was clear and blue, and the sun beat down intensely. There was little shade to be had—the only vegetation on the hilltop was sagebrush and pinion pine, nothing that grew high enough to offer an escape from the heat. The legend, according to Jefferson, stated that plants would only grow as the fire giant's heart healed, which would only happen when he saw true connections forming between living creatures. "So tonight should go some way toward covering this place in greenery!" he finished enthusiastically. "Find a place to settle down, ladies and gentlemen, and let's get started on your Vision Quests!"

CHAPTER 16

As the blue of the sky gave way to oranges and pinks and eventual darkness, Sam took hold of one end of a long, heavy log and helped to haul it uphill. The crater of the cinder cone offered little by way of substantial firewood, forcing the group to search farther down the slope where the ponderosa pines grew. Fortunately it was cooler on the hilltop, but Sam was still sweating buckets by the time he returned to the summit.

Julia Rose had been given the task of taking care of the water bucket, filled from the stream that wound its way down the far side of the hill. A tied muslin cloth hung over the inside of the bucket, filled with herbs that were infusing into the water. "Sara says they purify the water," she explained, catching the skeptical look on Sam's face. "Well, some of them do. Some of them cover up the taste of the iodine, so it's kind of a mix of mystical stuff and good old-fashioned science. Here, smell it—I think most of it's just mint."

She took up the ladle and poured a cup for Sam, who gratefully gulped it. He was far too thirsty to quibble about what was in the water. Besides, once he had tasted it, he had to admit that it was actually quite pleasant. The water was cool and sharp and the herbs made it sweeter and infinitely more refreshing. "Is there enough to go around?" he asked.

"Yeah, there will be," Julia Rose took his cup and refilled it. "Cody's gone to get another bucket. Have as much as you want! It's not like the stream's going to run out."

Sam took her at her word and drank another cup, then another, and then handed it back and went to help to chop the logs. Night was drawing in, and he had spotted a mountain lion earlier. He was not eager to find himself in the dark with predators. He knew that in all likelihood, Cody and the acolytes would have guns or tranquilizer darts—there was no way they would take the risk that one of their wealthy guests might get hurt. His little stint in the underground medical facility had begun to open his eyes to the ways in which this "back to nature" experience had been carefully sanitized. It makes sense, he thought.

Who would run the risk of being sued by one of these people? Sakura Ito alone could probably buy this entire state.

✠✠✠

Another hour found Sam sitting among the other delegates, cross-legged on the sand-covered stone. He was finding it profoundly uncomfortable. Already his lower back was aching, and he was yearning to stretch his legs.

The instructions for the Vision Quest had been simple. They were to spend the night sitting entirely still and silent on the hilltop, alert but unmoving, eyes closed, and becoming familiar with the sounds and sensations that surrounded them. They were to listen to the rhythms of their own minds and bodies as they breathed deeply, all inhaling and exhaling in time with one another. They would spend the hours of darkness like this, and then as the first rays of the morning sun crept over the horizon, they were to lie down and sleep for precisely one hour, no more and no less. Cody, in his role as fire keeper, would tend to the bonfire and their security. Sam wondered if the man ever slept.

"In your sleeping state, you are more in tune with the divinity within you than at any other time," Sara had informed them. "Such a long meditation will bring you as close as you can currently get in a waking state, and the subsequent sleep will take you deeper into yourselves, your subconscious, your divinity, than ever before. While you are in this brief sleep, you can expect to experience an intense dream. There are certain symbols that people tend to dream of, and the symbols you report help us to work out what stage you are in your own personal FireStorm and whether you are ready to progress.

"Some dream of the hunt, which tells us that your mind is eager to find and connect with your divinity. Some experience a feeling of floating in stasis, indicating that they require a little more time, some energy work, and some more connection work, before they will feel ready to progress to the hunt. Some might see the condor and feel themselves being lifted up in its mighty claws. That tells us that they feel vulnerable and scared, but that something deep within them is crying out to connect.

Others might dream of nothing but darkness. If this happens to you, it is vital that you let us know—it's not that it means anything negative, but it means that we need to give you a little extra help.

That darkness is the darkness of the fire giant's grief, buried deep within layers of volcanic rock, letting them cool above him. We have a duty to care for anyone who is in that state, but we can only exercise that duty if you communicate with us."

Sara had said nothing about what would happen if they fell asleep during the meditation rather than at dawn, but Sam thought that he might be about to find out. He half-opened his eyes in an attempt to keep himself awake, and as he peered out he could see that Dylan Thoreau, the CEO of KNCT, was sitting a little way to his left—and he was shivering. Sam, on the other hand, was finding the cool night air and the growing breeze extremely comfortable. It was the least discomfort he had been in since his arrival in America. Whatever Cody had used to treat his heat rash had worked wonders too. He had scarcely felt it all day.

It was so tempting just to fall asleep . . . Tomorrow night we'll be back in the teepees, I suppose, he thought. And then it'll again be too hot to sleep. But this is a perfect temperature. No, come on, Sam. You've got to stay awake. If you're going to write this book you need to at least make an effort to join in and understand this stuff. And to be honest, it's not been as bad as I expected.

I can sort of see why people get into this kind of thing. It is quite relaxing, and it wouldn't be a bad idea to take a little bit more care of myself. Not the whole works, I'm not going to turn vegan or anything, but maybe I should use this as an opportunity to give up smoking, or to cut back a bit, at least —nothing drastic. But I'm not getting any younger, and it might not be a bad idea . . .

As hard as he tried to plan his better, healthier future as a means of keeping himself awake, the delicious breeze and darkness enveloping him were simply irresistible. The air was heavy with the aroma of pungent herbs that Cody had thrown in large handfuls on the fire, and the crackling of the fire was lulling him into sweet, soothing memories of childhood. Darkness began to close in, and for a long time Sam did not know whether he was asleep, awake, or in a half-dream of being awake.

When someone pressed a cup into his hand and told him to drink, he did so obediently, not knowing whether he was in a state of reality or a dream state. As the sweet water slid down his throat and flowed through his body, a word bobbed to the surface of his consciousness from the depths of his memory . . . . Lethe, the amnesia-inducing water that flowed between the words of the living and the dead.

✠✠✠

The hunt began with the clash of cymbals and the sound of the horns. The sound shredded the silence of the moonlit night. It was followed by the leader's single cry, which was picked up by the serried ranks of hunters, and it carried as they began to run. It was without words, a primal communication, and a frenzied ululation. It meant only one thing: the hunt had begun.

The sand was hot under Sam's feet, and he barely felt the chill of the night air as his blood rose. His brother hunters were by his side, he could smell the sweat as they ran in a close-knit pack. Who they were he did not know, since every face around him was covered by a white mask of bone, as if the skin of their faces had been neatly and cleanly peeled away. He was one with them, united in purpose.

They matched the pace of their pounding feet to the beat of the drums, drums that seemed to be everywhere, all around them and inside their heads. The desire to break loose was rising, to free themselves from the drumbeat and run after their quarry.

Sam could almost taste the building adrenaline, the electric feeling that at any moment the pack would become an entity that could not be controlled or reined in. All they needed to get them to that point was the first sign of their prey.

There it was! The beast broke cover. It dashed out from a thicket of sagebrush and sprinted across the open desert. The hunters shrieked and howled. They surged forward, flowing downhill like molten lava, unstoppable and dangerous. The beast could be no match for their speed, their grace, and their beauty. It howled with fear as it fled. Its gait was ungainly, its form lumpish and slow. It ran toward a pine tree and attempted to scale it, but in vain.

The first of the hunters was nearly on the beast when it attempted to run again. It blundered through the undergrowth, whimpering as the thorns tore at its flesh. Then it fell, its weak joints giving up and sending it tumbling to the ground. A hunter pounced, her steely knife glinting in the moonlight as she raised it to strike the first blow.

The hunters circled their fallen prey as it lay there, clutching its bleeding leg. Their senses were heightened by the thrill of the chase and the faint metallic aroma of the beast's blood.

The first blow had been struck, and now they waited to see who dared to strike the second. The beast stared up at them, its chest rising and falling in short, rapid breaths. It wailed and babbled incoherently. At last it tried to drag itself along the ground in a desperate, doomed attempt to escape its fate.

It was not clear who struck the next blow. All at once, the hunters plunged forward. They closed around the beast, obscuring it from sight. Their ululations reached a fever pitch, higher and more piercing than before, so that the birds in the pine trees rose and flew away, calling out to one another in alarm. Bare arms rose and fell in a frenzy, knives slashed, and hot blood spattered across the skin of those who were at the kill. The others, Sam included, danced around the edges, waiting for their turns to plunge in and claim a piece of the prize.

He saw Sara, her black and gold mask singling her out from all the white skulls, drawing the beast's head back and slitting its throat, sending an arc of blood spraying out. Jefferson in his golden mask moved in and plunged his knife into its chest, prying the ribs apart to extract the beast's heart, which he presented to Sara, placing it in her elegant, tapered hands. What became of it Sam never saw, since the leaders moved away. It was time for the rest of the hunters to descend on what was left of the beast.

CHAPTER 17

S am woke up parched. His eyelashes were matted together and all in all, he felt as though he had been gently baked in an industrial oven. He rolled his aching body over and felt around for his waterskin. It was only half full, but it was enough to take the edge off the ache in his throat. He pushed a hand deep into his backpack, looking for the packet of cigarettes that he had stashed there. In all his many years of waking up hung over, he couldn't remember a time when he had felt quite as rough as this. Not since the last time he—

Right. Of course, he thought as he failed to find his smokes. Not since the last time I tried to quit smoking. That'll be it. Gingerly, he eased himself into a sitting position. His back twinged in a rather disconcerting way, apparently determined to remind him that forty was not far off.

"Good morning, Sam," said Purdue. He was sitting at the other side of the teepee, his knees pulled close to his chest. The folding tablet lay on the blanket beside him, showing the front page of the newspaper Le Monde's website. "You were starting to worry me."

"Why's that?"

"Because you've been asleep for the best part of twenty-four hours. It seems that something in the water didn't agree with you."

"What are you talking about?" Julia Rose was unconvinced. "Sam was just tired. And it's not like he's the only one who slept a long time after the Vision Quest. Plenty of people did. Sara said it happens all the time. It's how some people respond to an intense emotional experience."

Purdue peered at her over the top of his glasses. "Indeed, Miss Gaultier. It's also how many people respond to the aftereffects of hallucinogenic drugs."

Julia Rose rolled her eyes. "Some people just can't handle the idea of an experience they don't know how to explain.

You know, if all you saw was darkness, you should really talk to Sara about that. She'd be happy to help you."

"Please, don't think that I do not appreciate your concern, Julia Rose," Purdue adopted his most dismissively polite tone. "But I am perfectly capable of managing my own 'spiritual journey.' Far from seeing darkness, I spent that hour having a most pleasant sleep, during which I dreamed that I was falling from a great height—which is, of course, one of the most common dreams known to humankind and generally indicative of the dreamer being concerned about maintaining control of his own life. You can probably imagine why a man in my position might have such a dream. Admittedly, it is one that I have infrequently, but I do not spend a great deal of time worrying about it when I do."

As exhausted and sore as he was, Sam struggled not to laugh as he saw Julia Rose scowl. He felt a little sorry for her—being on the receiving end of one of Purdue's polite put-downs was not an enjoyable experience—but she had walked straight into it, and it would be a valuable learning experience for an aspiring journalist. She was not yet good enough at this game to come up with a sharp retort, so instead she pulled her boots on and went for breakfast.

"Sustaining yourself by crushing hopeful spirits?" Sam inquired, "or just not hungry?"

"Neither," said Purdue. "I'm sure Julia Rose will encounter more difficult people than me in her quest for journalistic glory. Assuming, of course, that she does not decide on a change of career and offer herself as Sara Stromer's latest acolyte."

"Sara does seem to have made quite an impression on her, doesn't she?" Sam mused. "It's funny. She seemed so hardheaded when I first met her, but there's definitely some hero worship going on there. Still, that doesn't answer my second question. Aren't you going to come and have breakfast?"

Purdue shook his head. "The diet here is not to my taste. Fortunately, I anticipated this and brought supplies of my own." Reaching into his bag, he produced a couple of cereal bars. "Would you care for one? I realize that they are not what you would choose either, but you might prefer them to what's offered here. I would certainly urge you to have one just now. You'll recover far quicker than if you eat the connection tent fare."

I never thought I'd meet someone who was even more scathing about all this vegan hippy food than me, Sam thought. He accepted the cereal bar and tore off its wrapper. Through a mouthful of dry, oat mush he said "So you really think there were drugs on the go during the Vision Quest?"

"It wouldn't surprise me," Purdue shrugged, flicking idly through the headlines on his tablet. "Most of these types of quests appear to get their results either through mood-altering substances or through some kind of mass hysteria. I can't imagine how they could be effective otherwise."

"I don't know," said Sam. "I would have said the same thing, but I must admit, I've been quite surprised by this thing. I'm still not convinced by their talk of bringing everyone together in some kind of massive, worldwide connection orgy—but they might be onto something when it comes to, I don't know . . . paying attention to the things around us, stuff like that." He felt foolish the moment he stopped talking. "I don't know. It's just not as excruciating as I thought it might be."

"You might change your mind about that 'worldwide connection orgy,' as you put it."

A tiny smile played around the corners of Purdue's mouth. "I think they might surprise you."

"What do you know?" Sam grinned, despite himself. Purdue's games were infuriating, but he could never quite resist being intrigued. "Is there something you haven't told me about all this?"

The small smile gave way to Purdue's customary smirk. "Oh, Sam," he said, "so much—as ever."

✠✠✠

They had barely finished their cereal bars when Kai, Purdue's bodyguard, appeared at the tent flap. "Incoming, sir. Cignetti-Dwyer."

Purdue did not pause to reply but immediately folded the tablet down to its smallest size. He reached forward and snatched up Sam's discarded wrapper, inserted the tablet and folded the plastic so that the whole thing appeared to be nothing but a half-consumed cereal bar. He shoved the little package into a side pocket of Sam's backpack, and then dived back into his previous position as if nothing at all had happened.

"No, I haven't heard from him in some time," Purdue said, as Cody came into the tent, "but do give him my regards if he contacts you again. How is he? Back in Siberia?"

For a moment Sam was confused. Who are we talking about? he wondered. Ah, right—Alexandr. Got it.

"Yeah, for now," he improvised. "He said that's why he hasn't been in touch for a while. He's living on the side of some mountain out there and the nearest net connection is days away. I'll tell him you said hello when I write back."

"Please, do. Oh!" Purdue reacted with surprise to Cody's presence. "I'm so sorry, I didn't hear you come in. What can we do for you, Mr. Cignetti-Dwyer?"

"No need to be so formal," Cody's permanent, gentle, understanding smile looked slightly strained. "You can call me Cody. I just wanted to come and check on Sam here. You ok, buddy?"

I was until you called me buddy. Sam bit his tongue and swallowed that response. "Yeah, I'm fine. Again. Thanks."

"It sounded like you had quite the vision," said Cody. "When we brought you back here you were kind of out of it, but you were talking a little bit about chasing something —hunters and leaders and searching for something. I guess you saw the hunt?"

For a moment Sam's brain thrust him back into that strange, intense experience. He saw the sweat-soaked bodies crowded around him and the ominous shine of knives being held aloft in the moonlight. Could that really have been nothing more than a dream? It had felt so incredibly real, yet Sam knew that it was something he would never have taken part in. " . . . Yes," he said uncertainly, "I did. But I don't know, maybe I wouldn't have dreamed about that if Sara hadn't mentioned it beforehand."

"Hey, it's possible," Cody spread his hands in a noncommittal, vaguely agreeable gesture. "If you don't think it means anything for you, just let it go. If you do, maybe you should see where it leads. That's the other reason I'm here. There's a separate ceremony tonight for the people who saw the hunt. Wanna come?"

Sam got the impression that this was not really a request so much as a mandatory event.

He nodded, feeling his hot eyeballs protest at the movement in his head.

"Great!" Cody clapped his hands together in a gesture that was a little too loud for Sam's liking at that moment. "I guess I'll see you there, then. Oh, and there was one other thing, while I'm here. We're just making sure that everybody is getting the full experience of cutting off from the outside world, so if either of you has anything you forgot to hand in, any phones or laptops or whatnot, you can give them to me now and I promise, there'll be no judgment. It's easily done—especially for a guy with as many gadgets as you, Dave! God, I'd be more surprised if you didn't forget to hand something in!"

Purdue arched a single eyebrow. "I seldom forget anything," he said. "But rest assured, Mr. Cignetti-Dwyer, so far I am not aware that I have forgotten to give to you any devices of mine. If I find that there is anything that slipped my mind, you can be certain that I will pass it on."

Judging by the look Cody was trying to wipe off his face, Sam came to the conclusion that he knew about the tablet. Why can't he just ask for it outright? Sam wondered.

I don't think he'd have a problem doing that for any of the rest of us. And it can't be just a money thing—there must be people here who are as insanely rich as Purdue, and I don't see Cody pestering them for their stuff. Something is preventing him from pushing too hard. I wonder what it is . . .

Cody did not say another word, but smiled and bowed out of the tent. Kai held out his hand to Sam for the tablet, which he took charge of.

"Good thinking, Kai," said Purdue when he was sure Cody was safely out of earshot. "Keep it in your possession for the rest of the day—I will reclaim it tonight, otherwise insomnia will be even less bearable than usual." Kai nodded, turned on his heel and left.

"I knew there was someone who didn't end up in our tent," said Sam, kicking himself for missing the detail earlier. "Where's he sleeping?"

"The tent opposite," said Purdue. "It gives him a broader field of fire, should his talents as bodyguard be required. Besides, I prefer to keep my distance where I can. The constant companionship does grow rather tedious, and presumably that works both ways.

He is also a more useful spy if he can see who is approaching the tent and let me know with a little warning. In fact, it can be—" He broke off as Nina entered, looking somewhat subdued.

"I was just down at the river," she said, barely pausing to greet the two men, "when it struck me—has anyone seen that Hunter guy since last night?"

CHAPTER 18

Anyone else who saw the hunt? Over here if you saw the hunt! Don't worry, ladies and gentlemen, this is not a test! Just go to whichever event matches the dream you had. If you saw the hunt, you're with Sara over here. Anyone who saw the condor, head over there and speak to Jefferson. Anyone who saw blackness, come talk to me. If you're confused, just stand in the center, and we'll help you in a moment."

Sam followed the direction of Cody's waving arms and walked toward the connection tent. Sara was waiting for them in the entrance, motionless and regal as usual. Quickly, he performed a head count of the others and checked where they were going.

Nina was shuffling reluctantly toward Cody. Sam could tell that she too was suffering the effects of nicotine withdrawal. Her shoulders were sloped, and she wore dark glasses in a vain attempt to counter the effects of the glaring sun on her aching head. She had told Sam and Purdue that she did not really believe that she had dreamed of darkness, but simply that she had fallen into the kind of dreamless sleep that accompanied exhaustion. Nevertheless, since that did not seem to be an option that was available and she was happy to admit that she was not ready to "connect" in the way that the FireStorm officials wanted her to, she went dutifully toward the appropriate meeting.

It had been impossible to ease her mind regarding Hunter. Sam had suggested that maybe Hunter had got up early and gone to help with breakfast or have a particularly long wash in the river. I hope that's the answer, Sam thought. He's a sweaty bastard, so he could do with it. Purdue had questioned whether he might have changed tents, or whether he might have been taken ill. "They must have some facility for caring for anyone who is taken sick," Purdue had said, and Sam had bitten his lip to avoid confirming that he was right.

Despite the rational explanations on offer, and certainly despite her dislike for Hunter, Nina remained concerned. She planned to keep an eye out for him during the day's events, and then ask Cody about him if she could not find him. Maybe he's had a sudden pang of remorse and gone to steal our cigarettes back, Sam thought, as he lost sight of Nina.

With him in the connection tent were Julia Rose and Henley Daniels. Quite by chance they were standing together, Julia Rose watching Sara intently, and Henley picking idly at her fingernails. Suddenly Sam was hit by a flashback, as violent and unexpected as a kick in the head. He saw a moment from his dream, a vision of Julia Rose standing over the beast. She was trembling, her breathing shallow and her eyes wide. Her knife was loose in her grip, until the black-masked figure that Sam knew to be Sara approached and wrapped her hand around Julia Rose's, guiding her as she plunged the knife into the beast's mutilated carcass. Sam shook his head, trying to expel the image from his mind.

Henley glanced up, noticing the sudden movement, and accidentally made eye contact with Sam. He gave her a smile and a friendly nod. She flushed pink and immediately dropped her head. That's weird, Sam thought. I wonder what's wrong.

Before he could give it too much thought, Sara clapped her hands together, commanding everyone's attention. "Initiates!" she cried. "Yes, I can call you initiates now. Anyone who has seen the hunt is and will forever be a part of FireStorm. Your own divinity within has called out to be a part of this exciting, exhilarating new movement, a more effective way of attracting the right people to us than any conscious initiation would have been. You are now ready to join us on a deeper level, to learn more about our ultimate goals. For this we must welcome you into the depths of our organization, deep in the heart of the fire giant's home."

With a flourish, she swept aside the reed mat that covered the floor beside her, revealing the outline of a trapdoor in the floor. She uncovered a button beside it and stepped on it, pushing down with all her weight. The trap slid open to reveal a dark hole in the group, a gaping invitation into the heart of the mysterious group.

✠✠✠

The dark hole led down to a door, beyond which lay a corridor. The delegates—or initiates, as Sara insisted they must now be called—were instructed to walk along it one by one, because each of them must face three challenges in order to enter the inner sanctum.

This must be where the medical facility was, Sam thought, as he emerged from the darkness to stand before the door. Though there must be more than one door down here. This one looked as though it had been there for centuries. Certainly it had been designed for smaller people than Sam to fit through with ease. Knotted, sandy wood twisted together with gnarled vines and roots. He could see the remains of a tiny barred window, but it was reduced to little more than a small slit now that the wood had expanded in the heat and shifted over the years. Sam peered through the remaining sliver. He saw no sign of the last initiate to go through, which meant that it was his turn. Taking a deep breath, he turned the wrought iron handle and stepped through.

Why am I so nervous? Sam asked himself, feeling his heart pounding in his chest. It's nothing. This is nothing to be scared of. It's just daft. I know it's daft. A few mind games in the dark, like asking someone to put on a blindfold and stick their hand in a shoebox full of jelly worms or something.

Ranged along the dimly lit corridor were three alcoves, one for each of the three challenges. Sara's instructions had been to approach each one in turn and not to move on until he was certain that the challenge had been completed. He stepped into the first alcove. He could not be certain, but he thought that the corridor grew dark behind him.

"When you face the first challenge, do not turn around," Sara had warned him. "Do not turn back or look away, not even for a moment. What you will see during the challenge, I do not know. But no matter what, you must keep looking into the pool. Do not flinch, and do not close your eyes."

The pool resembled a font, but hewn from stone, perhaps carved out of the volcanic rock. Hot water bubbled from a natural spring below the ground, filling the pool and spilling over onto the floor. The air in the alcove was hot and sulfurous, and Sam felt giddy as he held his head over the steaming water.

Gazing into the pool, Sam felt his mind beginning to wander. Amid the smells of brimstone and wet earth, he could have sworn that he smelled the herbs that had been thrown onto their campfires. He laid his hands on the stone wall in front of him for balance, leaning over the top of the pool, staring down. Slowly images began to form, somewhere between his eyes and his mind. He saw the hunt again, saw his own hands smeared with hot, dark blood, flaking off his skin as it dried. He saw the look on Nina's face as she had seen him again for the first time in that hotel corridor. He saw her as she had been in the submarine, tear-stained and desperate, ready to offer their surrender to the approaching destroyer, seconds before she had kissed him—like just before Björn pulled the trigger of the gun he had pressed against her forehead.

He saw Nina's face blending and changing into another, her hair lightening and face lengthening, flesh melting away and bone breaking through until she became Trish, who stared out of the water at him with disappointment in her one remaining eye. Sam felt his own eyes pricked by tears before the face changed again, darkening a little, and the flesh repairing itself until it was Sara who gazed at him from the water.

A high, sweet note sounded from elsewhere in the corridor. Instinctively Sam followed the sound, which led him into the second alcove. There he saw another rough-hewn pillar, but this time there was no pool. Resting on top of it was a large ball of polished stone, dark green in hue. "The stone is moldavite," Sara had said. "It is a powerful, transformative crystal that came to this world on a star that fell to earth. Borne here by a meteorite, now it serves to open a connection between anyone who touches it and the universe."

He followed her instruction to rest his fingertips on it. As with the previous challenge, he was to stay where he was and not let go of the stone, no matter what. He wondered what kind of challenge this could possibly prove, because the stone was inert, but he quickly found out. He gasped as the stone began to cool beneath his touch, rapidly draining the heat from his fingers until it became as cold as ice. Am I imagining this? Sam stared at the moldavite ball, trying to figure out how it could be manipulated. But before he could reach any kind of conclusion, he was distracted by the swift rise in temperature under his hands. The moldavite was growing warmer with every passing second, becoming hot— too hot. It was glowing beneath his fingers, but Sam refused to let go. Just as he began to find the sensation unbearable, it subsided. He left his hands resting on the ball until the high tone sounded again, beckoning him to the third alcove.

"Close your eyes for the third challenge," Sara had said. "Do not open them, no matter what. It is a test of endurance, much like the first two—but many people find it more difficult to endure. It will ask more of you, probe more deeply. Your task is simply to withstand it.

This time it was not just the corridor behind him that was plunged into darkness. As Sam stepped into the alcove, the dim light faded and died. As per Sara's instructions, he shut his eyes tight and waited to find out what would happen.

The first thing he felt was a light brushing sensation against his cheek, like a feather, or perhaps a spider's web. It tickled slightly, but it was not unpleasant. What followed was a gradual buildup, the brushing becoming a slightly scratchy feeling, which developed into the sensation of thin, bony digits pressing against his face. Evert instinct he had screamed at him to run, that he was having his face pawed by a skeleton hand, but he knew that he had to wait it out. The hand moved over his eyelids, down his nose, traced the shape of his lips—then without warning, two long, stick-like things pushed inside his mouth.

Sam forced himself to keep his eyes shut. He kept perfectly still, refusing to give in to the desire to open his mouth, to spit out the intruding fingers—if indeed they were fingers—or to gag. One of the fingers ran down the inside of his cheek, pushing it out—then, just as suddenly as they had arrived, they were gone. Through his closed eyes he could feel the change as the soft lights came back on.

That wasn't so bad, he thought, and followed the sound of the sweet music out of the corridor and through the far door.

CHAPTER 19

You're seriously telling me that no one else saw anything but darkness?" Nina raised a skeptical eyebrow. She had expected that there would be at least a couple of other people joining them in Cody's stuffy little teepee.

"What can I tell you, Nina?" Cody shrugged. "People see what they see. Though I have to say, we've had an unusually good crop of initiates here. They are some really receptive people. Sara and I both feel blessed to be working with them, with you."

It was a strange little tent, much smaller than the one that Nina shared with the others. As far as she could tell from the visible belongings, Cody occupied it alone. Where does Sara sleep? she wondered. I thought they were in here together. The air felt closer, staler, as if the tent flap was tied shut most of the time, trapping the stagnant air inside.

"So, go on then," Nina prompted. "Tell me about how disconnected I am and what I'm meant to do to fix it."

Cody made no immediate reply. He sat opposite her for a long time, legs crossed, hands folded in his lap, scrutinizing her. She tried not to give him the satisfaction of squirming in discomfort but stared straight back at him. He sported the beginnings of a wispy beard across his thin face, and for some reason this annoyed Nina. He reminded her of many of her students—arrogant, aggressively liberal, with all the assurance that came with a life of privilege.

She wondered if she was reading Cody correctly. Was he one of those trust-fund brats who had decided to make a career out of the buzzwords he had learned as a "bohemian" undergrad?

She had always hated his type. The ones who had grown up in large cities and gone to fancy schools, where they had learned that the world belonged to them; the ones who had never doubted a damn thing in their lives. She disliked him all the more for passing his carefully cultivated certainty off as a spiritual journey.

All of a sudden she felt homesick—not for Edinburgh, but for the West Highlands where she had grown up. There had been few people like Cody there. Perhaps if I'd known that there were so many of them in the world, I wouldn't have been so keen to work my way out of Oban, she thought. Perhaps I should just have stayed there. That way I wouldn't be sitting here today, in this tent with this idiot.

"Nina," Cody drew a long, deep breath and slowly blew it out. "I'm getting the sense that you are . . . how should I put this? That you're not entirely cooperative, you know? I'm getting the impression that you don't take all this entirely seriously."

"It's not really my cup of tea," Nina admitted, "but I'm doing the best I can. I'm joining in. I shared when you asked me to, and I sat all night on the hill. I haven't refused to do anything."

"You don't eat our food. You smuggled in cigarettes." The tone of Cody's voice was not one of accusation, but of pitying disappointment. It was perfectly calculated to push Nina's buttons.

"Yes, that's right," she said, forcing herself to smile. "I don't eat your food. It's not to my taste, so I'm eating supplies that we brought instead. It's not intended as a slight. And I was never informed that cigarettes were banned, or phones, for that matter. I'd have thought twice about coming here if I'd known."

Cody held up his hands in a placatory gesture. "It's true," he conceded. "We never made it explicit that you can't bring cigarettes here. I guess we should! We just kind of expect people to have done this kind of thing before and to know that it's not the kind of place where we welcome toxins. Although, if you need an alternative . . . " he turned away and picked up an ornately carved box.

Nina expected him to open it and offer her twigs to chew on or some kind of calming herb or homeopathic nonsense that she would have to accept politely and pretend to use. Instead, he lifted the lid to reveal a fat plastic pouch filled with high-quality marijuana.

A small box of matches and rolling papers lay next to the bag. "This stuff doesn't have any of that tar and nicotine and all the other crap that makes normal cigs so bad for you. And it's just great for expanding your mind! Do you want one?"

Nina wanted to say no. She had always been too much of a control freak—and frankly, too much of a small-town good girl—to experiment with even the mildest of drugs. Cigarettes and alcohol were as far as she went. Yet as she looked at the rolling papers, her fingers twitched involuntarily. She could feel the headache beginning to ease off as she imagined the sweet swirls of smoke filling her mouth and her nostrils, circling around her tongue as she prepared to blow a smoke ring. She knew her hand would only feel complete again when the thin stick was poised between her fingers . . .

Before she could complete the thought, her hand was out and she was accepting the packet of papers. Cody passed her a tiny bag of filters and watched approvingly as she constructed a joint. I don't know if this is meant to be just the same as making an ordinary roll-up, she thought. Oh, you know what—I don't care. Just as long as it takes the edge off of this bloody headache, it'll do.

"I'll join you," Cody offered, beginning to roll one for himself. "Technically I'm not supposed to, seeing as how I'm working, but nobody likes to smoke alone, right? It can be our peace pipe. We can hail a new beginning!"

Yeah, yeah, whatever you say, Nina thought, as long as it gets me a cigarette.

She lifted the joint to her lips, struck a match, and then took a long, luxurious drag as it caught light. Nothing in her life, she was sure, had ever felt quite so good.

✠✠✠

"True story," Cody said solemnly. He was lying stretched out on his blanket, drawing lazy smoke circles in the air as he talked. For the past half an hour he had been telling Nina exactly how he came to be involved with FireStorm. She had heard about his youth in Seattle, his studies in Vermont, and the life he had begun to build after college. He had set up a marketing company with his girlfriend, and within two years of graduation they had expanded and were both pulling in six-figure incomes. Two years after that, the girlfriend had left. Cody had been screwed out of his share of the company and left a brokenhearted wreck, embittered and discompassionate, until he attended a motivational talk given by Sara. His life had been changed, his attitude completely altered, and now he was barely recognizable as the same person. How orthodox, Nina thought. I wonder if they had a training montage.

"So you see," Cody insisted, "I know what it's like to be disconnected. I know. I was compartmentalized. There was Cody, the business man; Cody, the team leader; Cody, the boyfriend; Cody, the son—I thought they were all separate things and I tried to live that way. It was so stupid! People don't work that way. I couldn't see then that I was just one Cody, one complete, complex person. We only struggle with the boundaries of our various personalities because we create boundaries. And we don't have to! But we do—everyone does, Nina, at least until they learn not to. Look at you—how many Ninas are there?"

She thought about it. I don't know. Half a dozen? A dozen? The failed academic. The daughter who doesn't see her mum often. The secret romantic. The clichéd thirty-something fucking up her love life. The girl who got amazing exam results and was meant to go on to do great things. The over-qualified woman who doesn't have any kind of sensible future. But all of these things seem to fit together just fine. I can't say that I feel any kind of disconnect among them. They're just . . . me. She shrugged. "Several and just the one," she said. "Simultaneously, which is fine."

"Ok, let's try a different approach," said Cody. Nina thought she saw him suppressing a sigh. Under the slight buzz of the weed she had smoked, it made her want to giggle. "What are the qualities you prize most in yourself?"

This was much easier. She knew how to answer this one. "Intelligence," she said decisively. "Definitely intelligence and hard work, and tenacity. Loyalty, too—I stick by the people I care about."

"Great," Cody rewarded her with a wide smile. She rewarded herself with another puff. "That's really great, Nina. So you're intelligent, hardworking, tenacious, and loyal. But those aren't all that you are, right?"

"I suppose."

"When we find our strongest positive qualities, we can flip them over and find our strongest negative ones. For instance, you're highly intelligent but you're also capable of making some really stupid decisions—no, don't look at me like that. This isn't a judgment, it's an analysis. Stick with it. I promise you'll see where this is going.

You're hardworking, but that makes you resentful toward anyone who hasn't worked as hard, and it means that when you decide not to work hard at something, you slack off completely.

You're tenacious, but when you break, you really break. And you're loyal, but when someone does something to lose your loyalty, you cut yourself off from them completely, as you did with Steven."

Nina froze. "What did you say?"

"Relax, Nina." Cody sat up and laid a hand on her arm. She shook it off, nearly burning him with her joint.

"Don't touch me. How the fuck do you know about—"

"About the fact that you had a really long fling with a married man? And he wasn't just any married man, was he? He was a married man whose best friend happened to run an international arms ring, the same ring that killed Sam's fiancée and that nearly killed you, Sam, and Dave just two or so years ago?"

Nina was scrambling to her feet now, ripping open the tent flap and stumbling out onto the hot sand. In a split second Cody was up and after her. He grabbed her by the arms and turned her to face him. "Hey, what's the problem, Nina? We do our homework on everyone who comes out here, didn't you know that? The death of privacy is the most important step on the road to true connection, Nina!

We want to know you! We want to help you to know yourself. Isn't that great? Isn't it an amazing thing? But you're never going to have this amazing thing, this unity, this contact with yourself, if you don't work through this— come on. Come back inside. Let us help you to get out of this darkness, Nina!"

Cody's face was alight with the righteousness of his cause. Certain that he had won her over, he relaxed his grasp a little. She stared at him, indignant and confused. "Fuck off," she spat.

"You need more help than I thought," he said, shaking his head sadly. He began to pull her back toward the tent. The beatific expression on his face was completely at odds with his forceful grip on her arms. Nina struggled furiously, but she was no match for Cody. He was far taller and his muscles were firm and well developed. He was easily capable of lifting her off the ground and dragging her back into the tent against her will. Suddenly she felt that she was in real danger. I wish I had lied, she thought. I should have just pretended I'd seen the hunt and gone with all the others.

Sure enough, Cody lunged forward and wrapped an arm around her waist, hauling her upward.

She screamed, but he only laughed. "Nobody can hear you, Nina!" he yelled. "Nobody's close enough!"

She felt the sickening drop in her stomach as she realized that what Cody said was true. She could not see or hear anyone else. The flaps of the connection tent were wide open and she could see that there was no one inside. As far as she could tell, the campsite was now deserted apart from Cody and her.

In desperation she slammed her knee into Cody's groin. He dropped her, doubling over and roaring in pain. She ran.

CHAPTER 20

The white room was worlds away from the beaten earth and gnarled wood of the corridor that Sam had just left. For a moment he thought he was back in the Verbena hotel, with all its clean lines and highly polished surfaces. It was a large room, circular, like sitting inside a drum. The door blended into the wall when Sam closed it behind him.

A bank of seats formed another circle in the center of the room, and the initiates who had already passed the corridor of challenges were sitting quietly, scattered across the seating bank. The chairs themselves were little circles with low backs, capable of spinning like bar stools, and there was no screen or podium, nothing to indicate which direction the initiates should face. Sam selected a seat at random and could not resist giving it a quick spin around. He caught the eye of Sakura Ito as he spun and was pleased to see that he had made her laugh.

One by one, the other initiates completed the challenges and filed in. Sam counted the ones he knew. Christopher Slack, the British MP, who had recently been caught in a minor scandal concerning data protection and the sale of people's tax records to private companies, but had emerged almost unscathed after a more junior minister took the fall. Dylan Thoreau, whose star was rising rapidly as his social media network, KNCT, looked set to overtake Facebook. Ethan McCluskey, whom Sam had met previously, the man reputed to be the unsung hero behind microblogging.

Sam racked his brain for the details of the Chinese politician who entered next. He knew his name was Xiang Ma, and that he was a member of the National People's Congress, perhaps even the standing council, but Sam could not recall the exact nature of the political office he held. I'm slipping, he thought. There was a time when I'd have had all of these details at my fingertips. He remembered Seth Spencer well enough, though—the senator from Nebraska who had recently caused controversy by suggesting that everyone's full medical records should be available to their employers, freely and with no need to seek permission.

There were several others who were not familiar to Sam, except as faces he had seen around the campsite. He wondered whether they were also important people. He knew from talking to Purdue that there were other chief executives here, other powerful people in search of some kind of enlightenment. What are they experiencing? Sam pondered. I'd love a chance to interview a few of them, maybe compare their experiences to Jefferson's. I should speak to Paige and Henley too, find out how they've been doing—ah, speak of the devil.

Henley appeared in the doorway, looking a little shaken. She scanned the room, clearly looking for a friendly face. Sam gave her a little wave, and she rushed over and took a seat beside him. "Hey, Sam," she said, smiling faintly, determined to conceal her nerves.

"Hiya, Henley. How did you get on with the corridor?"

She replied with a one-shouldered shrug. "I don't know. It was kinda dumb, I guess. Like a crappy haunted house or something. Did you have something try to poke into your mouth at the end? That was just gross. I really hope they sterilized whatever that was. I kind of wish I would have been here when my mom did this, though. She must have pitched a fit. She hates anything unsanitary."

"I can imagine. So she's been down here before?"

"I guess. She and my dad talked about stuff that happened in the inner sanctum. It's cooler than I expected down here. I thought it was just going to be more sand and crap, but it's clean, at least. You know, when we—"

She was interrupted by another door sliding open, revealing Sara, now dressed in a sharply tailored linen suit. She strode in, followed by the acolytes. The door slid silently shut behind them. They took up a position to Sam's left, prompting a moment of shuffling as everyone repositioned their seats to face Sara.

"Welcome, initiates!" She threw her arms wide as if to embrace them all. "Congratulations on passing your challenges! I am so happy to see you all here—not a single one of you balked at the things you were asked to do. I applaud your bravery. Before we progress any further, we have to break the spell for a moment and attend to a few minor housekeeping matters." She slid one of the wall panels aside and produced a sheaf of papers. "First, if you have decided that you wish to proceed to initiation, we will need to get you to sign one of these forms. Just stay where you are and we'll bring them to you. Second, despite the fact that it's cooler down here—air conditioned, even!—it is still important to keep yourselves hydrated. So we will bring around some water for everyone, along with the forms."

Sara did not move, but the two acolytes wove through the seating bank, one handing out papers and pens, the other carrying a tray laden with small cups of water laced with the familiar sweet herbs. Once they had collected all the signed forms and empty cups, they spirited everything away, allowing Sara to command everyone's attention once more.

"Initiates," she began, "you have begun to understand the principles behind FireStorm. You know the mythology that underpins our ideology. You know that we believe in connection—complete, limitless, and absolute connection. We dream of bringing the whole world together so that no one ever has to experience isolation or loneliness, that crushing sensation of being on one's own in an unfriendly world. We believe that connection is the key to the end of war, of poverty, of all humankind's suffering. To know that nameless, faceless masses on the other side of the world are starving and dying is one thing. To know that individuals with whom you are connected are suffering is quite another.

"Could you look a man in the face and tell him that you are sorry, but there's nothing you can do about his pain? That you can do nothing about the fact that you have plenty and he has nothing?

Most of us could not—not if we knew the man, not if we were aware of his name, his age, his place of birth, his education, his family, his likes and dislikes, the suffering he has already endured, and the triumphs that have defined his life. If we knew the things that defined him as an individual, we could not help but see him as a real, live human being just like us, rather than as part of an amorphous mass. We would feel compelled to end his misery, because connection would bring us to a point where we believed we shared it.

"Imagine also the potential for our own growth! You are all educated people who have seen something of the world. You know the vastness of human experience and intelligence. You have all traveled and experienced other cultures, and I have no doubt that you have learned from them. But I am sure that you are also aware that there are many who have not been afforded that opportunity. There are people whose worlds are small, whose parameters are limited, whose minds have never been expanded the way ours have been.

"Time was when people in that situation would have been doomed to stay that way, to live out their lives without ever being taken beyond their existing limitations.

Even an experience like this would have been unavailable to them, because their limited lives would never have allowed them to achieve the excellence that marked you as candidates for this Mind Meld. But now, things are different! Now there is a way to bring connection to the entire world, and every single person in this room has something to contribute toward making that vision a reality. We can harness the power of technology to bring about the spiritual growth of the human race.

"Make no mistake—this will be a long and difficult journey. We can bring about this change, and I believe that we must—but there will be technical issues. There will be human resistance. It must be treated as a process, not as an overnight change. The first step alone will demand a change that people will find frightening until they learn to accept it. The first step on the road to global connection will be better explained by a man who has been working with us to develop the technology required to bring it about. Please welcome the man who will introduce you to the death of privacy—Mr. David Purdue!"

✠✠✠

Nina kept running until she reached the river. She could not see Cody when she looked over her shoulder, but the thought that he might be stalking her, tracking her like a predator, would not leave her. She wanted to get away from him, as far away as possible, until she was certain that the others were back at the camp.

That's assuming they come back, she thought. Where are they? How can a whole group of people just vanish like that? I don't know what's going on here, but this place is like some long, weird nightmare. I don't know how to escape. I don't know whether escape is even possible. But what I do know is that this is not a good place to be alone.

As a precautionary measure, she scooped up handfuls of the cool water and drank deeply. She wanted to put more distance between herself and the base—or at least between herself and Cody—and she did not want to risk finding herself far away from a source of water.

I don't want to get myself lost either, she thought. All I want to do is steer clear of Cody for a while, not end up as vulture meat. She looked toward the cinder cone they had previously visited, just a short walk away. That's probably my best bet. At least I've walked the trail before, and I know there are water sources and a few sheltered places there. I'll go that way.

By the time she had made her way to the cinder cone, she was absolutely certain that Cody was not following. Instead, she deduced, he must be waiting for her to return to the campsite. I have no idea what I'm going to do if the others don't reappear soon, Nina admitted to herself. This really wasn't a long-term plan. Well, first things first. I need to get out of the sun. I seem to remember that there's a little stream with some bushes beside it this way . . .

She followed the faint trail around the side of the hill, alert for any sign of movement. This was inhospitable terrain, and she wondered whether she had leaped straight out of the frying pan and into the fire. Perhaps I should have just stayed and found a way to deal with Cody, she thought. Or just dealt with whatever he had in mind. Out here . . . there's plenty that's less reasonable than Cody. I'm going to get myself eaten if I'm not careful. By coyotes. Or bears. Or snakes. Or spiders. Or scorpions . . . Oh, god, I wish I was back in Scotland . . .

Cautiously, scanning the surrounding environment with every step she took, Nina worked her way around to the little patch of bushes surrounding the tiny stream.

The patch was just big enough that she would be able to stretch out beneath it, unseen, safe from the sun and from any predator that relied more on sight than smell. Admittedly, that's really just humans, she realized, but it's better than nothing.

Picking her way across the rocks, Nina reached the bushes and pulled a couple of branches aside. Beneath the layers of leafy green there lay a dark shape. Ugh, not a dead animal, she hoped. I really don't want to have to share my space with a dead coyote. Or have to drag it out and get it out of sight somewhere. Please let it be nothing more than someone's discarded sleeping bag or something, otherwise I'm not going to be able to—

She never completed the thought. As she brushed the branches aside she realized that the black mass was cloth, and that the dead animal was in fact a dead man, a murdered man. It was a man who had been repeatedly stabbed and had chunks of his flesh torn off; a man whose black T-shirt she recognized; a man with whom she had shared a tent . . . Hunter.

For only a moment Nina stared. The scream that her soul was trying to make died in her throat.

Then she turned back toward the camp, ready to run back and get help—or, if not help in a meaningful sense for Hunter, at least a few people who could retrieve the body

A sturdy root hooked round her left ankle as she turned, and as she tried to launch into a run she found herself flat on her face on the sand. She opened her eyes to find herself staring into Hunter's empty eye socket, the eyeball already taken by a predator. The pain that surged through Nina's leg, originating in her ankle, was immense. It occurred to her that she might have broken a bone, or at least sprained it badly, but there was no time for that now. Fueled by terror and desperation, she ignored the pain. The campsite was visible on the horizon. All she could do now was hope that the others would have arrived back before she did.

CHAPTER 21

urdue? He's actually involved with these people? Sam was astonished. Then his astonishment made way for careful scrutiny and he quickly considered that the man was, after all, involved with the Order of the Black Sun. He seemed to have a penchant for clandestine organizations.

He tried not to gape as Purdue introduced himself, but fortunately any amazement that showed on his face could be easily explained when the walls lit up, revealing themselves as plasma screens. Throughout his talk Purdue referred to them frequently. Complicated diagrams drew themselves across the screens at the touch of his fingers as he talked about the world's booming population, the spread of the Internet, the ever-expanding popularity of social media, and people's increasing willingness to run their lives online. An image of the world flashed up, spinning before their eyes, and Purdue caressed the screen to bring them zooming in until they could pick out individuals on a busy street in perfect high resolution.

Sam caught barely a word of Purdue's presentation. He took in enough to know that Purdue had been involved in designing some kind of app that would revolutionize . . . something—social media, presumably. It was a new kind of app that would not only be found on computers, phones, and tablets, but which would eventually be present in every electronic device one could possibly think of, from sat navs to table lamps. Beyond that, Sam was lost. This was not his area of expertise, and he was still preoccupied with the revelation that Purdue was so closely linked to FireStorm.

In his mind he was busy reviewing every conversation he had had with Purdue since his arrival in Las Vegas, trying to fathom whether there were any clues he had failed to pick up on or whether he had fallen victim once again to one of Purdue's elaborate schemes. Jefferson had been only a puppet in this play, he assumed with an aching feeling of renewed betrayal, the indifference of Dave Purdue still fresh in his mind while he and Nina faced the Aryan's wrath on Deep Sea One.

✠✠✠

Nina slowed down as she approached the campsite. Once again she sheltered behind a rock and caught her breath, sobbing gently. It must have been a mountain lion, she told herself. It must have been. Even if someone wanted to kill him, why would they do that? He was barely recognizable. He was barely human . . . oh, god. What if that was deliberate? It can't have been. It can't. It can't. He must have wandered off and something got him. I knew something had happened, I knew it, I should have listened to my instincts . . . What if we could have saved him? Maybe if we'd gone out looking for him when I first realized that he was gone . . .

As hard as Nina tried, she could not convince herself that Hunter's messy fate had been accidental. Those were clean wounds, the kind that came from sharp implements, not teeth and claws. Her experience of looking at mutilated bodies was limited, admittedly, but she was certain that Hunter had not been eaten. No doubt he would be as soon as darkness fell and the nocturnal predators emerged. She tried not to think about it. Indeed, she tried hard to put the image of the sliced-up corpse out of her mind, but every time she so much as blinked she could see it imprinted on the inside of her eyelids.

When she was sure that she was not going to be sick again, she glanced over the top of the rock. In the distance she saw Sam disappearing into their tent. Hot tears of relief flowed down her cheeks, and she began the painful limp toward what she hoped would be safety.

※※※

"Ok, Purdue," Sam said, the moment they were both back in their tent. "I'm confused. What the hell's going on? What is this FireStorm thing all about? And I mean the truth, the real purpose, not the marketing blurb."

Purdue removed his glasses, pulled a scrap of microfiber cloth from his pocket and polished them carefully. "I can appreciate that it must be confusing, Sam. But surely you understand that this was simply too rich an opportunity to pass up—and by that I mean both the work itself, which has been fascinating, and revealing my involvement in this way. It was irresistible. My only regret is that Nina was not there to see it."

"You mean she didn't know?" Sam wrestled with the idea. If this was not the reason for her sudden intimacy with Purdue, then what was? And was she even aware that her affections were second to his ambition?

Purdue shook his head. "You know Nina," he said. "As dear as she is to me, keeping secrets is not her strong point. She has too much of a tendency to get over-excited and blurt out whatever she happens to be thinking."

"She's going to be raging when she finds out," said Sam. He would not blame her though. Discounting her innate fury, he would understand completely that she would be insulted to be excluded entirely, and more so because she was deemed untrustworthy.

"I know," Purdue smirked. "But in a way, that's part of the fun."

✠✠✠

"Nina! You made it back!"

Cody seemed to appear from out of nowhere. Nina's tears of relief were replaced by a gasp of fear. Although Cody wore his customary friendly smile, she could see the menace behind it.

"I've been so worried about you," he grinned, advancing on her.

"Stay the fuck away from me," she snarled, dropping into a defensive crouch. "My friends are just over there. If I scream, they'll be right over."

Slowly, deliberately, he took another step toward her. "And what exactly are your friends going to do, Nina? Look at you. You're injured. You're a mess. If I tell them that you're hysterical and I'm trying to restrain you for your own safety, I bet your friends will help me. You need help, Nina. Come on. Let me get you an ice pack for that ankle, at least." He held out a hand in a conciliatory gesture and continued to walk toward her.

"Did I not make myself clear?" Nina asked, lashing out, her fingers hooked into claws. "Stay. The fuck. Away. From me."

"Fine." Cody stepped back, his hands raised. "If that's how you want it, Nina. If you change your mind, you know where to find me. We're going to be out here for a long time, and your ankle's going to need attention sooner or later. How far have you walked on it?"

"None of your business. Why do you care?"

The look of disappointment on Cody's face was almost sincere. "Nina . . . I care about all of you. It's my job. It's also my privilege and my blessing as a connected human being. I'm just trying to save you from hurting yourself anymore."

"I don't need you to save me." Without turning her back on him, Nina inched closer to the teepee. "And if you think I'm going to be out here for much longer, you're mistaken. Now stay where you are. Don't follow me."

He made no reply but walked away, back toward the connection tent. With as much speed as she could muster, Nina dragged her aching leg toward her destination.

✠✠✠

The more Purdue explained about his involvement, the more confused Sam became. It seemed that Purdue had not, in fact, met these people prior to this trip. His entire acquaintance with them had been formed online, and it had all happened fast.

Just a few months earlier, they had contacted him to ask whether he would be capable of creating a new kind of mobile phone for them.

They wanted a device that would be designed with FireStorm at its heart, complete with apps that would feed into its social network, establishing a constant flow of information back to the organization from every user on the planet. It had to be user friendly, simple, and cheap both to produce and to sell.

Where most technology was intended to be expensive, to foster an air of exclusivity and a certain amount of geek cred, the FireStorm phone was to be for everybody. Its most basic models needed to be cheap enough to become the most popular phone in the developing world. The advanced models would retail at much higher prices, eventually capturing the market share that currently belonged to Apple, Research in Motion, and Google.

"They told me that they needed the device and its software to be capable of handling vast amounts of information," Purdue said, "because the intention is to collect every possible shred of data about an individual in one place. Imagine, if you will, a social network that handles all aspects of your life.

So far no one has managed it. Google has come closest —for many people, Google manages their email accounts, their calendars, their travel plans, and their Internet searches. Facebook has also made a valiant attempt. Either of these services allows you to log-in across multiple websites, collects information from the sites you log onto and the searches you conduct, then uses that information for marketing purposes.

"But imagine that one such service could handle everything—your diary, your formal and informal communications, the thermostat in your home, your dating site profile, your job hunting, your educational records, your medical records, everything! Imagine no longer having to enter anything in your diary, because the device in your pocket listens and makes entries on your behalf. It will tell you when your cat's next check-up at the vet is due, because it will remember what you were told at the last visit. If you use the device to scan an item at the supermarket, it will cross-reference that item with your medical records and warn you if there is a reason you shouldn't have it.

It will alert you if there have been any product recalls of which you are not yet aware. It will tell you whether you could get a better deal elsewhere and, if so, how far you would have to go to get it. It would not only record every purchase you ever made, it would also listen in and monitor how you spoke about them to determine what to market next to you.

"Of course, apps already exist that fulfill all of these functions—broadly, at least. However, not only would FireStorm provide something much more specific and individually tailored—it would also provide it all in just one app, on a device that had been created with the intention of ensuring that the FireStorm app ran smoothly on it."

Sam's mind was reeling. He was torn between wishing that he had got on board with modern technology and got a smart phone ages ago so that he might have had some idea what Purdue was talking about, and being extremely glad that all of this made little sense to him.

He got the gist—FireStorm wanted to harvest data, but on a massive scale and with the users providing everything freely in exchange for convenience.

How they planned to convert technophobes like him, he did not know, but he had little doubt that it would prove extremely popular if they were able to make it work—and with Purdue involved, he was certain there would be a way to make it work.

"It just so happened," Purdue continued, "that I had been working on something rather similar. Not just the device, because that part is comparatively simple—for me, at least. I had also been tinkering with a design for software that would allow for all of these things."

"But why?" Sam asked. "Why would you do that if it wasn't for anything specific?" Or was it? Judging by the sort of company Purdue had kept before, most notably organizations set on ruling the world from a minority, his question was mostly out of interest for Purdue's point of view. He had decided his own opinion on it.

"Why not?" Purdue looked genuinely perplexed by the question. "It was something to keep my mind occupied—a thought experiment, if you will. I needed something to take my mind off the misadventures in the Antarctic, and subsequently the unforeseen perils on Deep Sea One that resulted in unfavorable light with powerful people.

So I opened my folder of unfinished thoughts and selected one to work on. I've played with this idea on and off for years, which meant that Sara and her companions were able to bring forward the date of this Mind Meld by nearly two years. I think they were quite pleased about that."

"Right. Yeah. I'm sure they were . . . " Sam trailed off, his head too full of new information to offer more of a contribution. Surely there were ethical and legal considerations that would prevent any organization from ever accomplishing this kind of world domination? Surely they couldn't pull things together so quickly, or if they could, why would they require the smoke screen that was the Vision Quest? Still he was desperate to follow up on the details he recorded for Purdue's quest for the Spear of Destiny and when he was planning to pursue that devastating revelation to the world. Question after question lined up in his head, all equally eager to be asked, but as he opened his mouth to speak, Nina nearly collapsed into the tent.

✠✠✠

"Nina!" Purdue reached her first. She fell into his arms and he helped her down onto the floor. Her tank top was torn and smudged with dirt, and there was a long streak of brownish-red where she had wiped her hand after touching the partly-congealed blood. Her face was dirty and tear-stained, and most of her dark hair had escaped from its stubby ponytail and now hung in matted tendrils around her face. The pale skin of her arms and legs was covered in insect bites and scratches, and her left ankle was puffy and violently pink.

"Get her some water," Purdue took command, settling her on a blanket and dropping to his knees to examine the damage to her ankle. Sam grabbed a waterskin and pulled out the stopper, then held it to Nina's lips and helped her to take a sip. As he slipped an arm around her shoulders he could feel her trembling. He longed to ask her what had happened and to ascertain that she was unharmed, but evidently that would have to wait. Before anything else could happen, they would have to get her calmed down.

Only seconds behind Nina, the two acolytes burst into the tent. Without a word they pushed Sam and Purdue aside and began dragging Nina to her feet.

Sam kicked out at the legs of the male, knocking him off balance, while Purdue leaped up behind the female and attempted to pry her off. The duo had their hands full with Nina, who was lashing out in all directions, but reinforcements were on their way. Cody was right behind them, ready to take the struggling Nina off their hands and leave the acolytes to deal with Sam and Purdue.

"Freeze." They had not reckoned on Kai, always a strategic distance from Purdue. He materialized right behind Cody, and in a flash the barrel of his gun was pressed against the back of the young man's neck.

Cody relaxed his grip on Nina, but did not release her. "This is for her own good," he gasped, as he felt the cold metal on his skin. "She's a danger to herself. Let me go, and we can resolve this without getting our security involved."

To Sam's surprise, Purdue made a quick gesture at Kai and Cody was released. I haven't seen any security, Sam thought, but whatever they have, it's enough to worry Purdue. That's not good.

"Thanks," said Cody, as Kai holstered his weapon. "I'm sorry to have to do this, but I'm worried about Nina.

During our one-to-one session she attacked me and ran off into the desert. Who knows where she went? It's dangerous out there, and I think she's having some trouble staying stable. It happens sometimes. We do intense work with people, and it's too much for them. They struggle for a while. They need help. Especially considering what the poor woman had had to endure after almost losing her life on the North Sea."

"Fuck you!" Nina yelled. "I don't need your help."

Purdue and Sam both seemed perplexed by Cody's last statement. What did Nina endure after Deep Sea One? Why did neither of them know about it?

"Cody, if Nina says she doesn't need—"

"Sorry, Sam," Cody blocked Sam's attempted intervention, "but my options are limited. Nina physically attacked me. Either you let her come quietly with me, and we'll get her some help, or I call in our security team and then radio for the police. What do you think, Nina? Which is it to be?"

For a long moment, Nina looked at Purdue. Suddenly, as if someone had simply let the air out of her, she deflated. "I'll go," she said. As the acolytes led her away, she shot Sam and Purdue an imploring look.

CHAPTER 22

S ecurity?" Sam asked, the second Cody and the acolytes
were gone.

"There's a lot more to this place than meets the eye,"
Purdue said quietly. "I suggest we go somewhere a little
quieter and—"

Both men jumped as another figure appeared in the
entrance to the tent. Jefferson Daniels straightened up and
shot them his toothpaste commercial smile. "Hey," he
greeted them. "Was that Nina?"

Purdue nodded. "According to dear Cody, she is struggling
with the mental turmoil caused by her introduction to
FireStorm and needs to be restrained for her own safety."

"Ah," Jefferson nodded back sagely. "Well, it's not the first time, I guess. Remember how hard she took everything that happened in the Antarctic?" he blabbered unceremoniously, unaware of her emotional turmoil after her latest venture on the North Sea. "She's got a lot of trauma to work through. Thank god, she's in a place where there are people who can give her the kind of help she needs!" Blithely, he moved on, dismissing the subject of Nina and turning to Sam. "Sara sent me to find you, Sam," he said. "She'd like to talk with you—I think she's ready to give you that interview for the book! That'll be a great chapter."

"All right," Sam muttered, still preoccupied by listening to what was going on outside in the hope that they would be able to find Nina. "I'll come and talk to her a bit later."

"I think she was planning on talking with you now," said Jefferson. "Coming, buddy?"

Alarm bells rang loud and clear in Sam's head. First Nina was effectively arrested, and then Jefferson came looking for Sam? This can't be a coincidence, he thought. "I'll just get my Dictaphone," he said, crouching down to rummage in his backpack. As subtly as he could, he maneuvered himself into a position where he could make eye contact with Purdue unnoticed by Jefferson. "What should I do?" he mouthed.

Purdue, his face clearly visible to Jefferson, was not in a position to mouth back, but as he stood with his arms folded he shifted his hands so that he was pointing toward the door. It was such a slow, casual gesture that he could easily have passed it off as mere fidgeting, but Sam understood. He pointed to himself, then toward the door, mouthing "Go with him?" then waited. After a moment Purdue nodded, as if politely indicating that he was listening to Jefferson telling him about the plans for the next day's sweat lodge.

"Got it!" Sam dragged his Dictaphone from the depths of his backpack and got to his feet. He dusted himself off and gave Jefferson a smile. "Lead the way."

✠✠✠

Sara's tent was a far more sophisticated affair than the teepees. From the outside, Sam could not tell the difference, but the moment he set foot inside it hit him. It was cool and dark inside, and instead of reeds lining the floor there was a soft rug underfoot. Oversized cushions upholstered in silk were scattered about the floor—Sam guessed that they formed Sara's bed, in conjunction with the burgundy cashmere blanket that sat neatly folded nearby.

The air was thick with scent, but it was not the same earthy, herbal scent that Sam had grown accustomed to smelling during the FireStorm rituals. This was something darker, heavy with musk, laden with sandalwood and Melissa oil. It was, Sam had to admit, a powerfully erotic combination. The hairs on the back of his neck rose in a tingle of arousal.

It's gone quiet all of a sudden, Sam noticed. He turned to look outside, but as his fingers closed around the cloth of the tent he realized that it was considerably heavier than that of the teepees. It also hung in thicker folds, not stretched over the poles but cascading down from them luxuriously. All of a sudden he felt uncomfortably hot, though he could not tell whether that was the effect of the thick cloth trapping the desert heat or the unwelcome rush of libido that had him in its grip.

"Sam," Sara breathed his name as she entered the tent, her hand closing over his as she pushed the tent flap open. He leaped back as if her touch had given him an electric shock. Damn it! he cursed himself.

I hope she didn't notice that. One look at her dark eyes told him beyond a doubt that she had.

She strolled across the floor and selected two cushions, piled one on top of the other, and then arranged herself carefully on them. She was propped up on one slender arm, her long legs curled under her, and the curve of her hip jutting out enticingly under the folds of her ivory robe.

Feeling extremely awkward, Sam dragged a cushion to what seemed like a respectful distance from her and sat down. Sitting cross-legged seemed like the best option, and certainly the most comfortable, but he could never shake the feeling that it made him look like a six-year-old schoolboy.

"Where are my manners?" Sara's voice rippled through the pungent air. She rolled over and reached for an engraved silver bottle and two tiny goblets. "Would you care for something to drink, Sam?" She pulled out the stopper and poured milky-white liquid into the cups. The tang of alcohol hit Sam's nose, making him gasp. He had not realized how much he had missed it these past few days. There had been too many other things occupying his attention. Now it greeted him like the old friend that it was.

"It's pulque," Sara said, holding out the drink to him. "Have you ever had it before? Not that it matters if you have —I guarantee that this will be quite different. This is made like the old, sacred recipe, passed down through the generations from the Mesoamerican period to the present day. Legend has it that it's made with the blood of Mayahuel, the Aztec goddess of the maguey. It's a little bitter, but I'm sure that if you can enjoy a good whisky, you'll like it."

"Thanks." Sam accepted the drink, holding the small cup carefully between his fingertips. It was viscous and tasted of yeast. It could not compare to a decent dram, but it was not unpleasant.

"It's more common nowadays to drink it over ice, and in larger, less potent quantities," Sara told him, sipping delicately at her own cup. "But I prefer the old ways. Shorter. Stronger. Drink this from a beer tankard and you wouldn't just commune with the gods, you would move in with them permanently."

"We're not communing with the gods today, are we?" Sam asked, savoring the fermented aftertaste of the drink.

"It's not on my agenda," she smiled, pulling her dark hair out of its braid to let it spill freely over her shoulders. "Though I make a point of never ruling it out. Sam, I have to apologize."

"What for?"

"Two things. First, for dragging you here so abruptly. I told Jefferson that I wanted to speak to you, but I didn't expect him to bring you to me immediately. Second . . . I underestimated you. You've taken to our way of thinking much better than I expected. I anticipated nothing but resistance from you, but instead you've shown an openness, a willingness, that went far beyond my expectations. This might seem like a sudden change, but I pride myself on my ability to assess the alterations in people's characters and adjust to take account of them. I saw how you reacted when you heard us speak about the death of privacy, Sam. It made me think that you, alone out of all the initiates, are ready to be told more."

✠✠✠

Underground. Nina stared at the blank white walls of the cell. *They are holding me underground. There's a solid, crushing mass of earth above my head. There are no windows. There is no daylight. I can't get out of this room. I wonder how much air there is in here. Is there a vent? I can't see a vent. How am I going to get any air if there's no vent? But why would a vent help me anyway? All the air is far above me, on the other side of all of that earth. But there's got to be something, hasn't there? They can't have put me in here to suffocate me. But then, it's stuffy in here. And hot. Oh god . . . I can't think this way, I can NOT let myself think this way. Concentrate, Nina.*

She looked around for any sign of a way out. There was nothing. The walls were smooth, coated with some kind of white plastic. The floor was solid concrete, quite recently poured, judging by its almost pristine condition. She inspected the doorframe carefully, but it was perfectly sealed all the way around. There was no room to jimmy it open, even if she had an implement with which to try.

Slowly, deliberately, she took one deep breath after another and forced herself to focus on anything other than her confinement.

Picking a subject at random, she made herself list every pub in Edinburgh. The rules are that I have to recall the name, the facade, the first time I went there, and whether it's still open, she told herself. Let's pick a spacious one to start. The Pear Tree. The beer garden. The sky overhead. I was sixteen, hanging out with a bunch of students from Edinburgh Uni, pretending to be twenty-one. Drinking vodka and Coke and trying not to make eye contact with the doorman . . .

Yet even as she pushed her thoughts down that path and away from her fears, she could not prevent the tears from creeping slowly down her face.

❈❈❈

"How much has Purdue told you?" Sara asked. "I've no doubt he must have told you a little."

"Not much," said Sam. "He told me a bit more about the app—that it's not just social media for people who've done FireStorm. He didn't get a chance to say much more than that."

"He is a little less trusting than I am," she laughed. "But yet, the app is a little more than just social networking in the conventional sense.

What we are aiming to do, Sam, is revolutionary. After the death of privacy, once people have become used to the free and open flow of information, the world will be a different place. Information only commands a price because it can be kept confidential. Once everything is out there and no one has to purchase it, the value of personal information as a commodity will change irrevocably."

Sam was taken aback. "You mean you're not planning to harvest people's data so you can sell it yourself?"

Sara shook her head, causing her glossy hair to shift so that a single strand fell on her shoulder and lay in a gentle wave over the curve of her breast. It was distracting, and Sam was certain that she knew it.

"I can tell that trust doesn't come easily to you, Sam," she breathed. "And why should it? After all that you've been through. But don't you miss trust, Sam? Don't you miss feeling safe in the world you live in?"

Reluctantly, Sam allowed himself to consider the question. If he was honest with himself, he did miss the sense of security he had felt before Trish's death. It was nothing that he had ever felt on a conscious level while he still had it, but once it was gone he was acutely, painfully aware of its absence. Whether it was something that could ever truly be regained, Sam did not know. He sincerely doubted it.

"I know how you cut yourself off after she died, Sam," Sara continued, watching his reactions with hawk-like intensity. I know how close you came to drinking yourself into an early grave. The network of FireStorm might not be able to prevent tragedies—those are simply a part of life, albeit devastating. But we could make sure that you were never left to fall into despair again." Her fingers crept onto the exposed flesh of his arm and he shivered. The smile she gave him was that of a woman who was confident that she had won.

Yet the second her eyes met Sam's, her smile was interrupted by a flicker of doubt. He was not smiling back. Nor was his face the mask of nervous arousal or lust that she had anticipated. Instead his features had hardened, his eyes were flinty, and his mouth set in a hard line.

"I don't know," he said. "Despair seemed to me like the most appropriate response to what had happened. Maybe we'll just have to agree to differ on that one."

If Sara was wrong, she did an admirable job of concealing it. Her composure was instantly back in place. "I would never tell you that you were wrong to feel your pain," she said. "Please don't mistake me. All I am saying is that with us on your side, you would not have had to go through all of that and face the emotional aftermath alone."

It had been a long time since Sam had last snapped at anyone for presuming to know how he felt. After Trish's death, plenty of people had told him that they knew how he felt, or worse, that they knew how he ought to feel. It had taken him a while before he stopped feeling the constant undercurrent of fury at a world that had allowed her to be taken from him, and at the people who did not understand. But now it once again began to bubble up inside him.

"Sara," he said as patiently as he could. "I don't know if you've ever had someone you love shot in front of you. Maybe you have, in which case it's clear that we've got different ways of dealing with things. But if you've never seen the one person you actually fucking care about with their face half blown off, just take it from me—for some of us, it's an experience that can only be dealt with alone. The minute it happens to you, you're alone. And what you do here, for someone like me at least, wouldn't make a blind bit of difference. Now, before you go any further, I need you to tell me where Nina has been taken and what's going to happen to her. Until I know that, anything else you say about your organization is going to be a massive waste of your time."

CHAPTER 23

I wish I had never come, Nina thought, as she lay on the floor of the cell, staring up at the ceiling. She had no idea how long she had been confined, but she guessed it had been four or five hours. The white walls glowed at a consistent low brightness, offering no clue as to the time of day. She wondered whether they would dim or switch off at night. Somehow she suspected they would not.

Don't be ridiculous, she told herself. They're not going to brainwash you. This is just a stupid overreaction. At some point Sara's going to hear about it—Dave's probably arguing with her right now. I wonder if Sam tried to talk to her. Ha . . . Sam's probably in the next cell for breaking Cody's nose. No, if anyone's going to do the diplomatic stuff, it'll be Purdue. Then she'll need to hear my side of the story and Cody's, and I can tell her that I lashed out and ran because he grabbed me. That should worry her.

This is a litigious place; I can suggest that I'll sue them for harassment or something along those lines. I won't, of course. I couldn't afford to unless I let Dave help me, and I'm not doing that. But the threat should be enough to get her to back off and let us leave without any more interference. Well, assuming Dave doesn't mind us leaving. I'm sure he'll be all right with it. Even if he's not, Sam will—ah, no, Sam's here to work, isn't he? He probably can't leave. Well, I don't care. I'm leaving this place even if I have to walk across the desert alone. These people are seriously weird, and the more distance I can put between them and me, the better.

A small hatch in the door slid open. Nina leaped up, requests for the door to be opened tumbling rapidly from her lips, but she got no reply. She caught no glimpse of the person on the other side of the door.

Instead she saw a small tray being pushed through, containing a cup of water and a dish of what appeared to be greenish mush.

Suddenly aware of how thirsty she was she reached for the cup, but as she raised it to her lips she noticed the smell of the herbs and set it down untouched.

✠✠✠

Sam stormed out of Sara's tent and made straight for the river. The aftertaste of the pulque was bitter in his mouth. It was beginning to make him feel a little nauseated. Reaching the sandy riverbank he waded in, walking out until he was waist deep before dropping down to let the water cover his head. He opened his mouth and swallowed great gulps of the pure water, washing the taste away. He could feel the cool liquid all the way down his esophagus, spreading out from his throat as if it was charging through his veins.

As his body cooled, so did his anger—a little, at least. He stayed under until he could picture Cody's face without his hand balling itself involuntarily into a fist. Then he surfaced and made his way back to dry land, ready to go and find Purdue and make a plan to locate Nina and get the hell out of this place.

A sob from behind the sage brush caught his attention. Someone was sitting on the flat rock, trying not to be seen. He crept around the vegetation until he could see the person crying.

"Julia Rose?"

The young woman tried to abort her sobbing, but there was no concealing the distress on her face. "Oh, hey, Sam," she said with as much nonchalance as she could muster. "I was just, um, I."

She fell silent. Judging by the tension in her jaw, Sam was sure that she was biting the inside of her cheek to keep herself from bursting into tears. He was not sure what to do. Crying people were not his area of expertise. They stood in silence, Sam waiting for her to finish her sentence, Julia Rose battling to govern her emotions.

"Do you need me to, er . . . get anyone, or anything?" Sam floundered, hoping that he could help Julia Rose without provoking a flood of tears.

She shook her head vigorously. "What would be the point?" she asked.

"How do you mean?" Sam was nonplussed.

"There's no point," she said, avoiding eye contact and staring into the river. She picked up a handful of pebbles and began hurling them in powerfully, one by one. "I'll be fine. Just like always. Just give me time."

"Did someone do something to you?" he asked. First Nina, now Julia Rose, he thought. Is it just my bad luck today?

Again, Julia Rose shook her head and snuffled. "I told you, Sam, I'm fine. Just stupid is all."

"Hey." Sam crouched beside her on the rock. He desperately wanted to go and find Purdue, but the idea of leaving Julia Rose in this state made him feel a little nervous. Having helped her to get here, he now felt somewhat responsible for her. "Come on. You're not stupid. Tell me what's wrong."

She looked up at him, as if to confirm that he was serious. "It's totally stupid," she sighed. "I'm not even exaggerating. I . . . I was up at Sara's tent. I saw you going there and I followed you. I was going to listen, in case she told you anything she hasn't told me."

"And did she?"

Julia Rose laughed softly, a laugh that sounded half-desolate. "Yeah. Oh, yeah. And that's why it's stupid. I can't believe I listened to everything she said before. Dumbest thing I ever did. She's so full of shit, and I didn't even see it coming."

Sam attempted a comforting pat on the back. "Don't worry about it," he said. "Everyone gets taken in from time to time. I had the odd flicker of it myself! She's persuasive."

"I know," said Julia Rose, "but I usually know better than this. I was raised to have some street smarts. And I was so proud of myself for my objectivity! I was going to come here and uncover, I don't know . . . something. I was going to expose FireStorm as the new Scientology. Then what do you know, the minute I actually meet Sara, I develop some stupid girl crush on her and . . . I should have known better. There's no point in hero worshipping people. They'll always let you down."

As much as Sam wished that he could make the girl feel better, he was out of his depth. He tried to think of something comforting to say, but nothing came to mind—at least, nothing that wouldn't be a lie.

Rather than spin a line, he decided to concentrate on the practical. In his experience, that usually helped more than awkward attempts at comfort. Neither helped as much as a dram, but in the absence of any available drink he chose the next best option. "How much did you hear"?

"Plenty. Enough to remind me that when someone looks that slick and so put together, they probably got where they are by sticking it to someone." She shoved the back of her hand across her face, roughly wiping away the tears. "But don't worry about it. I'll get over my disappointment, just like I always do. And then I'll write my article, and maybe it'll keep a few people from pouring more cash and adulation into Sara's lap. Maybe it won't. But I'll still have tried. Even if the only place I ever get to post it is my blog."

She smiled, and Sam found himself returning it. There was something about her pluck and wry humor that reminded him of himself. "Look," he said, "I've got to get back to the camp—but if you've been following Sara as closely as I think you have, there's something I might need your help with."

✠✠✠

Purdue's long, thin fingers moved swiftly over the touch screen, swiping and tapping while Sam looked on and tried in vain to make sense of the endless strings of letters and numbers that flashed up. They were in the corridor where Sam had faced the three challenges, on the wrong side of a locked door.

"Is it going to take much longer?" Sam's impatience finally got the better of him. Purdue did not reply or look away from the screen but held up an admonishing finger while continuing to tap with his other hand. Sam turned to Julia Rose instead. "Are you sure there's another door in there?"

Julia Rose nodded emphatically. "I've never been through it, but I met Sara in here for a one-to-one session on the first day. Cody brought me in through this corridor, but she came in through a different door. You can hardly see it from inside—once it closes, it just kind of blends back into the walls."

Purdue gave a small gasp as the locking mechanism released and the door in front of them swung open. "There we are," he said, unfolding from his crouched position.

"Hurry now. We have only a few moments before the system corrects itself and locks us out again."

Sam, Julia Rose, Purdue, and his bodyguard all stepped through into the round room. Once the corridor door was closed the walls looked completely solid, as if there were no exits at all. Purdue reached into the pocket of his black shorts and pulled out a roll of red electrical tape, then felt for the outline of the door and placed a few small pieces of tape along it so that they would not become confused by the featureless walls. Julia Rose reached out her hand, ready to feel for the cracks that would betray the presence of another door.

"Don't!" Purdue's voice rang out in the empty room. Julia Rose froze, her eyes wide and her hand suspended in the air. "Don't touch anything," Purdue said. "Every surface that you see in here is a touch screen. Don't activate it. This will have to be a visual search."

Painstakingly all four of them pored over every inch of wall, spaced out at intervals and working their way around in a circle. Sam felt his eyes beginning to ache as he searched. The walls appeared seamless. Could Julia Rose have been wrong?

"I have it!" Purdue called. He beckoned the other three. The fissure in the smooth wall was almost imperceptible, with no discernible way of prying the door open. Purdue looked it up and down appraisingly, then began to wrap electrical tape round the tips of his fingers. At first Sam thought it was simply an unconscious gesture, perhaps a nervous habit, but as Purdue began to swipe at the screens with his covered fingers, it dawned on him. He was concealing his fingerprints. The screens must be able to identify users by their prints, Sam thought. That's clever . . . extremely creepy, but definitely clever.

"That should do it," Purdue said as the screen displayed a "Verification Pending" message. "Fortunately they are using screens not dissimilar to my tablet. I believe I know whose work this is . . . If I'm correct I must congratulate her—and thank her for not blocking the access code. We will know in a moment whether she did or not.

The system is set up to request three forms of identification. Fingerprints are the first. Easy enough to avoid by rendering them unreadable, but the second form is the iris scan, and the third is DNA, neither of which can be fudged without a little forethought.

I have authorization to access most areas of the camp, but no doubt they will be alert to the possibility of my attempting to release Nina. Ah!"

The message on the screen changed, replaced by the words "Access Granted." The door slid open, but this time only three of them passed through. Kai stopped in the doorway and wedged his foot against the sliding panel, jamming the door open.

The corridor that lay in front of them was lined with the same material as the circular room. With a few swift taps, Purdue was able to call up a map labeled "Solitary Reflection Units," which showed that there were four small rooms concealed behind the walls. Three were empty, but one contained a moving shape—a thermal image picked out in red, green, and yellow. Purdue tapped the figure and a panel opened up displaying her height and weight, the temperature within the cell, the time of her last meal, and the time at which she was next due to be offered water.

"Can you reprogram that?" Sam asked, pointing to the water timer. "Someone's meant to bring water in five minutes."

Purdue shook his head. "I could, but not without more time. We will have to do our best to get her out before anyone arrives." He stared intently at the screen, his fingers swooping and pecking as he tried a variety of override codes that might open the cell doors. Sam held his breath and counted the seconds as they passed.

Just as the cell door swung open, they heard Kai at the other end of the corridor. Someone had entered the circular room, and now he was speaking to them loudly enough for the rest of the group to hear. It was as much warning as they could have.

Sam made for the door to Nina's cell, but Purdue held him back. "Wait," he said. "We need to do this the right way, or we will trigger all sorts of alarms." He led Sam and Julia Rose to the cell door and stood outside. "Nina!" he called. "We are here to free you, but you must do exactly as I say. Come to the door, but do not step out."

Nina, looking small and fragile, did as she was told. It took some effort. Every cell in her body was screaming at her to run, to get herself on the other side of the door and not stop until she had open sky above her head.

Purdue reached out and took her hand. Her fingers closed gratefully around his. A yell came from the circular room as Kai prevented the acolytes from entering by the only means left to him. As the sound of the fight reached them, Purdue hauled Nina out of the cell . . . and threw Julia Rose in to take her place.

CHAPTER 24

What the hell, Dave?" Nina yelled, as Purdue
dragged her along the corridor toward the
circular room. "You can't just—"

"It's you or her, Nina," Purdue said, with alarming
composure. "They have no reason to be concerned about
her. You, on the other hand . . . "

He trailed off, distracted for a moment by the sight of
Kai battling the two acolytes. Despite their slight stature
they were both strong, and they moved with the speed and
grace of snakes.

They circled and struck, circled and struck, landing simultaneous blows that were paired to inflict maximum pain in both kidneys, the solar plexus and sternum, the windpipe, and the back of the knees. Grunting in pain, Kai lunged at one then the other until he caught one, the young male.

The female acolyte leaped onto his back, clawing at his face, but it did nothing to loosen his grip on the male. He twisted the young man's arm in two different directions, resulting in a sickening crack and a gut-wrenching scream.

Recklessly, Purdue slammed his hand against the door panel. There was no time for disguising his prints or any other trickery. He snatched his glasses from his nose and stared at the panel, willing it to scan his retinas faster, and then replaced them as he opened his mouth for the cheek swab. The sample stick protruded from the wall on a tiny extendable arm, jabbing quickly at his mouth.

They spilled into the challenge corridor, dashed along it and up the stairs to the connection tent.

It was still empty and the campsite was quiet as the sun reached its highest and hottest point, driving everyone to seek shelter.

Carefully, the trio crept across the sand. Where the hell are we going to go? Sam wondered. He wanted to ask, but Purdue seemed to have a plan, so he followed.

It did not take him long to work out their destination. Sam had not yet explored the tall rock formation where Nina and Purdue had sheltered just a few nights before, but it was the only visible structure that might provide them with shade and concealment. He wiped the freely flowing sweat from his face as they plodded through the sand. The spiky, scrubby bushes grabbed at his legs and tore long, thin lines into them. Beside him, Nina stumbled. Sam and Purdue both grabbed her arms and propped her up, ushering her toward the shade.

✠✠✠

"Henley?"

Half-hidden in the shade of the rocks, the girl raised her head to reveal a sulky, hurt face. "Yeah? What are you people doing here? This is my place."

"Just looking to get out of the sun, Henley," said Sam. "Are you ok?"

She gave a one-shouldered shrug. "I guess. This place sucks, is all. And you know what, you can tell my mom and dad. I don't care how much they love all this stuff. It's bullshit. I want to go home."

"Christ, you and me both," Nina sighed, collapsing beside her. "I wish I'd never come here." She turned her face toward the sky. It was too hot, even in the shade, and there was not even the slightest breeze to disturb the arid air. Nevertheless, it was the sweetest sensation she could imagine. Above her were miles of open sky, with not a wall in sight.

Despite wearing the lightest clothes he owned, a thin cotton T-shirt and pale beige shorts, Sam felt like he was melting. Beads of sweat trickled down the back of his neck, sticking his hair to his skin. The mental image of his waterskin, resting on top of his backpack back in the teepee, taunted him.

"Does anyone have any water?" Nina asked, as if reading his mind. "They gave me some when I was in the cell, but it had all that weird herbal stuff in it, so I left it alone."

"Good call," said Henley. "Mom says it's fine, but I think it's some kind of drug. She says it can't be drugs because it's just a plant. I told her that weed is just a plant too—I mean, she'd freak if she saw me with a joint but she's fine with me drinking that shit? So stupid. Besides, I don't think she ever saw some of the other shit they put in there." Her brow furrowed as she realized what else Nina had said. "Why were you in the cells?"

Sam and Nina exchanged a glance, noting that Henley did not seem even slightly surprised by the existence of the cells.

"I got on the wrong side of Cody," said Nina. "Although I don't think that's all there was to it. I think—no, Dave." She shook off the hand that Purdue laid on her arm. "I don't care if she runs to Jefferson. Or Sara. Or Cody. If any one of them tries to put me back in those cells, I'll claw their fucking eyes out this time."

"I'm not running to anybody," Henley said, twisting a lock of her dark blonde hair nervously between her fingers. "I don't trust anybody here."

Neither do I, Sam thought, trying hard not to watch Purdue suspiciously out of the corner of his eye. What is your game, Dave Purdue?

First you seem to be in with these people, then you're not, then you throw Julia Rose in the cell, and now we're following you and hoping that you've got a plan to get us out of here. I don't trust you an inch, yet for some reason I keep following your lead.

"Not even your parents?" Purdue asked.

Henley looked uncomfortable. "No," she said. "I mean, yeah, kind of . . . I don't know. It's Mom and Dad. Of course, I trust them, but they're just being so weird right now. It's been like this ever since Dad got into all this FireStorm stuff, and now Mom's drinking the Kool-Aid too. I don't get it, so obviously there's something wrong with me." She shook back her hair in a gesture of practiced defiance. "Well, whatever. I don't even care. I'll be eighteen in a few months, and then I can do whatever I want. I don't have to put up with this crap anymore."

Beneath the teenage bravado, it was clear that Henley was hurting. Even Sam, who prided himself on being as emotionally stunted as a Scotsman could be, could tell how upset she was. Her hands were shaking slightly, and the hand that cupped her crooked elbow had its nails dug deep into the skin of her arm.

Little deep pink crescent shapes speckled her tanned skin. A couple of the marks went so deep that they showed a thin line of red where she had broken through the epidermis.

A noise from the camp broke the stillness of the air. It was the sound of the gong in the connection tent, the one that Sam had only ever seen struck by the acolytes. If they were sounding the gong, Sam reasoned, it could only mean that they had overpowered Kai and that he was either in a cell or dead. He won't be dead, Sam told himself, battling the growing feeling of horror in the pit of his stomach. There's no reason to think that he's dead. If they overpowered him, he'll be in a cell. That's all. It's not good, but it would make sense.

"Anyway," Henley suddenly remembered that she had been attempting to ask Nina a question. "You didn't tell me what you did to get put in a cell. What was it?"

Nina let out a long sigh. "I'm not sure if I should tell you, Henley. Not because you might tell—I'm sure you won't. But it's just . . . it gets gruesome. There's something that happened, and I don't know if I should tell you about it."

"It's the dead guy, isn't it?" Henley met Nina's eye with a steady gaze, facing down her shocked expression.

"Dead guy?" Sam spluttered, an icy finger of fear suddenly running down the back of his neck. "What?"

"Over near the cinder cone. I saw him too." Although she was fighting to keep her tone calm, Henley's voice had dropped to little more than a whisper. "He's really messed up, but I think it's that software guy who knew Sara."

"Hunter," Sam said, hanging on to the one thing he was sure about. "His name was Hunter."

He could see it all in his head, so clearly. The beast being chased and cornered, people claiming parts of the body, the strange juxtaposition between reality and the dream state. "What happened?"

"Hard to tell," said Nina. "I found him when I was trying to get away from Cody. I just walked downriver for a while, and then I could see the cinder cone so I wandered over there.

Really, I was just waiting until there would be other people around the camp so it wouldn't be just him and me.

Then I saw . . . oh, god, he was such a mess. I think— well, I thought that maybe a mountain lion had gone for him. I don't think I'd even have recognized him if it hadn't been for the black T-shirt. There are only two people here who wear black shirts in the desert, and I was really sure it wasn't Henley. Anyway, I—Sam?"

✠✠✠

Sam lurched out of the shade and into the blazing sunlight, putting as much distance as he could between himself and the others before the contents of his stomach forced their way up and out. He did not get far before he was on his knees, retching and heaving, puking on the sand.

That wasn't a dream, he thought. They killed him. We . . . We killed him. I had a knife in my hand, I remember that, but did I ever use it? Did I get close enough to use it?

It doesn't matter. The point isn't whether I managed to stick a knife in the poor bastard or not.

The point is that I was there, screaming and baying with the rest of them. I was joining in. I didn't stop them; I didn't even try. It didn't even occur to me to try. And that's . . . that makes me just as much to blame as the rest of them.

And if they killed Hunter, what the hell is happening here?

Another spasm racked his body, but it had no more to give. He gagged pointlessly, bringing up nothing but a mouthful of bile and a slew of unwanted, guilty thoughts.

✠✠✠

There was no time for Sam to recount his memories of the hunt. Before he had finished throwing up, another sound had begun over at the campsite. Not the gong or the low, droning horn he had heard during his initiation, but a higher, more urgent horn. With a cold flush of dread he recognized the sound . . . the hunting horn.

"We have to go," he gasped, staggering back to the camp. "Purdue, what's the plan?"

"We must find Sara and Cody," Purdue said, pushing his glasses up the bridge of his nose.

"What?" Nina exploded, grabbing Purdue's arm in a tight, furious grip. "Are you fucking insane? I'm not going anywhere near them."

"But we must," said Purdue, his voice level, gently prying her fingers from his forearm. "I have something we can exchange for safe passage out of here. I can negotiate with —"

"No." Nina's face was a mask of fear. "You didn't see that corpse, you don't know what they'll do if they—"

"Why don't you take a car?" Henley asked.

"Car?" Sam repeated dumbly. There had been no sights or sounds that indicated the presence of a car anywhere near the camp. The thought crossed his mind that perhaps Henley was truly spoiled enough to think that there would be a taxi service tucked away in the far reaches of the Grand Canyon.

"There are cars?" Nina pounced on Henley's question. "Where are they? Can we get to them?"

Henley nodded. "Uh-huh. Well, I can. So if you want a car, you have to take me with you. Just get me as far as Vegas. I can make my own way home from there."

Nina opened her mouth to question the legality of taking a seventeen year old with them without her parents' permission, but Sam stopped her. "We can worry about where she's allowed to go later. We've got to go while there's still time. Henley?"

The girl nodded and beckoned them to follow. Sam stole a quick glance back toward the camp as she led them toward the river. He could see the FireStorm initiates congregating, passing cups back and forth between them. Some were writhing madly. Sam remembered visiting Pakistan in his early days as a journalist and seeing a man bitten by a snake. That man's strange dance of pain and poison had looked almost identical to what he saw now.

They waded their way along the riverbank, walking in the water to conceal their tracks. For a brief moment Sam was concerned that the noise of the splashing water might give away their position, but his fears were quickly eclipsed. The hunting horns stopped dead and for a moment there was silence from the camp. Then a heart stopping cacophony of shrieks and screams split the air, followed by the sound of many feet pounding on the sand as the hunt began its charge.

✖✖✖

"In here!" Henley yelled. They had reached the cinder cone where they had spent the night of the first hunt. Between the rocks, half hidden by the sagebrush, was a thin door. Brushing aside the plants, Henley fished out the key that hung from a chain around her neck and unlocked it.

Scratched, bruised, and bitten, the four of them piled into the room behind the door. The light was dim, and it took Sam a minute or two of squinting for his eyes to adjust.

When they did, he saw a vast hangar spreading out before them, stretching across the hollowed-out base of the mountain.

Housed within it were generators, presumably powering the underground rooms back at the camp, a number of industrial chest freezers, sacks, and barrels containing food and, best of all, a fleet of 4 x 4s.

Purdue was already on the case. He dashed over to the food storage and snatched up a large can of honey, then threw open the bonnet of the first vehicle he came to and tipped a generous measure of the sweet, sticky stuff into the engine.

"What are you doing?" Henley demanded. "We need that car!"

"We need one of them," said Purdue. "The rest are better off out of action. Sam, Nina, help me, please. Henley, does that key of yours open the door that will let us out, or will I need to access the computers?"

"It's my dad's key, it opens just about anything in this place." Henley stuck her chin out defiantly. "I stole it. Dad said he was going to teach me to drive while we were out here, but then he got too busy with all his FireStorm bullshit, so I was planning on teaching myself. I kind of know how already, it's not that hard."

Nina, limping as she carried cans of honey between the cars, yelled that she could hear the hunt advancing as she passed the door.

Sam doubled his pace, vandalizing the 4 x 4s as fast as he could, while Henley went to open the exit door and Purdue selected a vehicle to hot wire.

He settled on a large, sand-colored Zibar MK2 and climbed into the driver's seat to access the wires.

The engine roared to life as Henley twisted the key in the lock and the vehicle exit slowly eased open. Sam dropped the can he was carrying and went to help Nina, whose ankle was swelling rapidly and causing her to limp. She grabbed his arm to support herself as she made her way toward the car.

"Wait!"

The thin door swung open, revealing Sara with Jefferson at her shoulder.

"Daddy?" Henley's defiance suddenly deserted her and she wailed, running toward her father and allowing herself to be enveloped in his arms. "I'm sorry I took your key!" she wept. "Don't let them take me away! They said they were going to use me as a hostage!"

For a moment Sam stood dumbstruck, staring at Henley. Then Nina yelled at him to get in the car, and they sped out just as the rest of the hunters came tumbling through the door.

CHAPTER 25

Purdue slammed his foot down, grinding the accelerator pedal against the floor. The finely tuned engine offered only token protest, growling as they powered over the dune that lay beyond the exit. Sand sprayed up on either side of the car, showering the initiates who had given chase. Sam found it profoundly satisfying to see Cody get a face full of dirt. Of the acolytes there was no sign. Perhaps they're still restraining Kai, Sam thought. I hope he's all right . . . him and Julia Rose.

"Do either of you have a compass?" Purdue yelled over the sound of the engine. "No? Nina, could you—"

Before he could finish, Nina had anticipated the question.

While Purdue kept both hands on the wheel, working to keep control as they gathered speed on the uneven terrain, she plunged her hand into his pocket and found the folding tablet. Extending it to its largest size, she held it toward Purdue. "Map," he enunciated.

The tablet sprang to life. It lit up, a satellite view of their surroundings spreading across the screen. A green triangle marked the position of the tablet. Zooming in as far as she could, Nina could discern the shape of the campsite that they had built just days before. The level of detail was incredible.

"We're heading south," she said.

"Perfect," said Purdue. "That is exactly where we need to go. Though at some point we should reach the Colorado River, right?"

Nina checked again. "Yes. We can either head south and follow it around to Lake Mead, which will get us back to Overton and we can pick up the I-15 from there, or we can start heading southwest and save ourselves the time. Assuming, that is, that you want to get back to a main road."

"Ultimately, we need to reach any road that will take us in the direction of California." Purdue swung the vehicle around to take them southwest.

"California? Why are we going to—"

"Purdue, look out!" Sam yelled. A small, black, airborne device had appeared by the car window. For a second Sam thought that it would collide with them and instinctively began to duck, but it changed course, zoomed upward and vanished from view.

"It's a drone," Purdue stated flatly, "a scout, if I'm not mistaken."

"Why the fuck does a group of hippies need a drone?" Nina hissed. "What the fuck is going on here?"

"I doubt it will be just one drone, Nina," Purdue warned. "If I am not mistaken—"

"Yeah," Sam interrupted, "they've definitely got more than one." He watched as a thin, menacing line of black drones rose up over the dunes behind them, hovered for a moment, and then advanced.

As the first bullet sailed past the car and buried itself with a thud in the sand, Sam began to laugh.

They're shooting at us with toys, he thought, remote controls. I saved up my pocket money for something that looked like these when I was nine. How can this be happening?

"Hold on!" Purdue yelled, slamming his foot to the floor and spinning the car through ninety degrees. Sam grunted as Nina was thrown against him by the momentum.

"There's a canyon up ahead," Nina gasped, pulling herself back into her own seat and consulting the tablet. "North Fork or something? Should we be going this way? Can we hide?"

A bullet found its mark, slamming into the rear of the vehicle, burying itself deep in the chassis with a scream of shredding metal.

"We can try," said Purdue. "When I give the word, be ready to run."

Sam spun around and leaned over the back of his seat, scouring the back of the vehicle for anything that might aid them in their escape. It had obviously been equipped for possible danger—there were several shotguns piled on the floor. Deciding that they were worth having, Sam clambered precariously over the back of his seat, yelling a few words of explanation to the others.

There was little else to be had. Apart from the guns, all he could find was a can of petrol and a large disc that he recognized as a photographer's reflector, white on one side and silver on the other.

He had heard of photojournalists who had found themselves stranded in desert areas who had used these disks to signal for help.

Sam wondered whether that might be the reason for its presence, or whether it might just have been left behind by a photographer who had occupied the vehicle. Either way, he reasoned that the white side might be useful if they needed to deflect the harsh light of the burning sun. By the time Purdue yelled for them to jump, Sam had loaded himself with three shotguns under one arm, a couple of boxes of ammunition in his pocket, the petrol can in one hand, and the reflector in the other.

They ran for cover, diving into a patch of sagebrush. Purdue's eyes lit up when he caught sight of Sam's haul. "Give that to me," he said, reaching for the petrol can. He peered out from between the branches of the bush. "There are more bushes over there," he said, gesturing toward them.

"Run for those. Take the reflector with you. Hold it over your hiding place, silver side out. I will join you in a moment."

Sam handed him a gun, passed another to Nina, and then did as he was told. He and Nina broke cover just in time to see the scout drone circling, searching for anything it would recognize as a human shape. They scrambled into the bushes and he flung the reflector on top, just as Purdue had instructed.

Then they huddled together. Paying no attention to the thorns, Nina pushed the branches apart to see what was going on outside. She regained visibility just as the patch of bushes they had previously sheltered in went up in flames, and she heard Purdue's brief, triumphant whoop of laughter as he dashed over to join them.

"That should confuse them," he gasped, breathless with excitement. "Smoke will make things a touch more difficult for them! So will the reflector. But we will need to disable them. We have guns—but can either of you shoot?"

Sam shook his head. The truth was that he had always had a horror of guns, even before his unfortunate experience with the arms ring.

Several people had offered to teach him to shoot, but he had always refused, saying that it was a skill he hoped he would never need. Now, once again, he found himself wishing that he had accepted.

"I can," said Nina, loading her gun. "There aren't many advantages to growing up on a farm in the middle of nowhere, but that's one of them. I've never fired anything as fancy as this, but I'm sure the principle's the same."

She took Sam's gun from his hands and quickly showed him how to load it. "It's buckshot, so this is going to be more about luck than skill.

Just point, squeeze the trigger, and watch out for the kick. If we survive this, I'll give you the advanced tutorial another time."

I can do this, Sam told himself, clutching the shotgun as they heard the low growling of the line of drones. Having completed one pass, they were now returning for a second, seeking a clear view. Through the billowing smoke Sam counted five of them, but he was certain there had been more visible from the car.

He forced himself to calm his breathing, as he looked through the sight. A drone broke cover, bursting out of the cloud of smoke, and Sam's finger closed on the trigger.

Seconds later he shook his head and looked around to find himself in a different position, flat on his back and staring upward at a ceiling of twigs. The jagged branches dug into his back where he had landed on them, and as he pulled himself back into a crouch he heard the thin material of his shirt rip. The smell of spent gunpowder filled his nostrils. He could taste it, acrid and sulfurous in the back of his throat. The memories were trying to flood back, the vision of a half-destroyed face . . .

"I warned you to watch out for the kick," said Nina, with the faintest hint of a smile on her lips.

"You got one!" Purdue cried, pointing in the direction of Sam's shot. Sure enough, a tangle of metal and black plastic was burning brightly in the sand a short distance away. "Well done, Sam! I think it might have been the scout! Now, I need you two to keep shooting. I am going to attempt to jam their signal."

Gritting his teeth, Sam hoisted the gun to his shoulder again. He watched and waited until he heard the drones approach again, still seeking their target. He knew it was only his imagination, but he was sure that the snarl of the engines sounded different, as if the drones were becoming frustrated by their inability to find their objective.

He heard the noise of Nina's gun behind him, followed by her cursing under her breath as the shot failed to land. She fired again, and again, but before he could learn whether she had brought any of the drones down, he spotted one approaching and fired. His aim went wide, and only a small amount of shrapnel hit it, piercing its casing without incapacitating it.

The fire that Purdue had set was beginning to dwindle. Much of its fuel had burned away, reducing the bushes to glowing, smoldering ash that gave off a thin, tapering trail of smoke rather than the thick clouds it had offered before. The remaining drones were increasingly visible—and Sam knew that this could only mean that the drones could see them too.

Four—no, five, he counted. I must have miscounted before. That would be about right if Nina hasn't yet shot any down. But I thought she had, and I definitely did, and . . . oh, no.

Over the horizon, another half dozen drones rose into view, the outlines of the little places dark and menacing against the blue sky. We're never going to be able to shoot them all down, Sam thought. And even if we could, do they have more? Will they just keep them coming?

Crouched on the sandy ground at their feet, Purdue bent double over his tablet, whispering one instruction after another to it and jabbing at the screen. As the last of the thick smoke cleared, leaving them with only wisps for concealment, Purdue gave a muffled, hopeful exclamation. "Initiate program," he told the tablet, and Sam could hear in his voice the same persuasive tone he had once fallen for himself. He only hoped that the computer was as susceptible to Purdue's wheedling.

As one of the drones swooped toward their hiding place and began to fire, Sam took aim and went for the trigger again. It clicked, but did not fire. The trigger jammed. Sam swore under his breath and pulled again, but still it stuck. "Come on, come on, you little bastard!" Sam hissed at it as the drone's bullets hit the sand just a few feet from where they hid. The gun refused to fire. Sam yelled at the others to get down, throwing his arms over his head for protection. He closed his eyes and braced himself for the imminent hail of bullets.

Silence. Sam listened, but heard nothing. Is this it? he wondered. Am I dead? Is it over? He opened his eyes. There was still sand beneath his feet, and as he raised his head he saw that he was still in the bushes.

Not dead, then, he surmised. "Nina?"

"I'm all right." Sam heard her voice from behind him. "Dave?"

"I am well, thank you," Purdue's tone was bright and chipper. "All the better for seeing how well that little experiment worked. Look!" Unfolding himself carefully, he pushed the branches aside and got to his feet. Sam and Nina did likewise and looked around.

The scene was chaos. The desert sand was punctuated with the burning wreckage of the drones that they had shot down—one for Sam, three for Nina. However, the war zone image was interspersed with the comical sight of intact drones upended in the dunes, their noses buried. Once again Sam recalled the remote control helicopter he had owned so proudly when he was small, and how it had occasionally ended up crash-landing in his sister's sandpit.

"That will take care of them for now," said Purdue. "The signal will remain jammed as long as they are within range of the tablet. But there were at least two that fell into the canyon. If they survived the fall, they might well become operational once again. We should get as far from here as possible before that happens."

CHAPTER 26

S am rubbed his bleary eyes. "I'm sorry, folks," he yawned. "I'm going to have to stop the car and pull over."

"It's ok, Sam," Nina gave him an exhausted smile. "We're all exhausted. Purdue's been dead to the world for about twenty minutes now."

"Should we stop here?" he asked. "It's a bit open. Do you think I should find somewhere more sheltered?"

Nina looked out at the moonlit desert. There was nothing to see but an expanse of featureless, grayish sand. There were no trees, no high dunes to give them cover. "That could take a while. Besides, I have a feeling that if these people want to find you, you get found. Let's just stop here and get a couple of hours of sleep, ok?"

"Let's do that. Surely, we can't be too far from the road now."

Nina checked the tablet. "Not far. We'll reach it in the morning. Less than half an hour, I'd say, depending on what the terrain's like."

"If I never drive on sand again, it'll be too soon—bloody nightmare." Sam pulled the key out of the ignition and tucked it safely in his pocket. He pulled up his bony knees, curling himself as best he could in the driver's seat. Feeling something pushing his spine into an odd contortion and the seatbelt dock sticking into his knee, he wondered if he would be able to manage any sleep at all. Seconds later, he was oblivious to all sensation, fast asleep.

✠✠✠

Sam and Purdue were woken by the first rays of sunlight creeping over the horizon, flooding the car with harsh yellow light. It took Sam a moment to figure out where he was and what was happening. The conversation with Sara, the challenges, Julia Rose, saving Nina, the drones . . . he thought. Is it even possible for all that to have happened in a single day?

"Morning," said Nina. She looked exhausted. There were bags under her eyes, and her skin was dull. She had tied up her short hair as best she could, pulling it off her face and catching most of it in an elastic band, which highlighted the haggard look on her face.

"Morning. Did you get any sleep?"

She shook her head. "I couldn't," she said. "My mind kept racing, and I just couldn't. But it's all right. It's more important for you two to sleep. It's not as if I can drive at the moment anyway." She gesticulated toward her injured ankle, now massively swollen and painful looking.

"Ouch," Sam winced. "We need to get something on that —ice or a bandage maybe?"

"Ice would be great, if you've got some," she said with a wry smile, "but in the unlikely event that you struggle to find ice in the desert, I'd settle for being able to bind it. Got anything I can use?"

"I have an idea," said Purdue. "Wait there." He climbed into the back of the vehicle. They heard a gentle ripping noise, and then he reappeared with a long strip of black material.

"Thanks." Nina accepted it gratefully and began to roll it into a cylinder, ready to apply it. "What is it, anyway?"

"A strip of the upholstery from the back," said Purdue. "Would you like some assistance?"

"I'm fine, thanks." She began wrapping the ankle, wincing slightly as she applied pressure to the swelling.

"You never did get a chance to tell us what happened," Sam said.

Nina hesitated. The injury felt like so long ago, even though it had only been a matter of hours, a day at most. She was reluctant to remember the previous day's events. But she had questions of her own, and piecing together what was actually happening would require her to make her contribution.

Bit by bit, she told Sam and Purdue about her encounter with Cody—the reasons for her running away, finding Hunter's mutilated corpse, the fall that had damaged her ankle, her return to the camp in search of help, how Cody had intercepted her just minutes before he had turned up at the teepee to arrest her.

"There are so many things I don't understand," she said, gently massaging above and below the swollen flesh. "I still don't know what happened to that guy—Hunter, did you say his name was?

And I don't get why they didn't want to let me leave. I suppose they're doing something dodgy, but it's not as if I even know anything!

What do they think I'm going to do? Go back to the outside world and tell them that everyone here is part of a nefarious plot to find themselves?

I mean, I think they're creepy and exploitative and probably just after everyone's money, but that's not a crime, as far as I know. At least, no one cares when it's the Church of Scientology doing it. But if that's all that's going on, why do they have drones?"

Sam was suddenly rather glad that they had not yet had breakfast. Knowing that he was going to have to tell the others about the hunt made his stomach churn so violently that if there had been anything in it, he knew he would have brought it up. Haltingly he explained to Nina that there was indeed something sinister going on at the FireStorm base. He dredged up all the details he could remember regarding the hunt and shared them, holding nothing back. His words stuck in his throat as he recounted his own involvement and the memories of wielding the knife, of circling the dying man, baying like a beast as he waited his turn to slice at the prey.

He could not look at them. He did not want to see Nina's face as he described his behavior and the way that he had felt. After a moment of silence, he screwed up his courage and raised his head.

Purdue was watching him, scrutinizing him intently. Sam could read no judgment in his face, just a keen interest. He could almost hear the cogs in that finely tuned analytical mind whirring and spinning.

When he looked at Nina, he saw only anger. Her dark eyes were blazing with fury, her jaw was clenched tightly, and her slim hands were balled into fists. Her shoulders shook slightly. That's it, then, he thought. That's why I didn't fancy telling her about this. She's never going to look at me the same way again.

"Oh, Sam!" Nina lunged forward and grabbed him in a fierce hug. Startled, Sam gave a cry of alarm, but she did not slacken her grip. "How dare they?" she snarled through gritted teeth. "How fucking dare they do that to you, or to anyone? What the fuck is wrong with these people?"

"They have an agenda, Nina," Purdue said gently. "And it is increasingly evident that they will do anything to preserve and further it.

What happened to Hunter would, most likely, have happened to you had you continued to resist them. Their treatment of Sam, just like their treatment of every other initiate, is simple programming."

"Programming?" Sam asked. "Like hypnotism?"

"Essentially," said Purdue. "By training people to the point where they will follow a FireStorm leader without question, they exert considerable control.

The drugs in the water, the meditation that tips over into hypnotism, and the reinforcement of their message in all of Sara's little speeches . . . all of these things are part of their process. I would expect that sooner or later, they will also reveal that they have footage of all of these powerful people

participating in a hunt, which ended in the ritual slaughter of a human being. You can imagine the power that would give them. After the death of privacy they plan to—"

"Wait." Nina stopped him in mid-sentence. "The death of privacy? What's that? Why do you know so much about this anyway—oh, why am I even asking? You know everything. Of course, you do. You always do. But you never tell us anything. You don't give me a clue what you're about to drag me into! I suppose that I should have expected it after last time, shouldn't I?

I mean, after the first time someone almost gets me killed, I suppose I ought to learn, let alone a second time! This is strike three! So are you going to share? Have we reached the moment for your big reveal? Or is this not sufficiently dramatic for you?" In frustration, she slammed her fists down on the cushion of the passenger seat.

Based on what he knew of Purdue, Sam expected him to allow for a dramatic pause, and then reveal everything he knew with a smirk and a flourish. Much to his surprise, the silence that followed Nina's outburst was tense rather than anticipatory. Purdue's face was stark white, his mouth set in a hard straight line. He had only seen that look on Purdue's face once before, when the captain of the ship that had rescued them in the Antarctic had refused to abandon the survivors of the destroyer wreck. Then he had taken it for simple anger at not having his orders obeyed, but now he began to wonder whether what he was seeing was a look of hurt.

"As I have said before, Nina," he said with exaggerated precision, "I cannot talk to you when you are in this mood. I am going to see whether there is any water to be found. I suggest you two get out and walk a little before we move on. I am sure Sam will support you so that you do not damage your leg any further."

Purdue snatched a waterskin from the back, then climbed out of the car and stalked off across the sand. With a sigh and a shrug, Nina pulled herself across the seat and lowered herself to the ground, gingerly testing her ankle. She stifled a gasp as the pain kicked in, but she did not let it stop her.

"Is everything ok?" Sam asked, nodding in the direction Purdue had gone. He was trying his best to be tactful, but could not shake the feeling that it wasn't quite working.

Nina shrugged. "Who knows?" she said. "I probably shouldn't have wound him up like that, not if we're ever going to figure out what's happening. I'm just sick of being part of some game that I don't even know I'm playing. All I want to do is get to somewhere with an airport and go home. I'm so tired of all this."

"I know," Sam nodded. "I know exactly what you mean. I was just meant to come out here so I could help Jefferson write his book. This wasn't part of the plan."

"What irritates me is that I really don't know how far it goes." Nina's hand went to her pocket in an automatic gesture, searching for her cigarettes.

The change in her expression was barely perceptible, but Sam caught it. He knew how much the lack of a smoke would be annoying her. It was getting to him too.

"I don't know if I told you this," she continued, picking at the skin around her fingernails in lieu of being able to smoke, "but I think he might be the reason why I'm no longer working for the university. When I was using the tablet the other day an email flashed up from someone he knows at . . . well, I probably shouldn't name names, but let's just say that if I'd gone there I'd have spent a lot of time imagining myself in an F. Scott Fitzgerald novel. They were asking whether they should return the money he'd given them to endow a new fellowship because the candidate of his choice wasn't going to take it, or whether they had his permission to open it up to other people. They said that if Ms. Gould chooses to return to academia, they would be happy to discuss the creation of another place. Can you believe it? He'd decided he wanted to spend some time in America and was prepared to buy me a job here! Who does that?"

Sam considered it for a moment. "And all you had to do was sleep with him? Do you think he'd fancy me? If he wants to buy me a column in the Guardian, I'll let him do whatever he likes. If he can stretch to the New Statesman, I'll even go for kinky stuff."

Nina laughed and threw a handful of sand at Sam. "Fuck off," she said. "I read the rest of the conversation. He'd committed to giving them the money long before he asked me out. Besides, I think he gets off on manipulating people's lives more than he does on sex. I have a feeling that he might have been behind Matlock's recommendation that I go and do a fellowship elsewhere. Though Purdue must have known there was a fair chance that I would tell Matlock to take a running jump and just walk away from academia entirely—in which case I suppose this was his backup plan, just ask me out and then see if I'd come with him out here."

Sam could not help but feel a bit of reluctant recitation from Nina. He could not put his finger on it, but he had a hunch, as most hardcore journalists did, that she was either not telling it completely the way it was, or that she was keeping something else to herself. Something that played behind her eyes that her lips would never yield.

They reached a spot where a couple of small cacti grew. There was no sign of a source of water, so Sam pulled out his pocket knife and began sawing at the red fruits of a cactus, determined to plunder them for liquid.

While he did so, he filled Nina in on his own experiences—Jefferson's invitation, his strange first encounter with Sara and Cody, the brief moments he shared with Sara.

Then, haltingly, he tried to recount what Purdue had told him about FireStorm's plans to create a vast information-gathering resource that would control everyone's data and annihilate the world's concept of privacy.

"The death of privacy," Nina repeated the words, sucking the last of the juice from the prickly pear. "Yes, it sounds like his kind of thing."

"That's what worries me," said Sam. "He seems to have a plan, but . . . we don't know where we're going or why. Is he actually planning to escape, or are we just heading deeper into all this?"

Between the two of them, their last encounter on the North Sea oil platform and Purdue's fickle allegiance came to mind, but neither bothered to bring it up. It was still fresh in their minds how he became so obsessed with the Spear of Destiny that he abandoned all consideration—how the two of them were left entirely to their own defenses while Purdue was blind to their peril.

"I don't know," Nina sighed. "I wish I did. But what choice do we have? It's not as if you or I can do what Henley did and just change our minds. What was that all about, anyway?"

Sam swore as he caught his finger on the thorn-studded skin of the fruit. "I suppose she didn't think we'd make it. She's a strange little thing. Come on, let's take the rest of these and head back to the car. Mind your hands, they're sharp."

✠✠✠

By the time they arrived back at the car, Purdue was already there. He had flung the rear doors open and was sitting in the shade, the waterskins next to him.

"I found a small spring," he said, still sounding a little sullen. "I am not sure how clean the water is, and with no iodine or a means of boiling it, I would not advise drinking it. However, I thought it might be welcome for washing."

Sam wanted to snatch the full waterskin and empty it over his head, but he forced himself to practice some restraint. Handing Purdue a prickly pear in exchange, he took the container and carefully poured enough water into his cupped hand to splash his face and rub down his hands. It made him long for an icy shower, but it was better than nothing, at least.

At least the car has air conditioning, he thought. And now that we don't have any drugged initiates actively trying to murder us, we might even have time to figure out how it works. California, here we come . . . I just wish I knew why.

CHAPTER 27

When I-15 met I-40, Purdue finally agreed that they could stop for a break. He had been driving like a maniac ever since they hit paved roads again, his eyes fixed on the blacktop with a steady gaze, but at last he succumbed to Sam and Nina's persuasion that they would be too conspicuous if they remained in the Zibar MK2—particularly because it had a bullet hole in the rear panel.

They pulled off the Interstate in search of a replacement car and food. Of course, none of them had any cash, thanks to their belongings having been left behind at Parashant. This made Purdue crack his first smile in a long time. "I'm one of the richest men in the world," he chuckled, "yet I don't have twenty dollars for a few bottles of water and some sandwiches. What a sorry lookout this is."

Fortunately, though Sam had not used his petty pilfering skills since he was at university supplying his cupboard from the local pub, they remained serviceable. While Purdue went in search of a suitable new car at the far end of the car park, beyond the reach of the cameras, Sam and Nina browsed the convenience store. A cooler filled with shimmering bottles of pure, cold water stood tantalizingly before them, but their access was blocked by a bored-looking young man whose T-shirt, peaked cap, and lethargic shelf-stacking marked him as a member of staff. For all his apparent disinterest in the job, it was clear that stealing in front of him would not be wise.

Nina ran her fingers through her hair, smoothed down her stained T-shirt and smiled as she stepped toward him. "Excuse me," she improvised, drawing the young man's gaze away from Sam. "I'm sorry to bother you. I was just wondering if you knew where I could find a box of sticking plasters."

The youth eyed her suspiciously, as if wondering whether this was a practical joke.

"Isn't that what you call them here?" Nina rambled on, while Sam sidled closer to the shelves. "Elastoplast, maybe? You know, the pink stretchy things you put over cuts and grazes while they heal."

There was almost a flicker of life in the young man's eyes as realization dawned.

"Oh, you mean Band-Aids? Yeah, we got some, right over here. Say, are you Irish? That's a neat accent."

As the young man led Nina away, his interest apparently piqued by her speech, Sam seized the opportunity and grabbed a few bottles. He snatched up prepacked sandwiches at random, not even bothering to check their fillings, then searched the floor for a dropped receipt that would allow him to walk out, goods in hand, unchallenged.

He had almost made it to the exit when he saw something that made him spin around and rush to find Nina.

It was Cody.

✠✠✠

"You're sure?" Nina demanded, hastening her limping steps to match Sam's.

"Certain," Sam replied. "And he looked like he was searching for us."

"Well, I can't imagine what else he'd be doing here. Let's hope Purdue's found us a car."

Not only had Purdue found them a car, he had managed to find a spacious minivan whose owner had left a few belongings in the glove compartment. Among these was her wallet, which Purdue had taken and helped himself to the money in order to fill the fuel tank.

There was also, much to Sam and Nina's delight, an almost full packet of cigarettes. They were light cigarettes, but cigarettes, nonetheless.

"Looks like we're ruining someone's family holiday," Sam observed, climbing into the back and noticing the array of suitcases. He found and opened a capacious cooler. It contained enough cartons of juice, packets of dried fruit, and crackers to feed an army.

"I have their bank details," said Purdue, easing them out onto the Interstate. "I will ensure that they are suitably recompensed for the inconvenience as soon as we get home. Will that do? Now get some sleep, Sam. I will need you to take over driving in a few hours."

Sam finished his sandwich and stretched out on the back seat. His system was still flooded with adrenaline from sighting Cody, but he knew that their best chance of escape was to keep moving, and that would depend on one of them being awake and capable of driving at all times. Gradually, he felt his body growing heavy as he willed himself to sleep.

✠✠✠

Nearly ten hours later, not long after sunset, Purdue declared that they were almost at their destination.

"Are you sure?" Sam looked around dubiously. They were in Silicon Valley, he knew. He had seen enough signs to make him sure of that. However, the area they were currently driving through seemed desolate and abandoned. Street after street, he saw small McMansions that looked as though they had never been lived in. There were no cars in the driveways, no basketball hoops, no pools, and no trash cans out for collection. All the lawns were a little overgrown and the flowerbeds untended. As darkness fell, not a single window was lit.

"Yes, this is definitely the right place," said Purdue. "I remember visiting when these houses were being built, shortly before the crash."

"Let me guess," said Nina, watching a stray dog dashing through the empty yards. "The global economic crisis happened, then no one could afford these places anymore, and they've all sat empty?"

"It is true that they have always been empty, but not that no one could afford them. FireStorm was already considering establishing a base of operations in the San Jose area. It would be a technological base, rather than a place where they could recruit via their Vision Quests. When the world's economy collapsed, they simply bought up the lot."

"But I don't see a base," Nina was puzzled. "Is it underground?"

"In a sense." Purdue tapped Sam on the shoulder and pointed to a sign up ahead that read Pinewood Mall. "We need to follow that sign." He returned to his conversation with Nina. "What you see here is a sort of defensive border, Nina. The technology being developed by FireStorm is extremely sensitive—both in the sense of having to be protected in case it is tampered with, and in the sense of needing to be kept secret to avoid spreading alarm. As long as that base was operational, these seemingly innocuous streets acted as a corridor between it and the outside world. The approach of an unknown vehicle would trigger a massive security shutdown. Anyone who took a wrong turn onto these streets would find they had a chance meeting with a police car, and the police would politely check the driver's destination and set them on their way with a warning that it is not safe to drive around abandoned areas, even in predominantly middle-class Silicon Valley."

Sam gave a long, low whistle. "They've got the police under their thumb?"

"Sam, they have everyone under their thumb." Purdue's voice took on a tone Sam could not remember hearing before. He actually sounded somewhat defeated. Still, it was only there for a moment before he continued in his usual more upbeat way.

"Fortunately, now that this base has been replaced by a more remote—and frankly infinitely more suitable—option in Canada, only minimal security remains. Of course, FireStorm's idea of minimal security is still considerable compared to most places, but I am glad that we are not trying to infiltrate an operational base!"

"Wait," said Nina, "Why exactly are we trying to infiltrate anything? We've taken it on trust that we needed to come this far with you, Dave, but you really need to tell us what you're getting us into this time."

While listening to Purdue and Nina, in the shadow of his own thoughts, Sam observed something which tickled his cynicism about their relationship. He did not wish to entertain such notions, but the selfish part of him condoned it entirely. For two lovers, their interaction and discussion was significantly cool and impersonal. Even if it was just sex, there was no sign of any intimacy between them, not in speech or in body language. Nina's words, "that we needed to come this far with you, Dave," distinctly inferred that they were somewhat detached. Would she not come this far with him at all costs if they were a couple? Perhaps, Sam thought, he was just more romantic than he had thought he was to doubt their closeness.

"And I will," he said. "I was simply waiting for the apposite moment—early enough to give you all the necessary details, yet late enough that you will not have time to overthink things and become unduly nervous. Despite the fact that this base is abandoned, it is still used to store some of the servers that FireStorm will require in order to bring the full version of its network online. We must destroy those servers, otherwise the network will be launched at the end of the Mind Meld with the backing of all the powerful people they have recruited, and it will catch on swiftly.

"Within days, millions will have signed up. Within weeks those millions will find it indispensable. Within months, billions will be using it—almost the entire developed world, and it will have begun its spread into developing countries. Within a year, we will scarcely be able to remember our lives before we all used FireStorm, and within two years the death of privacy will have been achieved. By the time anyone begins to realize how foolish they were to hand over so much valuable information freely, it will be much, much too late."

✠✠✠

The long line of identical houses ended at a T junction, beyond which lay an expansive strip mall. If I didn't already believe Purdue's story about this place having special protection, Sam thought, that signage would convince me. It still reads Pinewood Mall! Surely it ought to be missing at least half its letters by now.

"Turn left here," Purdue instructed him. "We need to go to section D."

Section D of the vast parking lot, it turned out, looked remarkably similar to sections A, B, and C. The white lines had begun to wear away through time and lack of maintenance, and the whole place was completely empty apart from the minivan. Sam turned the vehicle around so that it was parked across four spaces. Despite the expanse of other spaces and the fact that the mall would never have any actual customers clamoring to park there, he still felt the faint thrill of wrongdoing.

"Really, Dave?" Nina groaned, raising an amused eyebrow at Purdue's chosen point of access. "This is where you stored the servers? If this is your idea of camouflage . . . well, you have an overdeveloped sense of irony."

Sam followed her gaze to the sign on the monolithic shop front ahead of them. Target. He laughed.

When they arrived at the double doors, Sam waited for Purdue to bring out his tablet and start cracking the access code, but he did not. Instead he simply marched straight up to the door, waited for it to open and walked through.

"What happened there?" Sam asked. "Shouldn't that have been a bit more of a challenge?"

Purdue shrugged. "No one else was ever going to get close to this place, and even if they did they would have to know exactly what they were looking for. Not everything has to be complicated, Sam."

He led the way into the shop. Their footsteps echoed through its cavernous interior. Despite the standard cheerful signs welcoming no-existent customers to retail heaven, the atmosphere was unsettling. Half-emptied boxes littered the aisles between the half-stacked shelves, as if at some point during the initial setup, the store had been evacuated and nobody had ever returned. That's probably not a million miles from the truth, Sam thought. I wouldn't be surprised if FireStorm had the resources to buy this place lock, stock, and barrel.

"We should take some of these," Purdue suggested, reaching into an open box and pulling out a baseball bat. He handed one to Sam and one to Nina, then took one for himself and gave it an exploratory swing.

"They might come in handy when the time comes to destroy the servers," he explained.

They crossed the store and made their way into the main walkway of the mall. The strange atmosphere was even more pronounced among the empty corridors. A food court occupied a suspended space above the atrium, its colored fast food outlets shuttered and unstaffed.

One of the escalators leading up to it had collapsed, presumably due to lack of maintenance, and had crashed down onto the children's rides below. A grinning sun hung lopsided, dangling from a single wire, the other snapped and hanging aimlessly from the Plexiglas ceiling. The remains of a giant pink plastic teddy bear lay crushed under the fallen concrete, its glassy, heart-shaped eyes fixed eternally on the distant JC Penney sign at the far end of the strip.

"Get down!" Sam cried, grabbing Purdue and Nina and pulling them to the floor behind a bench.

"What?" Nina whispered. "What is it?"

"I saw someone," he said quietly, "over that way."

"What did you see?" Purdue asked urgently, gripping his bat tightly.

"I didn't have time to make it out," Sam replied. "It was just a flicker of movement. But I think there's more than one."

"Ah." Purdue got up, shaking off Nina's whispered protestations.

They waited. Sam could hardly draw breath. Purdue stepped out from behind the bench.

"I see you!" he called, his voice growing a little fainter as he walked away. "You needn't think you can hide from us! Sam! Come here! I think you might be interested to see this!"

Reluctant and confused, Sam stood up. He could see Purdue standing in the open doorway of a branch of Urban Outfitters, gently slapping his bat against his palm. Expecting to see the acolytes at least, or perhaps a company of soldiers like the ones they had encountered on their first collaboration at the ice station, Sam sidled over to join Purdue.

Two men stood facing them, one tall and skinny with round glasses, the other a little shorter, with a more wiry build and sandy hair in need of a trim. Another figure stepped into view in front of them, this one small, female and limping.

"Us?" Sam said. "It was a mirror?"

"Correct," laughed Purdue, waving a hand at the wall of mirrors that lined the back of the unstocked shop. "Still, no matter—at least we know that you're vigilant. Come this way."

They continued through the mall until they came to an alcove containing a couple of photo booths. Purdue pulled aside the curtain of the first booth and laid his palm against the view screen. He bent his head and looked straight into it, then leaped back as the booth began to move, sliding aside to reveal a white door with a number panel.

Purdue tapped in a code and that door swung open too.

"That is why the entrance to the mall itself did not require greater security," he threw over his shoulder as he led the others through. "Even if someone was able to get here without being intercepted and find the correct booth, there is no way into the facility itself unless your handprint and iris scan are in the system."

What lay beyond the door was a long row of stacked servers in metal cases, towering over Purdue. The row extended into darkness, further than they could see.

"Is there a light switch somewhere?" Nina asked.

Purdue shook his head. "They come on automatically. We will simply have to work our way along."

"Right then." Nina hoisted her bat. "Let's get smashing."

✠✠✠

Sam gasped for breath. He heaved the bat up and took one last swing, sending a glittering cascade of shattered glass and plastic cascading to the floor.

"That should suffice," Purdue panted, lowering his own bat. "The data we have destroyed by annihilating these servers is crucial to the operation of the whole system."

"Won't they just rebuild?" Sam asked. "I mean, even if the servers are split up across different locations, surely they have a contingency plan for what to do if anything . . . well, if someone strolls in and smashes the place up, say?"

Purdue opened his mouth to reply, but before he could speak a light flashed on behind Sam and another voice rang out—a twangy, nasal voice that set Sam's teeth on edge.

"Sure, we have a contingency plan, Sam," Cody said, training his gun on Purdue. "Did Dave not tell you about this part? Honestly, I don't know what kind of game this guy's playing, but there is so much he hasn't told you. You can't take down the FireStorm network just by destroying some servers! We've got backups.

Of course, we have backups! And as long as we've got the activation keys, bringing everything online as planned won't be a problem." He took a few steps toward Purdue, holding out his hand. "Speaking of which—I'm sorry, Dave, but I'm going to have to ask for your key.

I don't think you can be trusted with it anymore. Now, are you going to hand it over? Or do I have to take it from you?"

CHAPTER 28

Nina felt the shiver of past panic take hold of her mind. She recalled the threat she felt on the mountain in Tibet when Walter Eickhart's goon pulled his gun and wasted Jodh, who was about to kill her. That same steely determination to survive pushed at the back of her head like an ice cold finger probing and with flashes of the barrel in her face overpowering the words of her therapist, the trauma reminded her that she was still alive. Behind her eyes something clicked, like the cock of a hammer, and she made her decision. With as much force as she could muster, Nina swung her baseball bat. She fixed her eyes on Cody's back, imagining him collapsing to the floor, winded, and giving them enough time to run.

Then he turned—only slightly, but enough to catch her

movement in the corner of his eye. He dodged, but too late. He tried to duck the blow. The solid chunk of maple connected with his head with a sickening crunch.

Cody dropped to the ground and did not move. As Nina stared at him lying prostrate on the carpet of broken metal and plastic, a thin trickle of blood coursed down his face from ear to chin.

It was Purdue who had the presence of mind to kneel and check Cody's neck for a pulse. They waited as his fingers probed the fallen man's neck. Seconds ticked by. He adjusted his fingers, double-checking. Then at last he sat back on his heels and shook his head. "I think you might have fractured his skull, Nina," he said, his tone soft, even while his words were blunt. "Good work. You had to do it."

"He's right, Nina," Sam said, slipping an arm around her trembling shoulders. "If you hadn't, he'd have shot at least one of us."

For several minutes no one spoke. Nina stared intently at the corpse. Then she shook off Sam's comforting arm, stepped forward and picked up Cody's gun.

"We'll probably need this," she said. "Now, what are these activation codes he was talking about. How do we get hold of them?"

✠✠✠

They strode swiftly through the empty mall, or at least as swiftly as Nina could manage, considering her injury. As they walked, Purdue told them of the three keys that could be used to activate the backup servers. They were essentially USB devices, each containing part of an encrypted access code that would not unlock unless all three parts were plugged into the same terminal. When used together, the three keys would reveal the passwords for the backup servers.

"If we have all three in our possession," said Purdue," we can take the whole thing offline once and for all. I can disable the most dangerous parts of FireStorm so completely that it would need to rebuild the code almost from scratch—and without me, that would take them years. The first will be easy enough to acquire, since it belongs to me. It is in my safe deposit box at the Verbena. The second belongs to Sara. I do not know who currently holds the third, but let us take care of the first two."

They found themselves back in Target, passing the long aisles full of half-stocked shelves. "Should we maybe take a few things before we go?" Sam asked. "I can't imagine the Verbena will be happy if we show up like this, and the last thing we want is for the staff not to let us in.

Between the sand, water, bits of plastic, sweat, and blood, we could all do with a change of clothes."

"Good idea," said Purdue. "It's a pity the running water was cut off when the place fell out of active use, but you're right. Being presentable will help us considerably when we reach Las Vegas. Come on. We must be quick—if Sara is aware that I am no longer on her side, and she must be by now, she will surely try to take back possession of my key."

Swiftly they plundered the shop. Sam rummaged in a box until he found a pack of white T-shirts that looked about the right size, then searched for the most lightweight trousers he could find. He slipped on a pair, aware of how odd it felt to be changing in the middle of an aisle. Assured that they fit, he grabbed another pair for luck. Purdue reappeared in linen trousers and a black shirt, marveling at the sensation of polyester in a garment that was not intended as sportswear. Nina had chosen long, flowing yoga pants to cover her ankle, but she was carrying a smarter pair of slacks and a blouse for when they reached LA. She had also found a first-aid kit and raided it for a proper ace bandage, which she now wore in place of the makeshift one.

"Wait there a second," Sam told her, and he dashed madly through the aisles. When he came back, he held a folding cane in his hands.

It was neon pink with splashes of lime green. Under normal circumstances she would have thought it the tackiest thing she had ever seen.

Now she accepted it gladly, leaning heavily on it as she hobbled out to the parking lot. Sam glanced at her as they stepped out into the sunshine and she shot him the most heartfelt smile he had seen in a long time.

✠✠✠

It was Cody's car that got them back to Las Vegas, another of the 4 x 4s from the FireStorm hangar. They found the keys still in the ignition. Cody must have been really confident that no one would find their way out here, Sam thought. This is a nice car. You don't just leave a car like this waiting to be stolen.

They drove hell-for-leather, Sam and Purdue alternating between driving and sleeping, while Nina kept a lookout for police speed traps. By 10:00 PM they had the lights of Vegas in their sights. They abandoned the 4 x 4 several blocks from the Verbena and hailed a cab for the rest of the journey, using the last of the cash from the minivan owner's wallet.

"So what's the plan?" Sam asked, as they entered the lobby of the hotel. "We get your key, and then head back—"

He was cut off by the approach of a tall, smartly dressed man with a businesslike smile on his face. "Mr. Purdue," the man said, extending a hand. "Welcome back."

"Thank you, Tyrone," Purdue replied, shaking the man's hand before dropping his voice to a conspiratorial whisper. "I must ask for a little discretion on this occasion. My friends and I need a room, but I would prefer if it was not my usual suite. And if you could charge it to Mr. Brodie's account, it would be much appreciated. And could someone please bring my safe deposit box to my room? "

"No problem, sir," Tyrone's professional smile was unwavering. He gestured to a bellhop who skipped straight to his side. "Show these guests to 414," he said, and then melted back into the crowds.

✠✠✠

"Oh, my god." Nina collapsed onto the massive bed, sprawling out like a starfish. "Please tell me we don't have to do anything else today. I just want to lie here and never move again. Well, not quite. I just want to have a bath, and then lie here and never move again."

"That sounds like an admirable plan," said Purdue, dropping into an armchair to pull off his boots. "Should we order room service while you bathe?"

"Mmm. That would be great, thanks." She dragged herself onto her feet, and then disappeared into the bathroom. Sam and Purdue heard the click of the lock, followed by the muffled sound of rushing water.

"There is a second bathroom in the suite," Purdue said. He opened his safe deposit box and took out the only thing inside, which was a small USB stick on a chain. "It adjoins the other bedroom. Do you want to bathe too?"

Sam, slumped in the chair opposite Purdue's, shook his head. "I'll wait until after we've eaten, I think. I'm not much of a one for soaking, and I don't think I've got the energy to stand under the shower just now. Just a little rest and some food, then I can worry about getting myself clean."

He sat with his eyes shut, half-listening while Purdue called room service and ordered steaks, fries, green salads with balsamic vinegar, dinner rolls, sparkling water, and a bottle of robust burgundy. Even the sound of the word "steak" set his mouth watering. It would be a welcome change from the lentil-heavy diet offered at the campsite.

"So what's the plan?" he asked Purdue. "We're staying here tonight, we're picking up your key . . . and then what? Do we destroy it before we go after the others?"

"It might be best if we do not," Purdue mused. "There are alternative methods in place in the event of anything happening to the keys. As long as the backup servers remain operational, destroying the keys alone will not be sufficient. First, we must get hold of all three so that I can wipe the backup servers. Then we will destroy the keys and leave FireStorm to pick up the pieces. I propose that in the morning, once we are rested, we collect Julia Rose's car from

the valet service here and make our way back to Parashant, where I believe we will find Sara's key—and perhaps a little information on where to find the third."

A pang of guilt shot through Sam as he remembered Julia Rose, trapped in Nina's old cell beneath the campsite. To his shame, he had barely thought about her since their escape. "We need to find a way to get her out," he said. "I don't just mean if she's still in the cell. I'm really sure she won't be—I mean, she was really cozy with Sara, so I'm sure they'd have got her out. But I don't like the way they sucked her in. She's young, and they shouldn't be preying on vulnerable young women. We need to get her way from Sara, if we can."

Purdue nodded. "I am surprised that she became quite so caught up in FireStorm," he said. "My initial impression of her was one of resilience, not vulnerability."

"Mine too," Sam said grimly. "But I think we were wrong, and I feel responsible for getting her into all this. So let's go and get Julia Rose and the key."

❌❌❌

By midnight Sam, Nina, and Purdue had all eaten and bathed and were wrapped in thick, soft robes. They sat around a small table sharing a twenty-five-year-old bottle of Talisker, discussing their plans.

"How dangerous are they likely to be?" Nina asked. "With Cody out of the picture, do you think Sara's likely to also be armed? And what about the acolytes?"

"To some extent," said Purdue, "Though I suspect Cody was their muscle. They have knives, we know that. I think our best hope is to try to isolate Sara and subdue her."

"I suppose that as soon as we get Sara's key from her, time won't be on our side," Sam speculated. "She'll contact whoever has the third key. Can we stop her from doing that?"

"Put her in the cells," Nina suggested. "I'm not keen on the idea of inflicting that on anyone, but it would buy us a bit of time. Mind you, that will only work if the initiates aren't around. Can we bide our time until the end of the Mind Meld?"

Sam shook his head. "They'll be waiting on Cody coming back. When he doesn't, they'll know something's wrong. Purdue, are they likely to figure out that we're after these keys?"

✠✠✠

"I should think so," Purdue said, with a hint of hollow amusement. "Sara is many things, but she is not stupid. Because Cody was able to pinpoint our destination, we can safely assume that Sara knew that I would attempt to destroy those servers. No matter how confident she is in Cody's thuggish abilities, she would be a fool not to take steps to protect the key. She will be ready for us. I am just not sure what form that will take. Perhaps more drones, hopefully nothing worse.

I was not directly involved in the development of the Parashant base, so I cannot speak for its aggressive capabilities."

"Are we out of ice?" Nina leaned over and looked into the ice bucket. "Damn it, we are."

"Then try drinking it properly," Sam teased. "Just whisky in the glass—no water, no ice, no nonsense. It's the only way."

Nina snorted. "Yeah. If you like the feeling of your throat burning. I'll just go to the machine and get some more. Back in a second." She pulled on a pair of white hotel slippers, grabbed the bucket, and reached for the door handle. "How do I unlock this? Is there a trick to it?"

Purdue crossed the room and tried the handle for himself. "It's not locked," he said, but the door did not budge. "Or at least, it shouldn't be. Perhaps I locked it without thinking." He pressed his hand against the plate above the handle, and then tried once again to open the door. Nothing happened, but Purdue's spine stiffened and his face went white.

✠✠✠

In one swift, fluid movement Purdue ripped a panel from the wall beside the door, revealing a touch screen. He pressed his fingertips against it, then his whole hand. When this failed to get the result he wanted, he cursed softly and began tapping and swiping rapidly. "Nina, call reception," he said, not looking up from his task. "Ask them to confirm whether this door is supposed to be locked."

Scrambling across the bed, Nina snatched up the phone and pressed zero. A few moments later she slammed it down again. "They said it's unlocked," she said. "They told me to try again." Purdue tried the handle once more, but to no avail.

"Can we shoulder it open?" Sam asked. He scanned the outline of the door, looking for hinges, and then remembered that it only slid. He banged on it with his fist. "It doesn't feel that solid. We should be able to budge it open."

"Try your handprint first." Purdue seized Sam's wrist and pushed his hand against the panel. The uncovered screen flashed red. The door stayed in place. "No, not you, either . . . They have your handprint."

"Who?" Sam asked. "FireStorm? Why would they—"

"I think they have someone in the building. Someone who knows we are here and is overriding the door controls to keep us contained. If they had deactivated the doors for the whole building the reception staff would be bound to know by now, but it appears that it is just us. The door should unlock at the touch of my hand. Indeed, when opening from the inside, any door in this place should respond to the touch of any hand—the correct print is only required to gain entrance to a room, not exit from it. I can only assume that they have overridden that command specifically for us."

Sam racked his brain, trying to think when FireStorm could possibly have acquired his hand print. He could not remember giving them any identifying information, but there was so much that was strange and hard to remember about the events of his time at Parashant.

An image flashed in his mind of warm, damp earth, dark walls, and a strange glow in front of him. The trials, he thought. When we had to put our hands on that orb and keep them there . . . That must have been it. Staring into the pool, being prodded in the mouth by whatever that was. Were they harvesting biometric information? I thought they were just hippies . . .

"Nina!" Sam called over to her. "You didn't do the trials, did you?"

Her eyebrow shot up. "What? Why the fuck are you asking me that?"

"Never mind!" he yelled. "Did you do them?"

"No, I—" she was cut off with a yelp as Sam dived across the bed and swept her up, carrying her over to the door. He pushed her hand against the panel. At last, the lock clicked. Sam yanked the handle and the door slid silently open.

"Sorry, Nina," Sam said, gasping a little from the sudden exertion. "I just wanted to spare your ankle. I hope I didn't —"

"Get down!" she yelled. Sam obeyed on instinct, just in time to hear something whistling past his head.

Purdue was less swift. The knife hit him in the left shoulder. He stifled a cry of pain as he pulled it out, then, with a snarl, threw it straight back in the direction from which it had come. He hit the female acolyte square in the chest. She fell to her knees, collapsed onto the floor and began to stain the pale hallway carpet with blood.

"I think," he panted, "we can safely say that they know we're here."

CHAPTER 29

P urdue!" Sam rushed over and crouched beside him. Blood was flowing freely from the open wound. Behind them Nina slammed the door shut again, and then turned to see her blood-soaked lover slumped on the floor. Without a word, she and Sam took hold of Purdue and stripped his bathrobe from him, then folded it a couple of times and held it against the gash in his skin.

"Keep that there," Nina said. "I'm going to call for help." She lifted the receiver on the bedside phone, picking up Purdue's folded clothes from the bed and tossing them to Sam while she waited for an answer. There was none. She hung up and pressed zero again, pulling her own clothes on with her free hand. The phone rang and rang. She tried 911. Instead of clicking straight through to emergency services, that number rang and rang. "They've cut us off somehow," she muttered, hanging up. "Let me take over. You need to get dressed."

Sam did as he was told. He dashed through to the other room where he had left his clothes and pulled them on, returning just in time to hear tapping on the door.

"Open the door, please." They heard Sara's voice from the corridor. "I would like to resolve this without any further bloodshed, but if you continue to resist I will have the hotel call the police. I'm sure they would be interested to hear about why there is a dead woman out here—especially because the knife in her chest has Dave's fingerprints all over it."

Nina, Sam, and Purdue glanced at one another. Sam saw the alarm in Nina's eyes and thought her expression must be a match for his own. With pain in his every movement, Purdue held up a hand, motioning them to be silent.

"Dave, I know you're injured," Sara's voice rang out again. "I'm sure you've already tried to call for help. Well, that won't work until we stop jamming your phone, so if you want to get a medical team here before you bleed out, let me in."

Nina nudged Purdue gently, and Sam watched them have a rapid, silent argument. She flicked her eyes toward the door and gestured at his wound, but he made a small, emphatic gesture with his open palm, refusing any suggestion that they should surrender in exchange for his well-being.

When Sara spoke again, the irritation in her voice was obvious. "This is not going to help, you understand. We can wait here until Dave finishes bleeding to death. Sam, Nina, maybe you'll wait it out a little longer than that. Maybe you'll stay in there a couple more days, who know? You can survive without food for a while. But I can keep someone posted outside your door constantly, and the moment you open it, we'll kill anyone we find and take the key. Or we just call the police and let them take it from there. There's no way for you to get out of this with the key in your possession if you want to keep your lives or your freedom. Give me the key. If you're prepared to promise us secrecy and give up the key, I can promise that you'll get out of here alive."

"Stall her," Sam whispered, leaning in toward Nina and Purdue. "We have to open the door, but you need to keep her talking. I'm going to get downstairs and get help."

"Sam!" Nina reached across Purdue and grabbed Sam's hand. He thought she was about to object to the plan. Arguments that it was the only option they had were on the tip of his tongue. Then she squeezed his fingers between hers. "Be careful," she said. "Don't get hurt."

"I'll do my damnedest," he promised. "I need you to open this for me."

I must be insane, Sam thought as he stood behind the door, waiting for Nina to press the panel that would unlock it.

I might be about to get a knife buried in my back. Or a bullet. Or god knows what else. They might just shoot us all as soon as the door opens. But if they don't . . . I hope I can run fast enough.

The door slid back. Sam exploded out of the room, knocking Sara and the male acolyte back against the wall. He tore along the hallway, pulled open the door to the stairs and ran down, his feet slamming into the concrete, grabbing the handrail to pull himself around corners. He was not sure whether he was being followed. He did not dare to check.

⚔⚔⚔

"Well, that's a futile endeavor, isn't it?" Sara strode into the suite, her usual elegant glide abandoned in favor of a stiffer, angrier march. "What does he think he's going to do? Get reception to call the police? Does he really think I don't have the hotel security primed to take him down the second he starts yelling about throwing knives and impossible lock-ins? Sit down, Nina."

She perched in the nearest armchair, the acolyte close behind her, and smoothed her closely fitted black skirt over her knees. Nina considered whether there was anything that she could use as a weapon, any heavy or sharp object that could be thrown, but there was nothing close enough that she could be sure of getting to first.

She sat on the end of the bed, helping Purdue to lean against the edge of it.

"I never should have made your invitation a plus one, Dave," she said with a tight smile. "Or at least I should have vetted your guest more closely. If I had known this woman was going to cause so much trouble, I would never have agreed to her coming. She's one of the few people that FireStorm can't help—one of those unfortunates who won't cope well with the new order when it begins."

"New order?" Nina spat. "Just how insane are you? How the hell did you get from large-scale data harvesting disguised as New Age nonsense to . . . this?" She gesticulated wildly at Purdue's wounded shoulder and the looming acolyte behind Sara's chair.

"Such a closed mind," Sara hissed. "You're so certain that things can never change. The world is in a mess, and it needs a strong vision to bring it back on track. People like you are the problem."

"Their vision is extensive, Nina," Purdue's voice was strained, as he tried to ignore his pain. "It's a complete restructuring of the world as we know it."

"Whether we want it or not? That's been tried before. I specialize in studying the people who tried it."

"Ah, yes," Sara's tone sparkled with forced brightness. "You're the Nazi history specialist. You, of all people, should understand how cheap it is to compare anyone who attempts to build a better world to the Nazis."

"You make it difficult not to," said Nina. Her hands were shaking as she held the towel and she knew that she should not be running the risk of talking back to Sara, but she could not stop herself. "It's not just your dodgy ideology—you're even appropriating the same symbols as they did." She nodded toward the brooch on Sara's lapel.

"Ah," Sara's slender fingers flew to the polished ebony. "The black sun. The energy capable of generating a better race. It's an ancient symbol, Nina, surely you know that? The Nazis were not the only ones to adopt it. If you're trying to suggest that the use of it indicates that our intentions are not good, well . . . that's an argument as spurious as suggesting that anyone who studies Nietzsche or listens to Wagner is hell-bent on genocide. Good ideas are sometimes co-opted by bad people, Nina. That doesn't mean that we abandon them. But we are wasting time here. Dave is in need of medical attention, I would think. And all he has to do to get it is give me that key."

✠✠✠

A little way down the corridor, Sam hauled open the door to the stairwell. Flights of steps stretched before him in both directions. He ran up at first, going far enough to conceal himself while he waited for the door to open again.

It remained closed. I'm not being followed, he thought. That's . . . good, I suppose? But if they're not following, they're still there. In the room. With Nina and Purdue. That can't be good. And if they haven't followed, it's got to be because they don't need to.

Because they know I'll go for help, but there won't be help available . . . shit. Well, I have to try. I can't stay here all night. Slowly, cautiously, he straightened up and ran lightly down the stairs, thanking whatever fates had deposited them on the fourth floor instead of the fortieth.

The double doors at the bottom of the stairs brought him out into the lobby, which was crowded with people even at this late hour. He looked at the long line of reception staff, wondering whether any of them were safe to talk to. Are any of them part of FireStorm? All of them, maybe? Damn it, I can't assume that anything is safe.

He walked up to the nearest receptionist and flashed his most charming smile, trying to conceal his nervous shortness of breath. "Hi," he said, "I wonder if you could help me? I think there's a problem with the phone in my room, but I need to make a call quite urgently. You don't have another phone I could use?"

The young woman smiled back blandly. "I'm so sorry that there's a problem, sir. Can I take your room number and we'll get someone to take care of it right away?"

"Room 515," Sam lied automatically.

The girl met his gaze. Sam could not decide whether he detected a look of doubt. "Room 515. Right. One of our engineers is on his way. Now let me help you with that call."

She picked up the receiver of the phone in front of her. "If you'll just give me the number, I'll be happy to connect you. It will, of course, be complementary."

Sam hesitated. If I say 911, and she's one of them, I'm dead, he thought. If she's not, I might be able to make the call and get us some help—but look at her. She knows. I can see it in her eyes. She's waiting for me to make that mistake.

"It's, er . . . it's a personal matter," he tried. "I can't really discuss it out in the open here. Don't you have anywhere a little more discreet?"

Her gaze was unflinching. "I'm sorry, sir, but I would have to get my manager to authorize that. Do you want me to call him? It's just that he's dealing with another guest and it might take him a little while to get here, so if your call is urgent . . . "

"Er, you know what, it's fine," said Sam, backing away. "I've just seen someone I need to talk to anyway. I'll just wait until the phone in our room's been fixed."

"Certainly, sir. Have a pleasant evening." As Sam sidled away from the reception area, he saw the girl pick up the phone. He wondered whether she was calling Sara, or perhaps someone else within FireStorm, or someone they had bribed or coerced. Of one thing he was certain: that call meant danger for him and the others.

✠✠✠

"How do we know you won't just kill him?" Nina demanded. "Or leave him to die?"

Sara tapped her long nails against the arm of the chair with growing irritation. "You don't," she said. "But Dave knows that he can trust me, even if he has abused my trust. Once I have his key, we can bring the backup servers online and undo the damage you three have done. You will have been no more than a minor annoyance. We won't be able to risk having Dave at the heart of the operation again, of course, but we would be prepared to keep all three of you on our peripheries. We can provide you with lives, employment, and places to live—in exchange for your loyalty. Gradually you would be able to work your way back into the fold. FireStorm is forgiving—as you would know already, had you embraced it."

"So you're offering to let us live under constant surveillance? What if we refuse? Is that the bit where we end up getting sliced up in the middle of the desert by your drugged followers?"

"That never happened, Nina," Sara lowered her gaze and stared directly into Nina's eyes. "You would do well to remember that."

"And you would do well to go fuck yourself," Nina snarled. "I know what I saw. And I know that you're a fucking psychopath."

Too late Nina realized that she had finally gone too far. Sara's jaw tightened. With great care and precision she crossed one leg over the other, smoothed down her skirt and spoke to the remaining acolyte. "This is getting us nowhere," she said. "Kill him."

✠✠✠

The door, Sam thought. There's got to be a phone on the street, or another building I can go to, or even just someone passing by who might let me use their phone.

He strolled casually toward the door. Just going for a late night stroll, he repeated in his head. Taking the air. Stretching my legs.

"Sir?" A tall, broad-shouldered man stepped in front of the door that Sam was approaching. "I'm sorry, sir, but we can't let you go outside just now." The blood froze in Sam's veins as he heard the words. "There's been a police incident on the street outside, and they've requested that we don't let anyone leave the building until they give us the all clear. For your own protection, sir. There are some things you might not want to see out there."

I'll bet, Sam thought. He craned his neck, trying to determine whether there was any truth to the man's story. Sure enough, he detected a slight flicker of a flashing blue light, but nothing more conclusive than that. There's got to be another way out, he told himself. He had seen an emergency exit in the stairwell, but it had been covered in signs warning that it would activate an alarm when opened. Sam was not sure that evacuating the whole building was the way to go. Pausing in the middle of the lobby, he looked around, wondering whether there might be an exit through the kitchens or the laundry.

Then an elevator dropped past him, descending rapidly into the bowels of the building. As it flashed past, Sam caught a glimpse of a face he recognized. Julia Rose.

✠✠✠

Nina screamed as the acolyte advanced on Purdue, his knife in his hand. A long stream of angry threats spilled from her lips. She saw Purdue raise his good arm, ready to defend himself as best he could, but she threw herself between the two of them and lunged at the acolyte with her cane.

By sheer luck, she caught him square on the back of the hand and heard a couple of the small bones crack. He dropped the knife and she kicked it away, so charged with adrenaline that she did not even register the pain in her damaged ankle as she moved. The acolyte spun around, ready to go after the lost blade, but Purdue leaped up and flung his good arm round the young man's throat, hauling him backward, giving Nina the split-second she needed to dive across the floor and grab it.

She held it out as she turned back to face the acolyte, prepared for him to have shrugged Purdue off and come after her, but he remained sprawled on the floor. The two men were grappling with each other. It was clear that Purdue would not be able to maintain his grasp for long, but he was putting up as much of a fight as he could. Sara sat by and watched, an expression of distaste on her face. On instinct Nina started to move toward her, planning to make the most of her distraction and do her some harm.

She got no more than two steps before another figure entered the room. Nina did not even stop to think.

She jumped behind the man, grabbed his arm and twisted it sharply up his back. Automatically he bent backward, giving Nina the opportunity to press her blade against his throat. She could see it nicking the skin. A fat red drop of blood welled up against the metal.

"Nina . . . " the man croaked. "What are you doing?"

She nearly let go as she noticed who it was, but recovered herself in the nick of time. "Sorry, Jefferson," she said, "but I don't have a choice."

✠✠✠

Without a thought for who might be watching him, Sam ran full speed toward the stairwell and dashed down another flight of stairs, past the spa, the gym, into the housekeeping area where only staff were permitted to go. At the entrance to each new level he stared through the glass panels in the doors, looking for any sign that the elevator had recently arrived.

As he set foot on the top step of the final flight, leading down to the empty laundry, Sam froze. The door below him had swung open and was now slowly falling shut, and someone was climbing the dimly lit stairs with tentative steps.

"Julia Rose!" Sam whispered, as soon as she crept into view. She jumped, gaped at him in terror for a moment, then turned tail and fled back downstairs. Sam went after her, catching her just as she burst back into the basement laundry room. "It's ok, it's ok!" He worked to keep his voice gentle, as she lashed out at him. Glad that he was taller and stronger, he pinned her flailing arms to her sides with as little force as he could. "I'm not going to hurt you. Are you all right?"

"Don't take me back to them," she pleaded, her breathing harsh and shallow, her thin shoulders heaving as she leaned against one of the industrial washing machines. "Please. Sam, you have to help me, they think I betrayed them. When they found me in that cell they thought it was my choice—that I'd sacrificed myself to let Nina go, because they'd go easy on me. Sara said—" Julia Rose stifled a sob, then composed herself again and plowed on. "Sara said that our little plan wasn't going to work, and they were going to make an example of me because she couldn't stand people who try to play one side against another. She thought I'd been faking it when I followed her, Sam!

She thought it was all just me trying to get a good story—but I meant it, I really did. I thought she was so . . . Anyway, she said I could make up for it all at the next hunt. Then they blindfolded me and put me in a helicopter and brought me here. I got away, but the chopper pilot's not looking so good and I feel so bad. That poor guy, what if he's . . . ? I didn't want to hurt him, but I had to get away, and now I don't know where I am or how to get out. Please, Sam. Help me."

Sam groaned and slumped down onto one of the oversized laundry bags. "That's not going to be easy. God, I'm glad you're all right, though. I felt really bad about leaving you there. Look, here's what's happening. Sara is upstairs and she has Nina and Purdue. I need to get help, but I can't get to the phones and they've got people who won't let me outside. We need to get out. We need to get them out."

Julia Rose was quiet, pensive, considering what Sam had just told her. She looked around at the piles of sheets and heavy cotton bags. "Give me your lighter," she said. "I know you have one, you always have one. Give it to me."

It was clear what she was about to do, yet Sam's heart was in his mouth in disbelieving anticipation. Her hand trembled as she took hold of the lighter. She walked across the laundry to the far end, selected a pile of sheets beneath a smoke detector, then flicked the lighter open and held it against the cloth.

"It's better this way," she explained, as she waited for the flame to catch. "If we just broke the glass on an alarm or opened a fire door—that would activate a different symbol on the alarm system than if it's started by genuine flames. This way they'll definitely evacuate." She watched with satisfaction as the flames took hold and a thin trail of smoke spiraled up toward the ceiling.

Sam dragged a few sheets from the nearest pile and laid them over the laundry sacks, making sure there were no gaps that could act as a fire break. The farther the fire spreads, the more time this will buy us, he thought.

✠✠✠

"Wait!" Sara held up a hand, stopping the acolyte in his tracks. "Let go."

The acolyte released Purdue without question. Nina tried not to let her hands tremble, afraid of both showing her fear and accidentally slitting Jefferson's throat. Purdue scrambled to his feet. He waved at Jefferson's left hand. "There!" he wheezed, trying to get his breath back. "There! In his hand!"

"What's in your hand?" Nina demanded, squeezing Jefferson's trapped arm.

"I was bringing these to Sara," he replied in strangled tones, opening his fingers to let Purdue see what he was carrying. "What's the matter?"

Without answering, Purdue snatched them from Jefferson's hand. Two small pendants attached to leather thongs dangled from his fingers. He squeezed each one gently, popping them open to reveal that they were truly USB devices. "We have them," he smiled. "All three. Now let us—"

Nina never heard the end of Purdue's sentence. Before he could finish, the air was torn by the screaming of the fire alarm.

CHAPTER 30

S ara's lovely face contorted into a snarl. "Go find out if that's genuine!" she snapped at the acolyte, and then turned her gaze to Nina. "You don't mind if we break up your little hostage situation, right? You want to know too?"

The acolyte pushed past, forcing Nina to relax her grip a little to avoid cutting Jefferson's throat by accident. Nevertheless, she did not let him go. "Jefferson, you need to give those things to me," she growled.

"Nina," Jefferson spoke through gritted teeth, trying not to move. "You can't stop this. It's important. It needs to happen. Just accept—"

"Jefferson, just fucking listen to me. I really don't want to hurt you, but I swear I will. Give them to me now."

"Jefferson," Sara's voice was soft and dangerous. She rose from her seat, pulling herself up to her full height and gliding like a snake across the floor. Nina deliberately repositioned the knife, drawing Sara's attention to the way the point was pricking at Jefferson's jugular. "Listen to me. These people are trying to destroy everything we've built. We can't allow that. There's no price too high, you know that. You know that."

Nina forced her hand to stay steady. It was trying to shake, wanting nothing more than to let Jefferson go. I can't do this, she thought. They're going to call my bluff. They know I'm not going to cut his throat. All they have to do is wait because in a moment or two we're going to have to get out of the building and I'm going to—

A flash of movement behind Sara caught Nina's eye. Purdue was on his feet, his hands closing on the sides of Sara's head. Swiftly, elegantly, he delivered a sharp twist. The crack brought the bile up in Nina's throat. She flinched, letting go of Jefferson.

Before Sara's body had hit the floor, Purdue reached out and pulled the keys from Jefferson's hand. He grabbed Nina and hustled her out of the room, leaving Jefferson behind. The last thing she saw as the door closed behind them was Jefferson dropping to his knees, calling Sara's name.

✠✠✠

In the dingy stairwell, Sam and Julia Rose crouched and waited. They could hear the fire alarm and the sound of people beginning to make their way down the brightly lit, guest-friendly stairs above. "We should stay down here in the staff area until there's a bit of a crowd in the lobby," Sam suggested. "No sense in moving too soon and making ourselves too visible."

When they judged that the evacuation was well underway and they would have sufficient cover as they left the building, they crept to the top of the "Staff Only" stairs and joined the flow of guests into the lobby. The receptionists were out from behind their desks and directing people out of the building, uttering calm reassurances that although this was not a drill, the fire department was on its way and that everything was under control. If only they knew how untrue that is, Sam thought.

"Excuse me," he called, collaring one of the receptionists. "I'm just a bit worried—I left my friends in their room and I think, er . . . One of them is injured, she's got a bad ankle, and I'm concerned in case she—"

"It's ok, sir," the receptionist smiled back, continuing to wave people past. "We have fire marshals who will do a sweep of each floor. They'll check each room. We won't leave your friends behind. Now I'm going to have to ask you to step outside."

Countless bodies surged past Sam, carrying him along in their wake. It was all he could do to keep sight of Julia Rose. The jostling crowd half-dragged him out of the Verbena and across the street. It occurred to Sam to look in the direction from which the flashing blue lights had come earlier, to see whether there genuinely had been an incident. Sure enough, there was a police car—though whether it had been there for some time or was newly arrived, it was impossible to tell.

Sam bobbed about in the mass of people, holding his head as high as he could, scanning the crowd for Nina and Purdue, and keeping a lookout for Sara or the acolyte or anyone else who would give him reason to run. *What are we going to do now?* he asked himself. *The hotel staff will find the dead acolyte. They're bound to notice that Nina and Purdue are both hurt. God only knows what's been going on up in that room. I've no idea whether they ever got those keys.*

And now we've set fire to the hotel, and I'm just hoping Nina and Purdue will get out alive and that I'll have figured something out by the time they do. And what about Julia Rose? What am I going to do about her?

Up on the fourth floor, Nina pulled Purdue's good arm around her shoulder and moved as fast as his stab wound and her limp would allow them to go.

"You're never going to manage the stairs in that state," Nina muttered, looking at the laceration. She half-helped, half-dragged him toward the elevators and hit the call button. "We're in luck," she said, as she heard the mechanism working. "They're still functioning." Purdue managed nothing more than a weak smile in response.

The doors slid open and they stepped into the bubble of glass. The elevator that had arrived first was the one that faced out over the street, offering a view of the Las Vegas Strip, the distant desert, and the crowd on the road below. That's good, Nina thought, we're in clear view of everyone, we'll be safe. I'm sure we will.

With stomach-churning speed, they descended. Nina hauled Purdue into position, ready to get him into the lobby and to the comparative safety of the crowd. The bell pinged and the sleek white doors opened, revealing a corridor instead of the lobby. Sara's acolyte was standing with a gun in his hand.

✠✠✠

"Nina!" The cry was out of Sam's mouth before he even realized it. High above him he could see Nina and Purdue being held hostage by the acolyte in the glass elevator. The distance was too great for him to see the gun, but the angle of the acolyte's arm told him everything he needed to know. The next thing he knew was that his feet were slamming against the road, carrying him back into the hotel, barging his way past the staff who tried to stop him.

He reached the elevator doors just as they parted. Nina and Purdue were on the other side, about to be marched out, but Sam seized hold of both of them and hauled them out.

The acolyte gave a yell and lunged forward but Sam hurled himself forward, putting his whole weight into it, and shoved the young man back against the glass.

"Go!" Sam yelled at Nina. Still pinning the dazed acolyte to the glass with one hand, he reached out with the other and hit the control panel, aiming for the highest floor he could. The doors closed. Sam felt his stomach drop as the ground fell away beneath them.

This is it, Sam thought, this is going to be the last thing I see. A man whose name I don't even know, silhouetted against the night sky and the bright lights of Vegas. I'm about to get shot in the face. Just like Trish.

✠✠✠

The handful of steps from the elevators to the door felt like miles to Nina. Adrenaline was preventing her from feeling the pain in her ankle too severely, but she was fully aware of the weight of Purdue slumped on her shoulder. He was trying his best to support himself, but the loss of blood was making him weaker by the minute.

"Just a few more steps, Dave," she encouraged him. "We're nearly out."

Cool night air surrounded them, welcome and refreshing. No sooner had they got out of the building than Julia Rose ran over and helped support Purdue. They slumped down on the nearest empty stretch of pavement, and Purdue immediately pulled out the tablet and began to unfold it.

"There's no time to lose," he said softly. "Nina, hold these for a moment."

He passed her the three keys while he pecked and pinched his way through his own security. His slender fingers flew at lightning speed.

"Julia Rose," Nina said, "you're the one with no injuries yet, so we need you to go and find us a cab. We'll get you out of here safely, but we need transport. The first one you see, bring it here. Tell the driver we'll pay ten times his normal rate in exchange for no questions asked." Julia Rose, eager to be far away from the Verbena, did not need to be told twice.

"I have it," Purdue whispered. "Now, the keys!" One by one Nina handed him the keys and watched as he deftly slid the thin connector into the barely perceptible ports on the tablet. As soon as the third one was in, it flashed a code—too briefly, Nina was sure, for anyone to memorize it.

But she had underestimated Purdue. He retyped the code as quickly and accurately as if he had been typing it every day for years, and then waited with bated breath for a response from the servers.

"It's done!" he cried, and began to raise his arms in a gesture of victory before the pain reminded him that he could not. He caught his breath as the pang of agony hit, but it did not take the smile off his face. "It's done, Nina," he planted a sudden, celebratory kiss on her lips. "The servers are cleared. Now all we have to do is—"

Overhead, there came an ear-splitting crash. Purdue paused in mid-sentence. He and Nina turned their gaze upward, toward the source of the sound, to watch what was happening to Sam.

✠✠✠

The barrel of the gun drew level with Sam's eye. There was to be no mistake, no room for error. This would be execution style at point-blank range, hopefully painless and mercifully quick. Sam refused to close his eyes.

He was not even aware of the impulse to move his foot. The acolyte had doubled up in pain before Sam even realized that he had kicked him. Instinctively he ducked, hearing the bullet whistle past his head. It struck the doors and ricocheted, hitting the corner of one of the glass panels. Fractures streaked across the exterior surface of the lift.

Seeing the gun on the floor, Sam shoved it away and sent it spinning into the corner, as far as it could go from the acolyte. Despite their adventures with the drones, he was not convinced that he could shoot a man so close using a pistol. He'd be on me in the time it took for me to aim, he thought.

The bell sounded and the doors opened to reveal the thirty-seventh floor. I was hoping that by the time we got here I'd be in a position to kick him out and go straight back down, Sam cursed his luck. But I'm between him and the door, and I don't want to risk letting him get near the gun again. Maybe I can negotiate with him. Perhaps if I can buy us some time . . . He hit the panel again, sending the elevator gliding down toward the ground, but this time his clumsy hands caught the neighboring panel too. A section of white plastic fell away, displaying a bright red fire extinguisher underneath. Perfect! Sam thought. A blunt instrument. That'll do me a lot more good than the gun!

By now the acolyte had recovered enough to stand up—or at least to reach a painful approximation to standing. He took a swing at Sam, who dodged and started babbling, trying to persuade the acolyte that there must be a way that they could reason things out.

The acolyte's fist pulled back, ready to land a blow on Sam that would break his jaw. Trapped in a corner, too tightly hemmed in to duck, Sam hoisted the fire extinguisher in front of him for some protection. The ring that sealed the extinguisher dangled before his face. He grabbed hold of it and pulled hard.

The extinguisher nearly leaped out of Sam's hands, but he got it under control and turned the fierce spray on the acolyte. It hit the young man square in the face, hurling him backward. He slammed into the damaged glass with the full weight of his body.

In sickeningly slow motion Sam saw the fractures grow in the glass. One broken section parted company with another, sending shards of glass tumbling down to the street below like partly thawed icicles.

He saw the acolyte's face become a mask of horror as he realized that the material that had been supporting him was gone.

Gravity pulled him gently out of the damaged elevator. He flailed, his hands seeking anything on which they could gain purchase, but they found only broken glass. His arms described one final, despairing circle as he fell, spattering Sam with a thin mist of blood from his lacerated fingers. Sam did not hear the acolyte hitting the ground, but the reaction from the hotel guests assembled outside made it clear that he had—and that his end had been messy.

Curled in the corner of the destroyed elevator, Sam waited to reach the ground. The seconds felt like hours.

✠✠✠

"Right there!" Nina yelled. "Stop right there, we need to get that man into the cab."

"You sure are lucky they ain't closed this street yet, lady," the cab driver remained surly, even despite the promise of a large payout. He did, however, comply with Nina's request and pull up right outside the doors to the Verbena, where Sam was staggering out.

One of the receptionists had run up to him and was attempting to steer him toward the ambulances that had arrived, but when Sam saw Nina open the door to the cab and beckon him inside, he pushed the receptionist away and dived in. He collapsed into the back seat next to Purdue.

"Where are we going?" he asked.

"North Vegas airstrip," Purdue replied, his voice little more than a croak. He pointed to the tablet. "I will have someone waiting. We can get somewhere safe."

"We're not going home?"

"We can't, Sam," said Nina, "not yet, at any rate. These people are dangerous, we've seen that. If Dave's got somewhere safe where we can hole up for a while, at least until our wounds have healed, we have to go there. We can figure out whether there's any lasting danger and plan our next move."

It was the right decision, Sam knew—the practical decision, the safe decision. But suddenly his heart ached for home and he wanted nothing more than to be back in his flat in Edinburgh, complaining about the heat and being woken in the night by Bruichladdich.

He turned to Julia Rose. "I'm sorry," he said. "I should never have let you come along. Look where it's got you."

"You couldn't have stopped me," she said. "Besides, I'm not going with you. Mr. Purdue just used that thing of his to wire me some cash, just like he's doing for the cab driver, so I've got enough to get home. He said it's enough to cover replacing my car, too—well, I don't think I'm gonna get it back now, do you? I'm going to hide out back in Minneapolis for a while. Pretend all this never happened."

She fell silent and turned her face away, signaling the end of the conversation. The dark glass reflected her face just enough for Sam to be sure that she looked considerably more frightened than she sounded. There's no point in arguing with her, he thought. If she doesn't want to go into hiding, we can't make her. She'll probably be safest far away from us anyway.

Sam's head was still buzzing with questions and adrenaline by the time they arrived at the airport. Purdue greeted his personal pilot, Gary, and silenced his concerns about the suddenness and irregularity of their trip with promises of obscene amounts of money. Gary took one look at Sam and Nina, looking as torn as his employer and shook his head. With a weak wave of acknowledgment they greeted him. Gary was thankful he was not involved in this pursuit of Purdue's, as he was last time when he almost did not get away alive.

While Gary introduced them to the only medic he had been able to acquire at such short notice, Sam said goodbye to Julia Rose. He waved until the cab was out of sight, bound for McCarran International in Las Vegas, and then followed Nina and Purdue up the steps into the charter jet.

Purdue was already stretched out in a reclining chair with the EMT tending to his wound, while Nina had collapsed into the nearest seat and was staring catatonically at the back of the seat in front.

Without a word, Sam dropped into the seat beside her. The engines roared to life. Automatically, he held out his hand for her to grasp during takeoff. She took it.

"This is going to take a hell of a lot of sorting out," he sighed.

The plane thundered along the runway, then soared upward, carrying Sam, Nina, and Purdue away from the horrors of the desert, into an uncertain future.

~ THE END ~

Nina and Sam return in

THE QUEST FOR VALHALLA

(Order of the Black Sun - Book 4)

Made in the USA
Middletown, DE
15 April 2020